Play Fake

LISA SUZANNE

PLAY FAKE
THE BRADLEY LEGACY BOOK 2
© 2025 LISA SUZANNE

Published in the United States of America by Books by LS, LLC.

This book is a work of fiction. Any similarities to real people, living or dead, is purely coincidental. All characters and events in this work are figments of the author's imagination.

Cover Design by Qamber Designs.

Also by Lisa Suzanne

Grayson & Ava

Spencer & Grace

Asher & Desi

Tanner & Cassie

Miller & Sophie

FIND MORE AT
AUTHORLISASUZANNE.COM/BOOKS

Dedication

For my three. ♡

CHAPTER 1

DEX BRADLEY

The Things I Live For

I stare out the window of my training room as my shoes slap against the treadmill.

This room has a killer view of Las Vegas Boulevard, which is why I stuck the treadmill in it. I can see from the Strat all the way down to Mandalay Bay from three miles northwest of the famed Strip. I can see the stadium where I play football to the south and the practice facility out the other side of my penthouse.

These are the things I live for.

What's waiting with my doorman?

Not something I live for.

"I have a Tawny Jade here to see you, sir," Milton tells me over the phone.

I knew I should've trusted my instincts and not answered when I was in the middle of a workout.

Tawny is a woman I messed around with for a few months awhile back. I haven't spoken to her since I broke things off. She was more invested than I was, so I ended it.

"What does she want?" I ask Milton.

"She'd like to speak with you."

"Give me a few minutes and I'll come down." I don't particularly want to quit in the middle of my workout, but I also don't particularly want to invite her up here, so I take the lesser of two evils. I slow my pace to a walk so I can catch my breath, and then I stop the machine.

I towel off and throw a shirt on as I think about today's date. Today is July first.

When the first of July hits, that's usually the signal that I only have another few weeks to do whatever the fuck I want. In less than four weeks, training camp will start and a new season will kick off.

So that means I have less than four weeks to live it up before I have to be on my best behavior again.

I'm *supposed* to be on my best behavior in the offseason as well, but there are a lot of things in life we're supposed to do that I just…don't.

I prefer to do what I want. I do what feels good, what feels right in the moment. What feels fun. What gives me a thrill.

Though to be honest, that feeling of the thrill has been dead for a while now. I haven't felt a genuine thrill since…

I think back, trying to search my memory for when. I guess since last season when I hit my career-high sack count. Every time I run toward the quarterback from the outside, I get a thrill. My job as a defensive end is to keep the play on the inside and not let it get to the outside, but those moments when I get to rush the passer are golden.

Off the field, though?

Maybe a high-stakes bet in one of the underground gambling rings I attend. Maybe that time I took part in a drag race on the Strip even though my team expressly prohibited it. I had a need for speed, and it was fulfilled in a safe, legal way.

The Aces fined me anyway.

What do I care? It's just money, and I got the thrill I was chasing.

It used to be women that gave me a thrill. A night here with a gorgeous blonde with legs that go on for miles, a night there with a brunette with perfect tits. I still have those nights when I want them, but the actual thrill of them wore off long ago.

It's not that I'm searching for something more permanent. It's more that the excitement wore off. I have a certain reputation around this town, and it's not exactly hard to score whatever woman catches my eye first. I think it boils down to the fact that the thrill was in the chase, and I no longer have to chase.

It's gotten boring, to be honest.

I spot Tawny from behind as she waits near Milton. She has the same long, brunette ponytail I can remember yanking on and the same shapely ass I recall pounding into from behind.

"Mr. Bradley is here to see you," Milton says when he sees me, interrupting whatever she was saying.

When she turns around, my eyes immediately move to the baby carrier she's holding that was blocked from my view when she was facing Milton.

"You have a kid?" I grunt.

"It's yours," she says. She presses her lips into a thin line.

Jesus Christ.

I need to sit.

When I broke things off with her, I told her it was because I wasn't interested in commitment.

This is sort of what I meant by that.

"So, what do you want? A check?" It's possible I'm not the most diplomatic when it comes to these things, but I can't imagine why she'd wait this long to show up and tell me about the kid. The kid must be a few months old. A year, maybe. I don't exactly do baby age math.

"I want you to step up and take responsibility." She purses her lips at me.

"No can do," I say.

Milton eyes me sharply. He's sort of like a father to me. At least in the respect that he takes care of me to some degree. He knows who to keep out and who to let in.

Usually.

I guess he let Tawny in.

He makes sure I get up to my place safely when I come roaring in drunk. He's a pretty good dude, really, but he's *not* my father, and he can shove his sharp look. I'm not here for him to judge me.

"What do you mean, *no can do?*" she asks.

"I mean, you chose to carry the kid and have it, and you didn't contact me. So you suddenly want money? Or what? I don't even have proof it's mine."

She sighs as if she predicted that's what I'd say. "Look, I don't have anywhere to turn. I don't have family who can take him in. I can't give a child the kind of life it deserves. You have resources that I don't. I've done my very best for the last six months, but I can't do it anymore."

"You think I can? You had plenty of time to take care of the problem." My voice is hard and firm, and I regret the words as soon as they're out of my mouth.

"I wasn't going to have an abortion, Dex." She rolls her eyes and stares me down. "Fine. I'll go the adoption route, then. I wasn't even going to tell you, but my friends made me. They said it's your blood and your right to know, so here I am. This was clearly a mistake. A deadbeat like you would never take responsibility." She spins to leave, but her words seem to hit their mark.

It's my blood. It's my right to know.

My blood. My legacy. The very thing my own father talks so goddamn much about.

My eyes edge down to the carrier. It marks the first time I've looked at it, and I see a sleeping baby with a blue blanket tucked around him and a blue hat covering his head.

"Wait," I say.

She turns back around.

"A *deadbeat* like me?" I say instead of the other shit she just mentioned. "You don't know the first goddamn thing about me."

A couple walks through the lobby, and they're sort of staring at Tawny and me as I throw some loud words at her.

"Would you like to take this conversation somewhere more private?" Milton suggests, and we both ignore him as we face off.

"I know you're too selfish to care for someone else," she hisses.

"Aren't you the one here looking to pawn a kid off on me?"

"Not because of selfishness. Because I don't have any money, Dex. And there are things you don't know. I can't provide for this baby, so I'm trying to do the right thing." She sounds genuine as she says the words.

We're both facing off without words when Milton breaks the silence. "Sir, if I may." Milton looks at me and somehow tries to be the voice of reason in this complicated situation. "Get the DNA test done. Have all the facts before you make your decision."

"How do you know it's mine?" I ask Tawny, letting Milton's words settle between us. It wouldn't be the first time someone tried to pin a kid on me, but the paternity results have always stated otherwise.

"Because it is," she hisses. "I didn't have sex with anybody else when I was with you."

I hate to admit that I believe her, but I do. I can't say the same. We weren't in a committed relationship. We were friends with benefits that met at the sex club where she bartends. I assumed she was fucking around the same way I was.

I blow out a breath. "I'll still need those DNA results, but if he's mine, I don't want him going up for adoption." That doesn't mean I know what the fuck I'm going to do. Maybe a family member will know. I have six fucking siblings. Someone might have some semblance of what to do, not that any of them have kids. Or maybe my parents will help me out.

I scratch that idea from my mind as soon as it enters.

I'll figure it out.

My phone rings, and my father is calling—speak of the devil. I send it to voicemail.

"Stop calling the baby *it*. It's a boy," she says quietly. "His name is Jack, after Jack Dalton, my favorite football player of all time."

A boy named Jack.

Named after my boss. The owner of the Vegas Aces. Her favorite football player…decidedly not *me*.

I never wanted kids. I never wanted commitment. I never wanted responsibility.

I just wanted to play football and live a life for myself.

I have no idea what to do here, but as I stare down at baby Jack, the boy who might be mine, something seems to shift. "I'll give you money," I blurt.

Her eyes whip up to mine.

"If it's mine. If the DNA results say he's mine, I'll give you money."

She purses her lips and shakes her head. "I don't want your money. I'm not your problem. This kid, however, is." She holds up the carrier for emphasis. "There's, uh, there's something else."

My brows crash together. "What?"

She clears her throat, and her eyes edge toward Milton. She lowers her voice. "I was caught carrying an unlicensed concealed weapon by an undercover cop."

"So?" I ask. "If it's your first offense, you should be able to plea that down to a fine. Is that why you're here? I just said I'd give you money."

She shakes her head. "It's not my first offense. I need to surrender tomorrow for the next two years."

I suck in a sharp breath.

"I'll sign over custody rights to you. I'd love to see him again when I get out if you're okay with that. I won't try to take him from you. I don't know what else to do, Dex." She whispers the last part through tears. I'm not convinced she wants to give him up, but she truly does seem to be in a situation where I'm the only logical choice.

My phone starts ringing again. It's my father. Again.

It's like he knows. He's pushing me to make a decision here.

I feel like I'm being pulled in opposite directions. The selfish side of me wants to tell her to get out and never come back. I was better off not knowing.

The other side of me, the one raised by the man who keeps calling me, wants to step up and be a man.

I just don't know if I have it in me.

I let my phone ring, the blare of it piercing as it echoes through the lobby.

Before I know what I'm doing, I speak words that come from some place other than my brain. "I'll have my lawyer draft up a contract. Did you plan on leaving him here with me today?"

She nods as she swipes a tear from her cheek. "I have some stuff out in my car. Food, diapers, that sort of thing. And I have paperwork."

"I can send someone out to help," Milton says quietly from behind his desk.

"Thank you," she murmurs as she stares down at the baby. I see the love she has for him, for this baby boy who is a stranger to me but who has my blood running through his veins—we think—and I feel a strange surge of gratitude that she took care of him to this point.

I guess I have no other choice but to take it from here.

CHAPTER 2
Ainsley Riggs

I Don't

I hold Jordan's hands in mine as I stare into his blue eyes. I didn't think it would really happen for me. It was my best friend who signed me up for this reality show and convinced me to do it. *Speed to the Altar*, sort of a mash-up of different reality dating shows that end with a wedding, wasn't on my radar. But when Ivy saw the casting call in Chicago, she convinced me to do it.

And now, four weeks to the day after I met Jordan, I'm standing at a chapel in Las Vegas wearing a wedding dress about to say the words that will bond us together for the rest of our lives.

It's bananas, right?

I'm only twenty-two, but the dating pool in Chicago was thin, I hated my job, and I needed some excitement in my boring life, so I tried it.

Who would've thought I'd actually end up here, an actual Cinderella story in the making?

Not me.

"Do you, Ainsley, take Jordan to be your husband?" the officiant hired by the production team asks.

I smile at Jordan, and I pause as instructed so the editors can insert an even longer pause for dramatic effect. "I do."

Jordan seems to falter at my words, my goofy grin, and the expression on my face over the total thrill that I fell in love on a reality show.

He's not smiling back.

That should be my first clue.

I'm too overcome with my own excitement to notice.

"And Jordan, do you take Ainsley to be your wife?" the officiant asks.

He presses his lips together, and I'm certain for a beat that it's that same dramatic pause.

But then something shifts in his eyes, and a pit drops down into my stomach.

"I'm not ready to commit to you for the rest of my life. I'm so sorry. I don't."

I gasp.

I wasn't expecting that.

At least it's just us in the chapel, unlike other shows that host weddings for entire families to witness this dreaded moment. Well, it's us in here along with the other couples and the production staff.

You know, just like a hundred people or so to witness my complete and total embarrassment, only for the entire world to witness it in a few months when editing is complete and this stupid show airs.

The world seems to spin too fast for me as everyone else in the room reacts with gasps of their own—except for Jordan and maybe like one or two producers who knew coming in here that he was going to say that.

That he was going to break my heart.

In four weeks, I fell in love.

And now, I'm running as fast as my heels will carry me out of this godforsaken chapel, through the hotel, and out onto the Strip, where I heave in gulps of fresh air that really aren't so fresh since it's July in Vegas and the traffic is heavy and reeks of exhaust.

I start to run.

To where? I have no clue. I'm in an unfamiliar town, and I have no idea where I'm going, but I do know I need to get the hell away from here.

Maybe Jordan said it as a joke. He was kind of a jokester that way, but I don't think he'd joke about something as big as *I don't*. Regardless, I ran out before he could explain, so maybe I'll never know.

Tears stream down my face, and I know the producers will want to talk to me. They'll want my reaction. I can't give it. Not now. I need a chance to compose myself before they force me into some corner and make me talk about how the guy I said yes to said no to me.

I cry harder, and I run harder.

I glance behind me, and I spot two of the producers just running out the front doors of the hotel as they look around for me.

When I spot them, I turn a corner. I have no idea if they saw me or not.

And when I turn that corner, I run straight into a wall.

It takes me a minute to realize it's not a wall at all, but it's a man built like one. He has a broad, expansive chest, and he must be well over six feet tall—six-foot-four, maybe? He towers over me at my mere five-five height, lifted a bit by the heels I'm running in.

"Oh, gosh. I'm so sorry," I mumble, and when I back up, the man takes me by the biceps to help steady me.

And when I look up at him as he towers over me, I gasp again.

I recognize him.

And my God, he's hotter than the last time I saw him.

Pull it together, Riggs.

"Dex?" I say, and he looks at me in confusion as if he has no idea who I am. I'm panting from running, and I'm trying to catch my breath, but he's currently taking it away even more.

"Are you okay?" he asks as he looks me over. I must look like a disaster. I was beautified by a huge staff, but now I'm just a runaway bride with tears tracking makeup down her face as her chin-length hair has already started losing the beauty the stylists created for the wedding.

"Dex Bradley?" I say instead of answering.

"Yes. I'm Dex Bradley. Do you need some help?"

He still doesn't recognize me, and I suck in a deep breath as I try to get the crying under control.

"Dex, it's me. Ainsley Riggs. Your little sister's best friend."

"Ains?" he says, stepping back and really looking at me. "Jesus. I didn't recognize you like that. What the fuck are you doing?"

"Running away from the altar," I say a little sheepishly. I suck in a deep breath to try to stop panting and regain some composure. "Long story, but I need to get out of here. Can you help me?"

"Of course," he says, and he taps something on his phone and starts walking back in the opposite direction he was traveling when I ran into him. He doesn't say anything to me, and I'm not sure if I'm supposed to follow behind him or not.

I do, and we're just standing around for a minute when I sniffle and say, "I'm sorry to have interrupted whatever you were doing."

"I was running," he says. He's not panting like I was.

"So was I," I say wryly.

More silence spans between us, and a couple minutes later, a car pulls up to the curb on the side street we're on.

"Get in," he says, and he gets in beside me.

"Where are we going?" I ask.

"Back to my place. Are you going to tell me what's going on?"

Oh, God. I'm going back to Dex Bradley's place with him? Like this?

This is *not* how I imagined running into my best friend's hot, pro football-playing older brother.

I've managed to get the tears under control at this point, so I launch into my story. "Ivy talked me into going on this new reality show that ends with weddings. Oh, God, Dex, this is so mortifying. I just said *I do*, and the guy I was about to marry said he didn't, and I took off running. The producers are probably searching the streets for me since they own this dress and I do not, but I can't face them. I can't answer questions in a corner about how I feel. I quit my job to do this. I've spent the last four weeks getting to know someone who seemed genuine but turned out not to be. What do I do now?"

I don't know why I lay the entire truth on him. I guess because I don't know anybody in this town except for him. I actually forgot he was here.

We don't *know* each other. Not really. I'm eleven years his junior, and he sort of came and went when he pleased by the time Ivy and I met. He was in his twenties when Ivy and I were in high school. He didn't give a crap about the teenager his sister was friends with. And I'm sure he still doesn't, yet here I am, throwing my entire life story at him.

"Fuck 'em," he mutters.

"Huh?"

"Fuck those producers. Fuck that guy that said no to you." He shrugs. "Not in the literal sense. Don't go have sex with them. But fuck them over the way they fucked you over. Lay low for a few days, and it'll blow over." He gazes out the window as he talks. "Everything always does, right?"

He seems lost in thought as he says the words, and I'm not sure what to say to that.

"Lay low where?" I ask instead.

He looks over at me almost like he forgot I was here, and he sort of narrows his eyes at me. He studies me for a few beats, and I feel my cheeks heat at his dark, mysterious eyes on me. He tilts his head, and then he asks, "How would you like a temporary job while I figure some things out? You can lay low at my place."

My brows push together. "What kind of job?"

"How are you with kids?"

I lift a shoulder. "Pretty good. I actually considered early childhood education as a major, but when I saw how much money preschool teachers ma—"

"Fine. You're hired," he says, interrupting me.

I clear my throat. "I'm sorry. What?"

"You're hired," he says, enunciating the words as if I didn't hear him the first time.

"No, I heard you. What's the job?"

The car pulls to a stop out in front of a large complex.

"I'll show you," he says. He gets out and holds out a hand to help me out of the back of the car.

He greets the doorman, who doesn't gawk at me even though I'm in a wedding dress, and he presses a button on the elevator. We head up to the top floor, and when we get out, he opens the door to his place.

It's a pretty sweet setup, but it's hard to focus on his penthouse suite when all I can focus on is the gorgeous woman crying as she hugs a baby tightly to her chest.

I have no clue what's going on, but the woman sniffles and tries to pull herself together when she spots us.

"Oh, um…sorry. I thought I had a little more time." Her eyes fall to me, and unlike the doorman, she gawks. "Who is she?"

"A runaway bride," Dex deadpans, and I can't help but laugh.

"I'm Ainsley. I'm Dex's sis—"

"She's my girlfriend." He interrupts me before I get the chance to say I'm his sister's friend and that I just happened to run into Dex when I was running away from my wedding.

I thought those words sounded absolutely frickin' ridiculous. But *she's my girlfriend* somehow steals the show.

My jaw drops and my stomach flips as he walks over and slips his arm around my waist.

"I was out for a run, and she was just leaving her photo shoot," he tells the woman. "Ains, this is Tawny and Jack. Jack and Tawny, Ainsley." He nods back and forth between us as he makes the introductions. "Ains, I know this is nuts, but I just found out I have a son about forty-five minutes ago. Tawny is, uh…heading away for a while, and she's leaving Jack with me. Can you help me out for a few days until I figure out a more permanent solution?"

My eyes grow even wider. Like, we're at the point where they may actually just pop out. I mean…yeah, I was interested in early childhood education, but that's a little different than actually caring for a baby. And his *girlfriend?* I'm still not over that.

I pull it together. For whatever reason, he wants her to think we're together, and he just grabbed me legitimately off the street to help me out, so I play along.

I fold my arms over my chest as I think through how to play this in the span of a single second. A girlfriend wouldn't exactly be calm to find out her boyfriend had a baby with another woman, right?

"You have a baby?" I demand.

"He's six months old, and I was with Tawny long before you and I got together," he says, and there's a begging quality to his voice.

"We'll talk about this later," I huff. I stride down the hall and search for Dex's bedroom. A girlfriend would know where his bedroom is, right? I end up in a bathroom.

He follows me.

Can I help him?

Probably. I have experience with babies despite my choice of profession. I come from a rather large family, just like Dex does, but I'm the oldest of five siblings. I took care of my littlest brother when he was born and I was twelve, so it's not like I've never changed a diaper or fed a baby.

My parents are both teachers, and they make very little money. We just barely scraped by each month, and it's why I chose a different path when I chose a major. I wanted to be a teacher, too, but I thought there'd be more money in communications. But when you're a communications major and you end up as a data analyst for an insurance company, you start out pretty much on the bottom rung of the corporate ladder.

It's a fairly large regret of mine. I sort of wish I would've just gone into teaching from the start.

I wasn't leaving all that much behind by going on *Speed to the Altar*. Ivy, yes—she's my best friend, but with me out of college and her still in it, we have different schedules. And my family, of course. I'm close with my parents and my four siblings, but I'm not supposed to talk to any of them about this until the show airs.

I guess I just liked the idea of having the chance to find a happy ending the nontraditional way. Instead, I just met another dead end.

But since I have nothing to return to and I need to lay low for a while, helping my best friend's older brother in his penthouse overlooking Las Vegas Boulevard seems about as good an opportunity as I'll come across.

"Down the hall," he says, and I walk down to what must be his room.

He walks in behind me and shuts the door. "I'm sorry."

I blow out a breath. This is nuts. Bananas. Totally over the top.

But the truth is, it's also an opportunity.

I need somewhere to hide, and that may be all he needs from me.

"I can help you. But I need help, too. I need to get my suitcase from my hotel so I can change out of this nonsense." I sweep my hand down the dress production chose for me. Next time I'm at the altar, I'd love to choose my own gear. If there ever *is* a next time.

"Oh, Milton can help with that," Dex says.

"Milton?" I ask.

"The doorman."

I nod. "Great. I, uh…don't have my phone, though. They'll want the dress back before they'll return anything."

Dex nods. "I'll grab you something to wear, and we'll get you your shit back. It might be a little big on you, though. Give me a minute."

He disappears, and I head back out to the woman with the baby in her arms.

"So where are you headed?" I ask brightly, trying to make conversation.

She bursts into tears again. "Jail."

Oh, jeez. What the hell am I getting myself into here?

CHAPTER 3
DEX BRADLEY

Tens of Billions

I don't know exactly why I said it.

Maybe it was the way she looked at me when she bumped into me on the street. Her eyes were so sad, but the recognition was immediate on her end. It often is. I'm a pro football player. It took me a second to place her, though.

She's not the quiet, shy, rather unnoticeable teenager who'd come over to hang with my littlest sister anymore. She grew into a gorgeous woman. She was made up for television, which might've had something to do with it, but they just highlighted whatever features she already had. I've learned over time that makeup can't hide what's inside, and despite her sadness when she literally crashed into me, there was something radiating from her that I don't experience much in this town.

Innocence, maybe. Purity and kindness. Maybe a little slice of *home*.

I shake it off.

I think I just wanted Tawny to believe she's leaving the kid in good hands, even if I'm not sure she is.

She looked shocked when I said *girlfriend*.

I was shocked I said it.

My phone rings again, and I know I can't keep putting my dad off, so as I look through my dresser for the smallest T-shirt and shorts combo I can find, I finally answer. "What?"

"Hell of a way to greet your old man, but I guess it's better than being sent to voicemail for the fourth time today."

"I'm busy," I say petulantly.

"I'll be quick then. I assume Madden let you in on the underground operations?" he asks.

I freeze. "What underground operations?"

"The casinos."

"Casinos?" I repeat. "What casinos?" I rifle through a drawer and find an old shirt that I know is too small for me, so maybe it'll be okay on her.

"*My* casinos," he says.

"What?" I choke as I freeze again, and I realize not for the first time how much I really don't know a goddamn thing about the man I call *Dad*.

"Madden actually kept his mouth shut, huh? I have an underground casino operation in Chicago. The feds are on my trail here, so I want your help starting one in Vegas. You have a ticket into the lives of the rich and famous out there, you know all the greatest places, and you're already involved in underground gambling rings. Do this with me and I'll make the bottom line very attractive for you. It'll be your part in carrying on the Bradley legacy."

"You know I can't. I have a season starting in a few weeks, and I can't get caught up in underground bullshit," I say. "Besides, you've got the Vegas casinos to contend with here. The only way you're setting up anything underground is with a hell of a lot of capital."

"In the billions?" he asks.

"Tens of them, at least."

"Done." He's flippant, and meanwhile, I'm sweating.

My brows crash together. He has that much money?

I feel like with tens of billions, all my problems could cease to exist. *All* of them.

"I'm flying out at the end of the week, and I'd like to meet with you in person to go over the finer details while I'm there," he says.

This is a terrible idea. I shouldn't get involved. But I find myself struggling with my loyalties. My father is always droning on and on about the Bradley legacy, and he's asking me a favor. The truth is that yes, I do know a lot of rich people in this town, and there's probably something in this deal for me, too. "Fine. Text me your itinerary, and I'll let you know when I can meet."

I cut the call there before he can guilt me into more bullshit, and I grab a pair of boxer shorts and a shirt.

That thrill I was looking for seems to be hitting me over the head today.

First I find out I have a kid.

Then I run into this woman I know but don't who's apparently going to play my girlfriend while I figure out this kid issue.

Then my father asks me to start up an underground poker ring? That third one has the potential to fire me up. The others feel like *situations* that need to be handled.

I head back out to the family room, and I toss the shirt and shorts to Ainsley.

"Thanks," she murmurs, and then she disappears down the hall.

"I guess I need to get going, but it's harder to say goodbye than I thought," Tawny says to me. She reaches into the purse she set on the table and pulls out a paper. "This is his birth certificate in case you need it." She holds it out for me, and I grab it from her.

I glance at the paper. There's no father listed, and Tawny's real name is apparently Theresa Jeffries. The baby's full name is

Jack Dexter Jeffries. She gave him my first name as his middle name.

Nobody calls me Dexter. I actually thought about legally shortening it to Dex since that's what I've been called my entire life. But my full name is Dexter James Bradley, and it's weird seeing my name on a certificate as someone else's middle name.

It's unsettling. Confusing.

It pulses a bit of unfamiliar emotion in me.

I don't like it.

She squeezes Jack tightly, and then she hands me another paper. "This one names you as the father and signs custody over to you. You can file for a new birth certificate with it. My lawyer has a copy of it as well. If you need me to sign any paperwork, you know where to find me."

I nod, and eventually she shudders as she hands Jack over to me. I'm awkward as hell as I take him from her. I think this marks the first time I've ever actually held a baby, and I cradle him, not sure what else to do with him. He wiggles a little, and I feel like I might drop him.

"Take better care of him than I could have, okay?" she asks.

I nod as I stare down at him, and he stares up at me. I spot something in his eyes like recognition, and the strangest sensation like *I know him* washes over me. I think the same sensation is washing over him at the same time.

I hear the door click shut as if Tawny—Theresa, whatever—just walked out, and as soon as the door clicks, Jack bursts into tears.

Fuck. What do I do?

I suddenly want to cry, too. I am completely out of my element here.

"Stop crying," I tell the kid.

He doesn't listen.

"Shh," I say.

Nope.

I walk around the room and bounce a little, but I've always heard that you never shake a baby, so I don't know how much bouncing is allowed.

"Fuck!" I yell.

"Okay, okay," Ainsley says, appearing out of nowhere in a shirt that's most definitely drowning her. "When a baby cries, it's usually because he's hungry, wet, or tired. Sometimes all three. When did he eat last?"

I shrug. Is she talking to me?

"Well, let's start there. Where's his bottle?"

"I wasn't kidding when I said that I literally just found out I'm a father like forty-five minutes ago," I snap. The kid is screaming his little head off, and what the fuck? Where did my peace and quiet go? The tranquil view of the Strip has been erased by this nonsense.

I shove the kid at Ainsley, and I run toward the room where we dumped all the baby stuff. I find the bag with a bottle in it. I procure it and hold it up as if I've just performed some sort of epic feat, and I hand the bottle to Ainsley, who looks much more natural holding a baby in her arms than I just did.

She takes the bottle from me and taps the top of it onto her wrist then shakes it before sliding it into the baby's mouth.

"Why'd you do that?" I ask.

"Checking the temperature of the formula. What's his name?"

"Jack," I say, relieved that I finally know an answer.

"Do you have a rocking chair?" she asks. I shake my head, and she sits on the couch. "Crib?"

I shrug. "Some little box thing Tawny brought over."

"Box thing? Show me."

I grab it out of the room I decided would be Jack's and show it to her.

"That's a bassinet, which will do in a pinch, but he's growing pretty big already. You'll want a crib for him. What about a baby monitor?"

I shake my head.

"Diaper Genie?"

"A what?"

"Start making a list," she says.

"A list?" I ask stupidly. "I wasn't expecting a kid, and I'm not planning to keep him."

"He's your *son*, Dex. You can't just give him away."

"Tawny did."

"You're panicking, and that's normal. But I can help you through this transition, okay?"

I blow out a breath. "I don't want to do this."

She stares down at the baby as he sucks down that bottle. "I know. But you have to."

I'm not convinced she's right just yet…but I think I'm starting to face facts.

Regardless, the kid needs supplies, so a few hours later, Target is making a delivery with all of these new products. Milton sends back the dress and manages to get Ainsley's luggage back, though she has to promise to interview with producers before they'll release her phone. We also negotiate daily payment while she's here helping me out.

So far, she seems to know everything about babies, and having her here is pulsing a sense of relief in me I wasn't expecting. And that's hard to put a price tag on.

I'm still not convinced this is real, but either way, I'll need these things for the next few days until I figure out the next step.

CHAPTER 4

Dex Bradley

Completely and Totally Incompetent

What the fuck is that noise?

I'm awakened from a peaceful sleep with…a baby crying?

I glance at the clock. It's three in the morning.

And maybe my sleep isn't exactly *peaceful*.

I may have had a drink or six before I went to bed.

I like a cold beer after dinner. Or, you know, a couple of glasses filled with whiskey while I stand by my windows looking over the flashing lights in the near distance as I try to figure my life out.

It all comes back to me as I sit straight up in bed, and I throw off the covers, wrestle into some shorts I have next to my bed, and move down the hall to see why I'm hearing cries.

Fuck, I need to piss. But if I know anything about crying babies, it's that I want the crying to stop…not that I have the first clue how to make that happen.

I stop short when I get to the doorway and see Ainsley in there, a nightlight illuminating her just enough for me to see what's going on. She's holding Jack and gently bouncing as he starts to calm. My eyes go to her ass, covered by barely-there short shorts that allow me a peek at the curve of each cheek.

I can't help it. I'm an ass man. I look at everybody's ass, okay?

I tear my eyes away and walk into the room. "Why's he crying?"

"Probably hungry. Can you warm a bottle the way I showed you?"

I'm honestly not sure if I'm capable of that, particularly not at three in the morning and also not when I have a boner from looking at my little sister's best friend's ass hanging out of her shorts, but I shake it off and head toward the kitchen, where I flick on the dim light under the microwave and try to remember what the hell I'm supposed to do.

I pull the bottle she mixed before bed out of the back of the fridge and set it in the bottle warmer, and then I head to the bathroom to take care of business while it warms. I feel like I'm sleepwalking. I'm used to a solid, uninterrupted eight to nine hours of sleep a night, and this ain't that.

I head back to the kitchen only to realize I never turned the bottle warmer on, and fuck, it's just stupid enough to make me feel completely and totally incompetent. One more little thing that makes me realize I'm never going to be successful at this, and it's probably not even worth trying.

Ainsley comes out into the kitchen presumably to figure out what the fuck is taking so long, but she doesn't say anything.

Her eyes flick to my abs, but they quickly move away.

"I forgot to turn the damn thing on," I admit.

She chuckles. "It's the middle of the night, Dex. No one would blame you." She's holding the baby on her hip, and now I'm getting a nice view of her from the front, where her braless tits bounce beneath a tight, gray cotton T-shirt in time with the way she's bouncing the kid.

I blow out a breath and force my gaze away.

This is Ainsley Riggs. My little sister's best friend. She's here to help me with the kid because she got caught up in a situation. She's not here for me to ogle her tits and her ass even though I can't seem to stop.

The bottle warmer thing signals that it's done, and I pull it off and test it on my wrist. It doesn't burn me, so I hand it over to Ainsley, who then walks over to the couch to get into a better position to feed Jack.

I stand awkwardly in place. My floor plan is such that the kitchen opens to the family room, and panoramic windows line my entire place, so there are views all around us.

Usually I'm the kind of guy who has all the answers, and when I don't, I go with whatever feels right.

Right now, though, I'm kind of at a loss. Nothing about any of this feels right.

Do I go with her and sit while she feeds the kid? Do I go back to bed? I opt for option two. I'm paying her well to take care of this kid, and part of the requirements of my own career include good sleep. Maybe not in the offseason as much, but I can't get too far off schedule. Right?

I mutter, "Thanks. Goodnight."

"Goodnight, Dex," she says, and she sort of singsongs it with her lovely voice as a soft lullaby to the baby as I exit the room.

Why, exactly, does it play on repeat in my head? That's anyone's guess.

When morning dawns, I head right for my workout room as I always do.

I get on the treadmill, slip my noise-canceling headphones on, and get to work.

My shoes slap the belt as I sprint to the beat of the music in my ears. I've done this workout enough times that I can gaze out the window and lose myself in the sweet feel of pushing my body to its limits. I stare at Las Vegas Boulevard from this distance, and my eyes zero in on the exact block where a woman from my past rounded a corner and plowed right into my chest.

I was giving Tawny a chance to say goodbye to her son. I went for a run. I'd left my place for an hour knowing that Milton was there watching to be sure she didn't slip out with any of my shit.

I needed to get out. I needed a chance to run as fast as my legs would carry me. I wanted to run away from the situation entirely, and on that very run, my goal was figuring out exactly how I could do that.

But then fate seemed to step in and put someone who could help me right in my path. The answer to my problems. Someone else who was running at the same time. Her ass in those shorts she slept in pops unwelcome into my thoughts.

The answer to my problems…or just the root of another one. Time will tell.

I finish my workout and towel off, and then I head into the kitchen, and I spot Ainsley on the floor with Jack, who's lying on his stomach on one of the little mats I added to my cart yesterday.

"You're up," I say as I move to the pantry to grab my protein powder.

"The baby was crying," she says, looking up at me. Her eyes land on my abs again for a beat before moving to my eyes. "We may consider either moving your treadmill or moving the baby's room."

"Oh, shit. I didn't even think of that. Was I loud?" I grab a cup down to mix my morning shake.

"You weren't quiet," she chides. "But it's fine. Best to start on a good routine anyway. I made a little schedule for him."

She checks on him, sees he's fine, and stands. She grabs a paper off the family room table and brings it over to me.

"I need to get over to production this afternoon so I can do my final interview and get my phone back," she says.

I give her a terrified look as she sets the schedule down. "Does that mean you're leaving me with him?"

"You're more capable than you realize."

"I still don't know how to change a diaper. What if he's hungry or shits or whatever?" I scoop out the protein powder into my cup as we talk.

"If you look at the schedule, I'll get him down for his nap, and hopefully he'll just sleep through until I get back." She nods at the paper in my hand I still haven't looked at, and I set it down.

"And if he doesn't?" I ask. I grab the milk to pour it into my cup.

"If he doesn't, then you step up, Dex. You can do this."

I don't even know what *step up* means. I don't know if I'm supposed to let him cry in his crib or get him out immediately or change him or feed him. I still don't even know how to fucking hold him, and I can't quite believe that this is my life right now.

The whiskey last night didn't even numb me enough to forget about it for a moment.

My reality shifted in the span of the last twenty-four hours, and I haven't come to terms with this new one yet.

I put the milk away and screw a lid onto my cup, and then I shake the shit out of it while I contemplate what to do if I need help while she's gone for a bit this afternoon.

I realize I'm already relying far too much on her, and this is only temporary. I need to figure out a more permanent solution to this problem.

"I guess I can always call on Milton for help," I say. "Or maybe Madden would know what to do." I think that one over. I'm not particularly ready to tell my older brother, the one person I've always looked up to, about this just yet. "Or Everleigh," I amend, naming my sister. She's only a year younger than me, and we've always been close.

"Or you just handle it," she suggests, and the way she gives me this sort of no-nonsense attitude is kind of, dare I say…sexy?

Fuck.

No.

Not sexy.

Just…demanding.

But she's eleven years younger than me. She doesn't get to be demanding with me.

"Don't say a word about this to anyone. I can do whatever the fuck I feel like I need to do, and I don't need you telling me otherwise," I snap at her, and then I take my protein shake and walk out of the room with it to go take a shower.

CHAPTER 5
Ainsley Riggs

Completely and Totally Intimidated

Have his abs always looked like they were carved by some artist who makes art that's not realistic? Because nobody's body has any real business looking like that. Is he some AI-generated creature?

That's twice in the last seven hours I've had the pleasure of sneaking a peek at his abdomen, and good Lord, those abs are something else.

Dexter Bradley was always something special to look at. He's the hottest of Ivy's older brothers, but he's really peaking here in his thirties. His body is out of this world, and he's got this worldly experience in the way his dark, mysterious eyes land on a person. It's enough to feel completely and totally intimidated.

I'm just here to help, though. I'm not here to study his abs or feel intimidated by him. It's a job and a place to lay low when I was desperate for both of those things.

Desperate for Dex Bradley I am not.

I just got dumped on what will be on national television in a few months…or national streaming, anyway. International, probably. Hell, I don't know how this works, but I can't imagine it's going to cast *me* in a very positive light when I'm made the laughingstock because Jordan wasn't ready for marriage.

At some point, I'll have to face Jordan. Today, likely. Before or after my interview with producers. Definitely at the reunion show in a few months. But at least it feels like I have something to come back to now. I didn't have that when I ran out of the chapel yesterday. I was alone.

Was that really just yesterday? It feels like forever ago.

And now that I've had a minute away from the cameras and producers pushing me in a certain direction, I can see I was never really *in love* with Jordan. I think I was in love with the idea of being in love, but considering the only tears I shed were from embarrassment as I ran from the chapel, I'm not convinced it was really *love* that I felt for him.

I certainly wasn't ready to *marry* him. I thought I was, but as the saying goes, hindsight is twenty-twenty.

And in hindsight, it's pretty damn clear to see that I was desperate for a path to my happily ever after, and that's why I took a nontraditional approach to try to get there. I had people who wanted to make good television telling me I was ready, he was ready, and we were perfect together.

But today, I can see that I still have plenty of time ahead of me. There's no rush. I'm only twenty-two. Sure, my parents got married at twenty. My mother is a mere twenty-one years older than me. My aunts and uncles all married young, too.

But that doesn't mean I have to take the same path. I guess I've just put a lot of pressure on finding the one and having kids at a young age since my parents did, and it's possible—probable, even—that's just not the way life was meant to be for me.

Instead of focusing on any of that, though, I can't seem to stop myself from being a little angry with how Dex just stormed out of the room. I get that this is new and scary for him. It is for me, too, honestly. But he's acting like a child and not giving himself nearly enough credit. He's stronger and more capable than he thinks he is, but he's already decided he isn't.

I guess somehow it's up to me to make him see what he's capable of.

I'm pretty sure he's made up his mind, though. He doesn't seem like the type of person who ever wanted kids. He's too selfish, too into the pleasures of life rather than sacrificing for someone else. I don't know him very well, but I know enough to know that. He already said that me being here is temporary until he can figure out a more permanent solution.

And then what?

This poor, sweet baby goes to live with strangers who don't share his blood, and I just…go back to Chicago?

None of that sounds right, to be honest. I realize Dex is a stranger to him, but I see a lot of similarities between them. They both have brown eyes, dark hair, and are prone to throwing tantrums. They both rely on everyone around them to clean up their messes—which makes sense for a six-month-old. Not so much for a grown-ass man.

And maybe that's the *why* in all this—why I agreed to be on a reality television show when it's fully not at all who I am. Why I agreed to come to Vegas for this. Why Jordan said no. Why I ran.

Maybe fate was at work all along, and I was always meant to plow right into Dex's chest at the exact moment when he needed me.

Fine, it's a little far-fetched. Fate doesn't work like that in real life. But a girl can daydream…especially about those abs.

I get Jack down for his after-lunch nap, and Dex is standing by the windows in the family room when I walk out. I take just the briefest moment to look out over that view with him.

It's gorgeous. I can see all the hotels along Las Vegas Boulevard, and for a girl from Chicago who never left the eighteen-hundred-square-foot modest home she shared with four siblings and two parents, staying in a place like this, even short-term, is pretty damn exciting.

I sigh. "Jack is down, and I need to get going."

He glances at me. "Milton said he'd set up a ride for you."

I open my mouth to protest, but he holds up a hand and turns back toward the window.

"Please, it's the least I can do for what you've already done for me. I'm sorry I walked out earlier. This is just all…a lot." He doesn't turn to look at me as he says the words.

"I know it is, Dex. But you'll learn." I keep my eyes out on the view, too. I feel him turn to study my profile, and I refuse to be intimidated by it. "You got this. You can do hard things."

"What if I don't want to? What if there are other answers out there? What if this was never meant for me?" He's quiet as he says the words, and frankly, I'm shocked he's being so vulnerable with me. He sounds like he's truly at a crossroads and not sure what to do.

I'm careful to keep my eyes out on the view rather than giving away what I'm really thinking—just as I'm careful with the words in my reply. "Only you know how to answer those questions. Now that you know about him, are you going to step up and take responsibility? And if not, what's the other option? Could you give him up just like that and never think of him again? If you truly could do that, then you already know the answer."

He's quiet a few beats, and then he whispers, "What if I can't do this?"

I finally turn to look at him, and his anxious eyes meet mine. I lift a shoulder. "What if you can?"

He sighs.

"It's not going to be easy, but maybe you'll even surprise yourself. And I'm here to help you," I say.

"Yeah, but for how long?" he asks.

"As long as you need. I already walked away from Chicago, and it's not like I could find anything as a communications major that's paying me what you are." I smirk a little at that, and he chuckles. I glance at my watch. "Let's talk more when I get back. I need to get to this interview."

He nods, and then he surprises me by setting his hands on my shoulders, and he sort of squares off at me. "You got this, Ains. You can do hard things, and I think you might even surprise yourself."

I clench my jaw as I fight back tears. He just threw all my own clichés right back in my face, and somehow, they're simply everything I needed to hear.

"Thanks, Dex."

"Go get 'em, champ." He drops his hands from my shoulders.

"Champ?" I ask, and I can't help a giggle.

He shrugs. "Go be a champion."

"You don't do pep talks for women very often, and it shows."

He chuckles. "Okay, wildcat."

I wrinkle my nose.

"Vixen?"

I cross my arms over my chest.

"She-wolf?"

I tap my fingers on the opposite arm.

"Warrior Queen?"

I raise my brows. "Ooh, that one. I like it."

"You got it, WQ." He nods resolutely.

I roll my eyes. "We need to work on your nicknames."

"Duly noted. Now get to your interview and be the warrior queen you are and we'll work it out later."

I laugh. "Deal. And Dex?"

He looks at me with raised brows.

"If Jack wakes up, you'll be fine."

He draws in a deep breath through his nose and lets it go slowly. "I got this."

I nod. "You got this. And so do I."

He nods, and I head out.

I'm completely and totally intimidated in a different way when I walk through the front doors of the hotel where the entire staff of the show has been working and filming for the last month. I head toward the conference room where we've been taping our confessionals, and the first person I spot is Jen, the producer who always interviews me. She raises her brows and gives me a pointed look at the same time.

"I can't believe you ran and didn't even give us the courtesy of filming it," she says rather than greeting me with a salutation like a normal person.

"I'm sorry."

"It's fine, but since you broke your contractual obligations, you won't receive your payment."

I press my lips together. It wasn't much, a small amount meant to offset the fact that many of us quit or left jobs behind to be here. Enough to cover some of our lost wages, I guess. But not as much as Dex is paying me to help out with Jack.

I'd like to think that's not involved in my motivation to convince him that he should keep his son close, but the selfish side of me has to admit some hard truths.

I like it here in Vegas. I like it at Dex's place. I even like Jack already. We're bonding even though we just met yesterday. I don't have anything to return to in Chicago except for my group of friends, and even there we're losing touch. I only see Ivy a few times a month at best, and she's my closest friend. The others scattered after we graduated from college.

"If you're already not paying me, do I still need to do the interviews?"

"Viewers will need the closure to your storyline, and if you don't do the interview, you'll look like a bitter little girl who didn't get her way," she says.

I'm not sure what prompted me to think we were friends because her words show me how very much we are not. "Fine. Let's get this over with."

She nods to the chair for me to sit in, and we have our own little corner where she can fire questions at me with four cameras catching my every move from different angles.

"Why'd you run?" she asks first.

"I was embarrassed that I thought I was in love and said I'd marry him only to have him say no."

"Restate the question," she reminds me.

I sigh. "I ran out of the wedding because I was embarrassed that he said no when I said yes. I know now that I was never really in love with him, and I'm not just saying that to save face. I've thought a lot about it since I ran out twenty-four hours ago, and the moment I stepped away from the cameras, I realized the truth. He's not really what I want. I fell in love with the idea of love, and I thought Jordan and I could get there. I thought maybe we'd spend our first year of marriage falling for each other even more, and we'd eventually travel together to our happy ending. But things work out the way they're supposed to, and I've already formed a plan for what comes next."

"What's the plan?" she asks.

"I'm going to stay here in Vegas and see what opportunities await." I look up and feign dreaminess, and I hope that's all she wrote.

Nope.

She asks me about a hundred more questions, and I'm at the interview for a solid three hours.

Jack will be up by now. He'll be hungry.

I need to get back…but at the same time, I need Dex to see that he can do this on his own. I just don't want him to think I've abandoned him.

Jen finally gives my phone back to me, and I realize I don't have Dex's number to let him know I'm on my way. But the car Milton sent me in is waiting for me, so I hop in and head back to whatever the future holds for me.

CHAPTER 6

DEX BRADLEY

Peepee Teepee

Where is she?

It's been ninety minutes since she left, and the kid is going to wake up soon.

I've done my best to be as quiet as possible, but I've already decided once she's back and he's not in his room, we'll move his room so it's not so close to my weight room.

I don't know what else to do with myself, and I still need a solution to this problem. I decide to call my sister—not the one Ainsley is friends with, but Everleigh, the one who's only a year younger than me.

"Hey Dex," she answers.

"You sound tired."

"Thanks?" she says like a question. "I'm not tired, just busy." She's firm and to the point, which makes me think she doesn't have time for this conversation. "What do you need?"

"Nothing," I mutter. "Call me when you're not so busy."

"No, wait," she says, probably correctly reading that I was about to hang up. "Talk to me. Why are you calling? You never call."

"I, uh…I have a bit of a situation."

"A situation? Do you need to lay low at Madden's place until camp starts? I think he's in San Diego for now."

"I just spent the last month laying low there." I blow out a breath but don't let her get on my ass about not calling her while I was in town as long as I was. "I guess I got a woman pregnant around fifteen months ago."

She gasps.

"She had the kid, and then she got arrested, and she dropped the kid off with me while she does her time."

"Oh my God, Dex," she says. "When did all this go down?"

"Yesterday."

"Whoa. Okay, so you have *a kid?*"

"Yeah. And I have no idea what the fuck to do with it. Help."

"I'm an auntie?" she asks softly, and she sounds nearly emotional over it.

"Focus, Ev. I need help."

"Shit, Dex. Okay, do you know anyone who could help you out?" she asks.

"I actually ran into one of Ivy's friends who was looking for a job. Long story short, she's been a fucking lifesaver while I try to figure out what to do."

"What do you mean, *figure out what to do?*" she demands, and she's even more no-nonsense than Ainsley.

"You know…find a more permanent solution," I say.

"Like a nanny?"

"Like someone who can take him," I mutter.

"You don't want him?"

"Jesus. Why not get straight to the heart of the matter?" I realize that's my sarcasm biting, but I don't really know any other way. I clear my throat as I try to figure out what I *do* want. "Look, I never said that. But I only have a few weeks to figure this out. Keeping him, raising him…I'm not convinced it's the best option for either of us."

"Him?"

"Jack. He's six months old. His mom just surrendered herself to jail for the next two years, but she signed sole custody over to me before she left when she dropped him off yesterday."

"Oh, Dex," she says, and she sounds sympathetic. "You can't just give him away. He's your baby. I didn't want this huge crisis at work, but it's still my issue to take care of. You know what I mean?"

"Yeah, you've got work to do. I get it."

"No," she says firmly. "That's not what I mean. I mean, just because something lands on your lap that you didn't necessarily want doesn't mean you have as many options as you seem to think. It's your responsibility to take care of your child. What does Dad always say about legacy? What would Mom and Dad think about you just giving someone away who has the Bradley blood running through his veins?"

"I knew I should've called Ford instead of you."

"The reality is the same either way you look at it. I'm happy to help however I can, but I think if you set aside your fear for a second and really take a look inside, you know what's right and what's wrong in this situation," she says. Her words are tough, but her tone is gentle. "I wish we were closer so I could hold my nephew."

"Come visit me," I suggest.

I hear some rustling through the baby monitor. He might be up soon, and Ainsley isn't back yet.

"I'll try. It's been hard to break away from work. But now that there's an actual reason besides my dumb big brother, maybe I'll prioritize Vegas."

I laugh. "Thanks, Ev. You always know just how to make me feel better."

"I figured that was why you called. Listen, you'll be fine. No parent knows what they're doing when they first have a kid.

Yours is just, well, six months older than most kids are when parents get started."

"And there's often a significant other in the equation," I mutter.

"Valid point, but we play the cards we're dealt. And knowing how you've always been a little scrappy but managed to pull yourself up more than once, I think you've got this under control, too."

"Scrappy?" I repeat. "No one has *ever* called Dex Bradley scrappy."

"No one except his baby sister."

I can practically see the smirk on her face. "Well, thanks for nothing."

"Dex, seriously, if you need anything, call me. I'll do whatever I can to help."

"Thanks. Don't say a fucking word to anybody about any of this." I end the call before she gets mushy and says something stupid like she loves me, and as much as I hate to admit it, I think she *did* help.

Reality hasn't set in yet, and maybe it won't for a while. But I think she might be right.

As much as my first instinct was to figure out a solution to this problem, it's entirely possible that I myself am the solution.

It's a little over an hour later when he's crying, and I'm *trying* to change his diaper, but the kid is wiggly as fuck. I don't want to damage any of the family jewels, so to speak, so I'm careful to wipe him the way I watched Ainsley do last night, but then the kid decides he needs to take a piss.

There's no ready, aim, fire. It's just fire.

The piss arches straight into the air and right onto my shirt, and I don't know what the hell I'm supposed to do, so I panic for a few very wet seconds before I use the fresh diaper I was trying to open up, and I cover his entire area with it so at least I'm not still getting pissed on by my own kid.

He stops crying, at least. And now he's giggling.

He's fucking laughing at me as I pull the wet diaper away to inspect the damage.

The table is wet. The pad I have the kid on is wet. I'm wet. Jack is wet.

And he still isn't wearing a goddamn diaper.

I pull his clothes all the way off, and I make sure he's secure on the table before I pull my shirt off and toss it on top of his wet clothes. My shorts got a little on them, too, so I pull those off as well.

And that's how Ainsley finds us after three hours away. She peeks her head into the baby's room, sees Jack on the table naked and giggling along with me standing there in my underwear cursing my entire existence.

Her eyes are wide as she looks to me for my reaction.

"How was your interview?" I ask calmly.

She bursts into laughter.

"That good?"

She walks into the room. "What happened?"

"I was trying to change him, and he pissed all over me. Kid's got good aim, that's for sure."

"Just practicing for writing his name in the snow in a few years." She shrugs.

"He's got me for a dad plus four uncles. He doesn't need to practice quite yet, and there are plenty of guys who can train him."

"My mom said there's a thing called a peepee teepee to cover little boys up so they don't do that."

"Peepee teepee?" I repeat. "Jesus, I have a lot to learn." I stare at the mess on the table and muse, "Do they make those for adults?"

She shrugs. "Just seems like one more thing to get in the way. Kid or adult."

I laugh. "Will you get his diaper on while I go get some clothes?"

She shakes her head. "You get his diaper on. I didn't mean to interrupt."

I clench my jaw. I'm not used to being so goddamn far out of my element, and it makes me uneasy. I'm used to living life how I want. I'm not used to having to ask for help. "I don't know how."

"You do. Give it a try."

"I did, and I got pissed on," I hiss. She's close enough that she'll take over if I walk out, so I do.

I'm paying her to do this for me, not to make me feel like I'm incapable of doing it myself.

I take a quick shower to rinse the smell of urine off and pull out some clean clothes, and when I'm dressed, I find her and Jack in the family room on another play structure. This time Jack is sitting upright and slamming his hands on a part of the play gym that starts playing a song every time he hits it, so we're getting the same note on repeat since he's hitting it over and over while she absently scrolls her phone.

Truth be told, I'm starting to get a headache, and I'm not paying her to scroll. I'm about to snap about that when she looks up at me.

"Can we take him to a playground?" she asks. "Fresh air would be good for him, and then we won't have to listen to this nonsense. I found a few nearby we can try." She flashes her phone at me to show me the proximity of all the playgrounds nearby.

I'm glad I didn't snap, and her question goes another long fucking way to make me feel like a dick.

I'm hoping at some point I can get my shit together, but it doesn't seem like that day is today.

CHAPTER 7
Ainsley Riggs

Birdie

I can't help when my eyes edge over to the speedometer in his car.

He's going sixty-two. Sixty-two! The speed limit here is forty-five. There is literally no reason he needs to be weaving in and out of traffic and changing lanes every two seconds to get one car ahead. We're just out on a leisurely drive to take the baby to a park, and he's driving like his wife's going into labor and he's going to miss the birth or something.

But I refuse to be a backseat driver, especially when he seems to be easily angered by my words.

I can't imagine *why* he's angry, but it seems like he keeps storming out of the room like a child whenever I'm around. Either that or he uses sarcasm as a shield. I'm getting the sense he doesn't really know how to ask for help, but I'm also trying to get him to see that he's perfectly capable of all the things he thinks he can't do.

It's a weird line to straddle, and we're all just doing our best. Me included.

The tires screech as he comes to a stop on the side of the road by the park, and I walk around to the driver's side to get the baby out of the back of the car, where he's happily cooing in his car carrier.

I won't get into all the swearing that occurred as Dex installed the base for the car carrier, but there was definitely some colorful language before the task was complete.

I unbuckle the baby and grab him into my arms, and I remember hearing once that you're supposed to narrate to babies so they can hear your voice and start associating sounds with words, so I chat with him as I carry him toward the playground.

"Do you see the blue slides? There are three of them. Two are straight, and one is twirly. Do you want to go down the twirly one on my lap? I've always loved twirly slides, and there's nobody else here, so we can do whatever we want."

Dex is a few feet behind us. "Are you talking to me? Because if you want me to ride your lap, I won't say no."

My cheeks heat in total mortification that he thought I was issuing an invitation to him. I wasn't. In fact, I haven't issued that particular invitation to *anybody* yet, let alone a very experienced bad boy who's eleven years older than me. "I was talking to the baby."

"Why? He can't understand you." He shrugs, and if he's embarrassed by his sexual innuendo from a moment ago, he doesn't show it.

"The more he hears words, the more he'll start to understand them," I mutter as I try to pull myself together. Honestly, not looking directly at him helps.

"I guess that makes sense."

"But to address your other question, I don't want you to ride my lap," I say, and as soon as the words are out, I have literally no idea why I said them.

My cheeks turn pink.

"Really?" he asks, genuine surprise in his voice. "Usually when I offer, I don't get such a quick rejection."

I press my lips together. "You drive too fast, drink too much, and throw temper tantrums. I'm good."

He narrows his eyes at me. "And you're my little sister's best friend who's way too young for me anyway."

"Good. I'm glad we're on the same page." A hummingbird chooses that moment to flap his wings at a million miles per hour and hover beside me, and I duck down and pull the baby in closer to me to protect him.

"What the fuck are you doing?" Dex asks me.

"Protecting the baby!" I practically scream.

"From…a hummingbird?" He's laughing at me, and I don't care. "It's gone now. You can stop freaking out."

"Look, I was attacked by one once, okay?" I say as I straighten, and my cheeks are burning again.

"Hummingbirds don't attack humans."

"I had on a bright floral shirt when I was a kid, and I was standing near a feeder. It landed on me and scared me. Now you know my most embarrassing secret. I'm terrified of hummingbirds. And butterflies." I purse my lips and try once again to pull it together, this time as I look at him.

Dammit. It's a huge mistake, especially when he grins at me.

That smile is really something else. It's like it's lighting up this entire playground.

"Okay, Birdie."

I roll my eyes. "I liked Warrior Queen much better."

"But this one just fits you so much more." He shrugs.

"I hate you," I mutter.

"No, you don't," he retorts, and honestly…he's probably right about that.

I hand the baby to Dex, and he holds him awkwardly as I climb up the play structure since the only way to the top is via a rock wall or a ladder. "Hand him up to me," I say.

"How?"

"What do you mean, *how*? Just hand him over." I bend down over the side of the structure since I'm up high, and he sort of lifts him up as ungraciously as he can. I grab hold of the baby and pull him up toward me, and then I sit on the twirly slide, put Jack on my lap, and slide down.

Dex is waiting at the bottom for us, and even he smiles when he sees the look of glee on his son's face at his first ride down the slide on Auntie Ainsley's lap.

Jack giggles and kicks his feet, so I hand him off to Dex once more and climb back up. I motion for him to pass him over again, and again, I end up reaching over and grabbing him before we slide down.

Dex is waiting at the bottom for us again.

"Do you want to slide down with him?" I ask.

"That's okay," he says, and I don't push it.

Instead, I go down the slide probably thirty times with Jack on my lap, and then we move over toward the baby swings, where we buckle him in and take turns pushing him. "Did his mom ever take him to the park?" I ask.

He shrugs. "I have literally no idea what she did with him."

"I'm sorry, Dex. I can imagine how hard all this has been on you, but he's in good hands now."

He presses his lips together as if he doesn't really believe that to be true. "Yeah. I got lucky when I ran into you."

I elbow him. "I meant you."

We're both wearing sunglasses, and he glances away from me. I take the moment to study him. He's a broody, grumpy, really, really freaking hot bad boy pro football star.

And I'm his little sister's best friend and new live-in nanny.

And after his little sexual innuendo earlier…the idea of sex is front and center in my brain.

I'm a virgin, not that I'd ever admit that to Dex in a million years or for a million dollars.

I've had boyfriends, but none that seemed worthy of something so important. But I've held onto it so long now that I sort of just want to get it over with.

You know…with a broody, grumpy, hot bad boy who knows *exactly* what he's doing.

Like Dex Bradley.

CHAPTER 8

DEX BRADLEY

With or Without You

When my father said he wanted to see me, I immediately told him I'd meet him at his hotel. I'm not ready to admit everything to him yet when it's still so new to me. I've only known about the kid since Sunday, and I promised my dad we could meet up on Thursday.

The problem is that he wants to talk about illegal activities, so it's not like we can just head to a restaurant and chat over steaks. He was a little offended I didn't invite him to my place, but I don't really give a fuck about his feelings any more than he gives fucks about mine.

Hotel it is.

Ainsley and Jack are at home, and so far, nobody is the wiser to my little situation. After my talk with Everleigh the other day, I guess I'm starting to warm up to the idea that he's going to be around, but I'm keeping all options and avenues open. And that's really the root of why I'm not ready to tell my dad about him just yet.

Or any of my other siblings—provided Ev didn't tell anyone as I requested before I hung up on her. Or the press.

I'm not even totally sure why I'm meeting my father. I already know what he's going to say, but he'll do it in person in a more convincing way where it's harder to say no to him. That's how he operates. He's not here for business—at least not *legitimate* business. He's here to run this by me and get me to sign off on it before the season starts.

He has no idea that I'm being crushed by the weight of everything else around me, and he's just piling on more.

But maybe this is the exact distraction I need. The thrill I've been chasing. The excitement of Vegas, where *I* get to be the house that always wins. It's those conflicting sides pulling at me again—loyalty to family versus my own needs.

So I'm here to hear him out.

I knock tentatively on his hotel room door, and he opens it a second later as if he was standing by waiting for me. He's got a suite, and the main living area has a conference table where he already has his plans mapped out.

"I know you're a busy man, too busy to do dinner with your old man, so I'll get right to it," he says, laying on the guilt trip thick before he gets underway.

It's all so predictable.

"As you know, building a legacy is something I hold in the highest regard. It's why I started Bradley Group, and it's why I carefully and quietly started building something off the grid to create generational wealth for the Bradley family. But Chicago has limitations that Vegas simply doesn't."

"Dad, if you're running an underground casino, you'll need to be even more careful here," I point out. "Vegas already has casinos that operate *legally*, so what do you have that will attract people to an underground operation?"

"That's the thing, son. We'll start as a private lounge. High rollers. Invite only. Your connections, like we talked about. All aboveboard. All legal. But that's just the front for the backroom operation we'll also be running. That's the one that'll earn us respect here in this city. That's the one that'll put us on the map, and before long, we won't just be running some private club. We'll own the entire goddamn Strip." He grins proudly, as if he's the first guy who ever came up with this plan.

"The entire Strip is already spoken for. You've got Wynn, MGM, Caesars. We can't compete with those huge names."

"You don't think Bradley could fit right in with those? Look, they each started somewhere. I did my research. One of them started with a small investment in a hotel downtown when he was twenty-five, and now he owns hundreds of acres of land on Las Vegas Boulevard plus hotels around the world." He shrugs. "Why couldn't that be us?"

"Because you said it. He started with a small investment in a hotel downtown a million years ago. Not with a shady private club covering an illegal poker room." I shrug back at him, and he hates that I'm so much like him.

Except I'm not. We're different. I may like chasing thrills, but I'm not about to risk my contract over a stupid idea like this one.

Except if it's underground, theoretically nobody would ever know. Right?

Probably not, since the feds are already on his ass.

My phone starts ringing, and I send it to voicemail when I see it's my publicist. I'll call him back when I'm on my way home.

"Look, the plans are already in place. I'm doing this with or without you, Dex. With would be better. I'd love to cut you in on the action and the profits, which will be huge. There will be energy and excitement, and I know you live for those thrills and risks. You know people out here, and you have connections here that I don't. It'll benefit us both to have you in on it, and it will all be yours once you retire from the game."

I press my lips together. I want to say no. I want to stay out of the illegal, shady shit he's doing.

But I'm tempted.

His words about thrills and risks hit exactly where he intends for them to.

And aside from all that, I don't *hate* the idea of setting up a legacy for my own kid. I wasn't ever planning on having one, but now that I do, pending the results of the DNA test we had done yesterday, I want to set up the sort of future where he doesn't have to worry about being pressured into doing shit like this for his father. I may be like my dad in a lot of ways, but I don't want to be like him when it comes to parenthood.

Not that I have the first clue about what I'm doing…but if I'm setting up a legacy for my kid, I want him to know that he can take it or leave it, and I want him to be able to make decisions for himself.

Besides, just because my father starts it with illegal activity doesn't mean I have to run it the same way once it's mine.

I have a kid to think about now, and it's an interesting dynamic to be here with my father, who *doesn't* consider the needs of his offspring. I guess this is one way to set the kid up financially, anyway.

I already know I'm going to agree to my dad's terms against my will in the end anyway. That's just what he does. I decide to just skip past the next level of guilt trips and whatever hidden threats he has and get to the point. I should get back home anyway.

"Fifty-fifty split on whatever clients I bring in," I say to him.

He makes a face as if to say I'm crazy, his brows rising and his lips twisting as if he's holding back a laugh. He shakes his head. "No. I wasn't even going to offer you a percentage. A monthly paycheck instead."

I fold my arms over my chest. "No deal. You need me more than I need you."

He rolls his eyes, which is his own defense mechanism when he knows he's been outsmarted by one of his kids. I've outsmarted him enough over the years to read that signal.

"Fine," he mutters. "You get five percent plus a monthly paycheck."

"I don't want the monthly paycheck. I want forty percent of profits, not a cent lower, and I get access to the books." I know how he works. If he's willing to open an illegal gambling ring, he's willing to screw over his own kid.

He sighs. "Twenty percent. It's the highest I'll go."

I press my lips together and shake my head. "No deal." I stand to leave, and when he speaks next, that's when I know I've got him.

"Twenty-five, no books."

I turn to look at him. "Books, thirty-five. And you operate it all without me. I just swing by when I can. Final offer."

"You'll need to bring all the whales."

I nod. I was going to anyway. Of course I'll bring the whales—those with lots of money to burn. The more money that runs through this club, legal side or not, and the more I take from them, the more I line my own pockets.

He sighs and looks out the window. "Fine. Done."

After he amends the paperwork he brought along spelling out the details of the *legal* private club that he'll turn into his lawyer plus the contract that'll stay between us in good faith, and after the ink is dry on my signature on all that paperwork, I say, "I would've taken thirty." I smirk.

"I would've given you forty." He mirrors my smirk right back at me.

Fucker.

CHAPTER 9

Ainsley Riggs

You Look Nice

Dex is quiet when he returns from his meeting, and he doesn't say much about what happened, but he does go straight for the liquor cabinet and pours himself a healthy glass of whiskey before he stands by his window looking out over that gorgeous view. It's nighttime now, and the lights glitter in the not-so-far distance, casting a glow that makes it look simply magical.

"Jack go down okay?" he asks.

"Yep. He's starting to like his baths since we gave him those squeaky toys."

"Not terribly sorry I missed out," he murmurs, and I laugh.

"I don't blame you. I can't say I escaped without a headache."

He glances over at me. "You okay?"

"Oh, yeah. I'm fine."

"Hey, so my publicist wants me to get more involved with some charity stuff after, uh, a little scandal went down a while back. Would you want to go with me to an event tomorrow night? I know it's short notice, but he got me in and said I should bring a date."

Holy. Shit.

Did he just ask me out on a date?

And…he doesn't have anyone else to ask?

"What about the baby?" I ask.

"We can find a babysitter." He shrugs.

"I'd love to go." I really wasn't expecting this. I figured he'd sort of hide me out here with the baby, but I guess he did tell the mother that I'm his girlfriend, so maybe he wants to push that a step further and be seen in public with me. I decide to ask because I'm nothing if not direct. "Are you just wanting to be seen with me because you told Jack's mom that I'm your girlfriend?"

I wish I would've asked before I agreed to go.

He doesn't seem affected by my question. He keeps his gaze focused out the window. "Yeah."

"Oh." I try to hide the disappointment I feel in that. He wasn't asking me on a date after all. Not really. "We should probably tell Ivy about what's going on since presumably the press will be there."

"I don't want her to know about the baby yet." He takes a sip from his glass.

"Then how do we explain why we're together?"

He sighs as he turns toward me. "Good question. I guess we could just keep it vague. Say we ran into each other and you're helping me out with some stuff around the house while you lay low after your reality show ordeal."

I bite my bottom lip as I think it over, and then I nod. "Yeah. That could work."

I don't particularly want to call her just yet since she'll want to know all the details about my appearance on the show. I'm still technically bound by an NDA, which I can conveniently blame for pretty much all of it. But I miss her, and I miss my family. I'm fairly close with my mom, dad, and four younger siblings. Claire is only three years younger than me, and Holly is five years younger. My two brothers, Carson and Henry, are fourteen and twelve, respectively, and I spent a lot of hours babysitting the two of them when they were little before I started playing volleyball and the sport ate all my after-school hours.

"I'll just text her," I say. "My parents, too."

"Mm," he murmurs, and he continues his brooding.

"What should I wear tomorrow to the event?"

He clears his throat. "It's formal, so a gown if you have one."

"I don't."

He nods as if that's no issue at all. "I'll have Milton send up a selection of designer gowns in the morning. What's your dress and shoe size?"

"Stop, Dex. I can't possibly let you do that."

"Why not?" he asks, nearly affronted at my rejection.

"Because it's too much money to spend. Designer gowns are a waste of money."

"You're in a new tax bracket, sweetheart. Get used to it."

My jaw drops. "Are you serious right now?"

"Yes. If you're attending charity events with me, you need to dress the part. If you think they're a waste, keep them all and donate them to a women's shelter when you're done wearing them. Now what's your goddamn dress and shoe size?"

I huff out a sigh as I give him my details since the donation thing isn't a bad idea, and then I head to my room to draft a text to Ivy. As it turns out, the content of the text to my best friend is harder to come up with than I thought.

I stare at what I drafted, and eventually I click the send button.

Me: *Done with the show, can't talk about it. I randomly ran into Dex and he needed some help. Since I don't have a job at home anymore, I'm staying here for a bit. Miss you so much. Xo*

My phone rings less than thirty seconds after I click send, and I know I'll regret it, but I pick up.

"Hey, Ivy!" I answer, faking a cheerfulness I don't feel.

"Fuck this *can't talk about it* bullshit. Spill the tea, babe!"

I laugh. "I really can't."

"When you say you're *staying here for a bit*, do you mean Vegas? Or my brother's place?"

I clear my throat. "Both."

"Okay, so that tells me you're not living with whoever you were with on the show…unless they make you live apart. Did you get married?" she asks.

"I really can't talk about it," I say. "I'm sorry."

She lets out a frustrated breath. "Fine. What did Dex need help with?"

"Just like some stuff around his place. Picking up, that sort of thing."

"You're his housekeeper?"

More like his nanny, I think to myself. "Something like that, I guess. I'm going with him to some charity thing tomorrow."

"Ew, Ains. He's, like, so old."

I laugh. "And so not my type. It's not a date. I'm just being the wholesome foil to his bad boy."

"Well, be careful. Nothing is sacred to him, if you know what I mean."

I do know exactly what she means, and how two siblings could have *such* different values is a total mystery to me.

Like me, Ivy's a virgin too.

Dex is decidedly not.

Neither of us is waiting for any particular reason. It's unusual in this day and age, maybe, but neither of us found anyone worth giving it up to.

I'm two years older than her, and she's going into her senior year of college while I've got a year of work under my belt already.

"Nothing to worry about there. Believe me." I'm starting to wonder if I'm saying it to convince myself, too.

Because there's definitely an attraction there on my part, even if he'll never see me as anything more than the hired help.

Though the next evening, I feel his eyes on me as I walk out into the kitchen in one of the ballgowns Milton gave me to try on. I kept several of them for future events at the suggestion of Dex, but this one is just a simple black A-line dress with a plunging neckline that sinks down into a banded waist, and he's looking at me like I'm walking into the room naked. His teeth are sort of bared, and he looks…hungry.

Maybe I'm seeing what I want to see and he's just looking at me with normal eyes. Or maybe he's just actually hungry. Maybe I'm hungry, too. I mean, I'm *hungry*-hungry, like for food, since I haven't eaten since breakfast. But when I look at him, I think maybe I'm hungry for something else.

I don't know.

I don't exactly have a lot of experience with this sort of thing.

I wore darker makeup tonight, and a glittery barrette is holding back a French braid down the side of my hair that ties back into a curly bun. I don't often put in the effort with my shorter hair, but when I have the time, I love trying out different hairstyles. Meanwhile, Dex has probably gotten used to seeing me with no makeup and air-dried hair.

That's probably why he's looking at me like that. He doesn't recognize me.

I almost don't recognize myself.

Milton's sixteen-year-old niece, Madison, was able to babysit for us on short notice, and he's right downstairs should she need anything. The baby is in good hands, and I'm learning more and more about Milton and how he's a pretty good dude.

I take Jack from Madison and give him a squeeze since I've become the closest thing he has to a mother over the last week—a scary thought indeed—and then Dex asks if I'm ready.

I nod, and we head out to the elevator. He's quiet as we step on, and I wonder what the night has in store for us.

"You look nice," he says awkwardly as the doors seal us into privacy.

"So do you."

He clears his throat. "I meant to say beautiful. Not nice. You look beautiful, Ainsley."

My cheeks burn at his compliment and the way his voice gets all raspy when he says my name. I force myself to remember that this isn't a real date. He lied to Jack's mother that I'm his girlfriend, and his publicist wanted him at a charity event. That's all this is. "Thank you."

But when we arrive on the red carpet and he grabs my hand, it suddenly doesn't *feel* like that's all this is.

"Dex, who's your date?" some reporter yells.

He looks over at me, and I look up at him. We ignore the people yelling at us, and I'll be dubbed the mystery woman in the tabloids by morning.

I kind of like being Dex's mystery woman despite what I told Ivy.

Tonight's charity event is Vegas-themed, and it features both gambling and drinking. We start by heading over toward the bar.

I've seen Dex with a drink several times in the week I've been living with him, but as for myself…I'm not much of a drinker at all. I hate the way wine tastes, and beer is disgusting. I can tolerate a vodka and Sprite if it's heavy on the Sprite and has a cherry or three thrown in, and so that's what I ask the bartender for.

Dex opts for straight whiskey, and I'm not the best at hiding what I'm thinking. He chuckles when he sees my nose wrinkled in disgust.

"You don't like whiskey?" he asks.

I shake my head.

"You've probably only ever had the cheap shit. Try this." He hands me his glass, and I take a sip. As I do, I realize how very much it's something two people might do on a date.

But he's right. The sip I take is smooth, where the whiskey I've tried before had a bitter aftertaste and a gross burn as it slid down my throat. This one pulses a warm feeling through my entire chest.

Sort of like Dex is starting to do.

We take our drinks and head over toward one of the poker tables, where Dex proceeds to teach me how to play Texas Hold'em. We watch at first since the tables are full, and he explains each part of the game to me. The goal is to make the best hand with two cards you're dealt down and the five cards the dealer has face-up.

Someone loses all their money and gets up, and he nods to the chair as if I should sit.

"Dex, I don't have any money," I whisper to him.

"I got you. You're just sitting in for me."

I narrow my eyes at him, but he's insistent. I take the seat.

He stands behind me and gives me instructions as he talks about what to do with each round of betting, and I can smell him this close to me.

It's more intoxicating than my three cherry vodka drink.

On my first hand, I'm dealt two low cards, and nothing matches. I fold my cards after the first three community cards are dealt per Dex's instructions.

On my second hand, I have a queen in my hand, and the dealer flips over a queen. I glance up at him and he raises his brows as if to tell me to stay in this time but not to get crazy just yet.

I end up winning the hand with my two queens.

We go again and again, and I'm starting to get the hang of it when I'm dealt a pair of kings.

The dealer turns over a pair of twos in her first three cards.

I glance up at him, and he tells me to raise the bet.

The fourth card is dealt face-up, and it's a king.

I have a full house.

"Go all in," he murmurs.

I turn back and look at him with a question in my eyes along with a bit of fear.

The dealer is showing a two of hearts, a two of spades, an ace of spades, a four of spades, and a king. If someone has the three and five of spades, they'd beat me.

I realize the chances of that happening are slim, but this is also why I'm not a gambler. There's still a chance someone could beat me.

All in is over two thousand dollars. That's more than my biweekly paychecks were at my dumb old job.

But he's telling me to do it.

He raises his brows. "What's it gonna be?"

I shove all my chips toward the dealer. "All in."

The man two seats away from me also says, "All in." He looks familiar, but then everybody here does. It's a charity event made up of local athletes, celebrities, and millionaires—three things Vegas has no shortage of.

He raises his brows and looks at Dex, and it's clear they know each other. It's also a clear pissing contest.

"The fuck you doing?" Dex asks him, and I twist around and practically see steam coming out of his ears.

"I'm playing poker. What are you doing?" the man asks him.

"Teaching my girl how to play."

I preen at his words. He just publicly called me his girl. That has to mean something.

"Your girl?" he scoffs. The man glances at me a little lewdly, and I'm sure I don't like it.

"Yeah. My fucking girl."

"Fucking sounds about right when it comes to you," he mutters.

And that's it. That's the straw that breaks the camel's back. Or Dex's back.

Before I can even take a breath to figure out what the hell is about to happen, Dex's hand is balled into a fist, and it connects with the man's face. The man is up and out of his chair in a second, ready to fight back.

"Dex!" I scream as anxiety pierces me at witnessing actual violence in front of me, and just as the other man is about to throw a punch back, a group of large men seems to appear as if out of nowhere. One grabs Dex and holds him back while someone else holds the other man back. Security I hadn't even noticed comes running through the room, too.

"He threw the first punch," the dealer says, nodding at Dex.

Oh my God. I'm freaking mortified. Dex punched him because of some rude comment he made about *me*, about *us*, when we're literally nothing more than practical strangers who happen to share a bit of history.

"Come with us, sir," the security man says to Dex. I'm up and out of my chair, game and apparently the two thousand dollars be damned, and the guy Dex punched starts yelling after us as we're guided out toward the ballroom exit.

"It's a charity event, man. What the fuck is wrong with you?"

"Dude, what happened?" another guy asks, following us toward the ballroom exit.

"It was nothing," Dex huffs. He rips his arm away from the security guard, who's guiding him out by the elbow. "Get your paws the fuck off of me."

"My brother is going to rip you a new one," the guy who followed us says.

Why would his brother care?

"Whatever," Dex mutters.

"I'll try to smooth it over for you first," he says.

I'm beyond confused, and I'm not even sure how to ask the questions that are on my mind, but for now, I keep my mouth decidedly shut.

"We're going to have to ask you to leave, sir," security says once we're at the hotel exit.

"Yeah, yeah, yeah," Dex says. "Fuck off."

"Get out," one of the burly guys says, and he sort of pushes Dex, who's already a live wire.

"Dex, come on. Let's just go," I say, and I tug his arm, not really sure how to deal with this situation. He lets me pull him out the front doors, and then we're standing on the sidewalk as we look at the cars still arriving at the event.

It just started. It's so early yet that people are still arriving. I'd barely even touched my drink. I didn't even get to the cherries yet.

"Did you want to call Milton and have him send the car?" I ask.

He presses his lips together and stares at me for a beat.

"Do you want me to order an Uber instead?" I ask, trying to figure out what he wants here.

He shakes his head.

I sigh with frustration. "Come on, Dex. Let's just get out of here. Let's go home and call it a night."

He shakes his head again, and I feel way out of my depth here. I'm not sure how to deal with a dude who just punched another dude. He doesn't think before he acts. He's got a temper, and he doesn't give a shit about consequences. He lives his entire life without thinking through the consequences, actually.

Maybe he needs a walk. He needs to cool off. Or…

"Are you thinking of going back in there? We just got kicked out." I hear the begging in my own voice. I just want to get out of here.

Instead of answering, he grabs my hand. "Come with me."

He starts walking down the long sidewalk toward Las Vegas Boulevard. Soon we're in a crush of people also walking along the Strip on a Friday night.

"Who was that guy you slugged?" I finally ask.

"Jensen Bybee. I've known him a long time. We played in college together, and we were always battling for a starting position. He's a defensive end for the San Diego Storm now. We've never gotten along." He shrugs.

"How come? Because of the starting thing?"

"Nah. Because he's a dick who makes comments like that. And, you know, I slept with his girl once."

"Dex!" I chide.

He holds his hands up. "I didn't know who she was when I slept with her."

"And who was the guy who said his brother would be mad?" I ask.

He glances at me. "Do you watch football?"

I make the face of the awkward emoji with my jaw clenched and a forced, unsmiling face. "Not really."

"Well, if you're living with me, you will."

"How long am I going to be living with you?" I ask.

He glances at me. "Until the kid is eighteen?"

I laugh, but then I get serious when I realize he's maybe not joking. "You're kidding, right?"

"Of course. The guy who said his brother would be mad is Asher Nash, a tight end for my team. His brother is our head coach."

"Ohhh," I say, drawing out the word as it all seems to come together. "Will you get in trouble?"

"For punching an asshole at a charity event?" I nod, and he shrugs. "Maybe. Probably. Who knows?"

"Don't you care about the consequences of your actions?"

"A monetary fine was worth hitting that douchebag for what he said." He presses his lips together with a bit of finality, as if that's that on that.

We keep walking until we head inside the New York–New York Hotel and Casino.

"Where are you taking me?" I ask.

"You'll see."

I follow him through the casino, and we head up an elevator until we're standing in line for… "The roller coaster?"

He shrugs. "Life is full of choices and consequences. They'll be there whether we worry about them or not. Sometimes you just have to let go, say fuck it, and enjoy the ride."

"By riding a roller coaster?"

"By chasing a thrill. By having some goddamn fun once in a while." He pays for two tickets, and I guess I'm doing this whether I want to or not.

CHAPTER 10

DEX BRADLEY

Fuck It

We climb the lift hill toward the peak of the roller coaster with the fake New York skyline to one side and the real Vegas skyline to the other. Instead of watching the hill or either skyline, I'm watching her.

She's something else. She's no-nonsense when it comes to Jack, which is probably exactly what I need. She keeps trying to convince me I can do this. She didn't yell at me for hitting Jensen. She wanted to go home, but she came with me anyway. And now we're on a roller coaster where I'm teaching her to take more risks in life since she's trying so hard to teach me to step up and take responsibility for my actions.

Maybe we could each use a little of what the other has. Maybe we could rub off on one another.

I never saw her as anything more than my little sister's best friend until she walked out in that black dress tonight—barring the ass in the nighttime shorts incident, of course.

The neckline plunges down to her waist but still manages to keep her covered, and all night I've wanted that dress to slip out of place.

Is that so much to ask? Just a tiny peek of her tits?

I raise my hands into the air when we get toward the top, and when she sees me do it, she does it, too. And as we lift over the top of the hill and start the descent down the one-hundred-forty-four-foot drop, I hear her scream, "Fuck it!"

It marks the first time I've heard any curse word drop from her lips, and it was at my own instruction. I yell it along with her, and we're both laughing as the roller coaster whips through twists and turns and glides along a loop, flipping us upside down.

And through the whole thing, that dress stays right in place.

When we get off, she throws her arms around me. I stand stock-still for a beat, surprised that she's touching me but reveling in the feel of her warm body pressed against mine. I slip my arms around her waist and hold her close as I breathe in her soft lavender, and just as a pulse of need darts through me, she pulls back.

She pushes to her tiptoes and presses a kiss to my cheek. "Thanks for making me do that. It was exhilarating."

I don't think I've been kissed on the cheek by a woman since…

The last time I was at home and my mom did it, maybe? Probably not. Mom's not real affectionate.

But it's so wholesome. So sweet. So…not what I was wanting out of this night.

I shake it off. I'm just horny, that's all. It was the rush of the fight and the roller coaster. She's right. I don't care about the consequences of my actions, but acting on whatever it is that I seem to be feeling tonight would be a total mistake. She's here helping me, and I will only fuck that up by acting like I usually do.

I need her help. And as I think back to my conversation with my publicist and that wholesome kiss she just gave me, I think I need her help in more ways than just the one.

Vinny, my publicist, told me I need to project a more wholesome vibe. Punching a dude probably isn't that, but I'll call him and explain why I did it. When he spins it that I was just defending my girl…boom. Wholesome.

Exactly the vibe we're going for while maintaining some semblance of honesty, too, since I don't see Ainsley as the kind of girl who would be okay with getting caught up in a lie. Other than the obvious one that I told Tawny.

We head down to the casino and walk around a little, and I spot a little pizza place. "Are you hungry?" I ask since we missed dinner at the event.

She nods, and we sit together and eat pizza.

"Remember when I told Tawny you're my girlfriend?" I ask after we each dig into our first bite.

She nods.

"I hope you were okay with that. And with being seen with me tonight. The press is going to assume we're together, and I didn't really warn you about that before we went."

"It's fine. Actually, it could really help me since the show I was filming didn't exactly end with me looking the best," she says.

"I'm sure you looked as beautiful as you always do," I say quietly.

Her cheeks redden, but she shakes her head. "I said I'd marry him, and he said no. It was pretty devastating."

"Then maybe I ask you to marry me and you're already engaged to someone else when the show airs." I shrug.

She chokes a little on her bite of pizza. "What?"

I chuckle. "Look, I don't know how to spin this baby thing. I didn't tell my publicist about him yet, but he said I'm not getting as many sponsorship opportunities lately because my reputation has taken a dive. I got into some trouble a couple months ago, and even though we took care of it, I guess it looked pretty bad."

Her brows crinkle together. "What happened?"

"Nothing. It was stupid. Vinny, that's my publicist, he told me to lay low, so I stayed in Chicago at Madden's place a while. And that meant no income in the offseason. I'm back now, and hardly anything is coming in. He told me to work on my wholesome factor, and I think you could be my ticket to that."

She looks nervous at my words. "What do you mean by that?" she asks, giving me a bit of side-eye.

"I just mean if we're seen together and we're giving off the impression that we're a happy little family, it could mean more opportunities for me. And you, too—for the reason you just said."

"But what does a happy little family mean?"

I shrug. "Mom, dad, baby. Or husband, wife, baby."

"First, I'm not Jack's mom. And second...husband, wife, baby? Dex, this doesn't sound like you."

I twist my lips. She's absolutely right about that. "I guess it's another example of saying fuck it and just living life instead of being worried about the consequences. Didn't you go on a show to get married? Would it really be so bad to try it for a few months?"

"Are you so serious right now?" she gasps.

I shrug. "The idea just came to me over pizza."

"It's nuts, Dex. Bananas."

"You're right. Forget I said it. Though ice cream with nuts and bananas doesn't sound bad." I glance at the ice cream place across from where we're sitting.

She tilts her head and stares at me for a few seconds. "You would look like a rebound. Nobody would believe it's a legitimate marriage."

"You're right. Dumb idea." I push it a little further, and I don't even know why. "Even though we've known each other for years and years and could easily explain away the rebound thing. You always had a thing for me. I always had a thing for you...when you turned legal age, of course. We could make up a whole story. You came to Vegas and knew exactly who to call when that show didn't pan out the way you thought it would. All that shit's fake anyway, right?"

"We're not allowed to imply that."

"Didn't they already revoke your paycheck?"

She stares at me thoughtfully as she chews her lip for a few beats. She's actually thinking this through. "The show is in edits, and I'm not sure when they're airing it. But what if I was married to a pro football star when it came out? I wouldn't look like such a fool then, would I?"

I press my lips together. "Will they film a reunion show?"

She nods. "They're filming in three months."

"Maybe that's when we make it official, then."

"You're joking right now. Right? Because you're Dex, and I'm Ainsley, and this would never, ever work."

"We don't need it to work, Ains. It's a business arrangement."

"For how long?"

I twist my lips. "Until the kid is eighteen?" I say again, and she giggles. I'm not sure I'm joking.

"You're still nuts and bananas."

"If you keep talking about my nuts, we may have to make business personal."

Her cheeks turn a bright shade of red along with her nose, and I might just have to keep making comments like that only to see her adorable reaction.

Wait.

Wait just a fucking hot second there.

Did I just use the word *adorable* in my brain?

Fuck.

Maybe I *am* nuts after all.

She purses her lips as she stares at me, and then she nods resolutely. "Fuck it."

"Fuck it?" I ask.

She nods. "Let's do it."

My brows shoot up. "You want to get married?"

"I left Chicago expecting to get married in Vegas. So what if it's not the original route I took? Someone I know is trying to teach me to take more risks without worrying about the consequences, so fuck it. Let's get married."

"Let's get married," I echo.

I guess we're really doing this.

CHAPTER 11

DEX BRADLEY

Violence Isn't the Answer

"You gotta be fucking kidding me," I mutter as I study the citation.

"Sorry, Dex," Milton says.

I slam the piece of paper down on his desk. "It's not your fault Jensen Bybee is a dickwad. The fucker had it coming."

"I'm certain he did, sir," Milton says.

I'm fucking livid, but there's not much I can do. He wants to press charges like a little bitch, and he's only doing it because my court date is in six weeks when the season will be underway. He's doing it to get a rise out of me. I'll pay him back by kicking his team's ass on the field.

"It's fine, Dex. Consequences, remember?" a soft voice by my side says tentatively. "It's a misdemeanor. You didn't hurt him, but he has the right to press charges."

I clench my jaw. Her truth-telling skills are on point and also unnecessary at the moment.

"Let's just get upstairs," I huff, and I take the citation with me to hand over to my lawyer to see if there's something he can do to handle it.

I shouldn't be surprised that Coach has already texted me that he wants to see me in his office in the morning. I'll be there. I don't have much choice.

But tonight with Ainsley—after we left the event—just felt so *fun*. It felt oddly…freeing. Like she grounds me in a way nobody else ever has. Like she is holding me responsible in a way nobody else ever really believed I was capable of. Like she cares about me and sees me. And that's why it's so strange that it feels *freeing*.

If anything, she's trying to restrain me and get a handle on me. But it's like knowing I can be myself and have her as the safety net I've never had.

I need to shake all this off. The lavender, the black dress, the neckline, the kiss on my cheek. All of it.

Except somehow and totally out of nowhere, I just agreed to be her husband, and that sort of throws a wrench into shaking any of it off.

I give Madison a couple hundred bucks for watching the kid, who's sleeping soundly in his new room far away from my weight room, and we bid her goodnight.

I bid Ainsley goodnight, too, before I do something stupid like strip her out of that dress and see what she's hiding underneath it, and instead, I head toward the shower to take it all out on my dick.

And I pretend like I don't moan her name as I jizz all over my hand.

I don't feel any better when morning dawns since I spend the night tossing and turning, though I must fall asleep at some point because a glance at the clock tells me I need to get to Coach's office pronto.

I brush my teeth and throw on some clean clothes, and I bolt to the kitchen to grab a protein shake I can drink on the way.

"Good morning," Ainsley says from her spot on the couch where she's wearing glasses and reading a book to my son.

It should stop and give me pause. My son with the woman I agreed to marry last night.

I can't pause, though. I need to get the fuck out the door so Coach can yell at me.

"Morning. I have to meet with my coach. I'll be back in a couple hours." I rush out the door without waiting for a reply, in part because I'm having mixed feelings about how *adorable* (fuck, I hate that word no matter how fitting it is) the scene in the family room was, as I'm starting to regret our conversation last night.

I feel differently this morning, and I'm thinking about the consequences for once in my goddamn life. It's a bad idea to marry a girl I'm starting to have feelings for.

I realize how little sense that makes, but it is what it is.

I arrive at the Complex, the name of our practice facility, and I navigate toward Lincoln Nash's office. He's standing outside the office talking with his secretary, and he waves me in when I walk up.

"Talk to me, Bradley. What went down last night?" he asks once he's shut his office door and he's sitting behind his desk.

"Jensen Bybee opened his stupid mouth and pissed me off, so I slugged him."

"Anyone ever teach you that violence isn't the answer?" he asks.

"Says the man who tells me to put the quarterback on his ass every week."

"You think sarcasm is going to win you favors?" he asks.

"You literally once told me to choke somebody."

He flattens his lips. "On the field, Bradley. Listen, you'll likely get dismissed in court, maybe a fine. Jack is pissed, but he'll get over it. The team decided to fine you as well, and you'll need to take anger management classes that we can probably work in if you stay an hour after practice for a few days."

I wince when he says the name *Jack*, and it doesn't slide by my eagle-eyed coach.

"What? Why the face?" he asks.

I contemplate how much to tell him. He's a father, a coach, a mentor. He's here to support his players. He called me in to both check on me and inform me of my punishment.

He might have some insight as to what I should do in my situation.

I blow out a breath.

"What's going on?" he asks.

"Last week, a woman came by my place to see me. She had a baby, a six-month-old, with her, and she claimed he's mine." It sounds ridiculous as I say the words, and it only gets more far-fetched as I continue. "She had to surrender herself to jail, and she's going away for a couple years. She signed the kid over to me and left him with me. I don't know what the fuck I'm supposed to do with a kid, and I'm trying to figure out the next step."

"Do you have proof he's yours?" he asks.

"Not yet," I admit. "We submitted a test and are waiting on the results."

"Good first step. What will you do if it comes back negative?"

I hadn't really thought about that. I guess the answer is pretty obvious. If he isn't mine, he goes to the real father or to Tawny's next of kin.

"It won't," I say. "The kid *looks* like me. He acts like me, too. Stubborn as fuck."

"Whines a lot?" he guesses, and then he chuckles at his own jab. "Do you have help?"

"Yeah. My little sister's friend happened to be in town and she's good with kids. She's helping me out for now, but I'm not sure how temporary that situation may be. She was with me last night."

He presses his lips together and nods. "Still, why the face before when I mentioned Jack?"

"Jack. That's his name. The baby. His mother named him after her favorite football player of all time…Jack Dalton."

He bursts out laughing.

"I think she was trying to make my life as awkward as possible, honestly."

"Success. Listen, if you need a good babysitter, or even a nanny, Jolene and I can come up with some resources for you. And clothes. Joey has outgrown all his baby stuff, and my wife was just talking about wanting to pass them on to someone else. Lots of Aces gear in there."

"I'll take whatever you have," I say.

"So the next step you referred to a bit ago doesn't mean you're trying to find someone else to take him on?"

I lift a shoulder. I'm still not completely sold on that, but reality is starting to set in. And the more I see Ainsley with my son, the more I see them both becoming more permanent fixtures at my place.

Or maybe I'm just nuts and bananas, as Ains would say.

We finish our conversation, and I end up confessing what Jensen said that made me punch him. Coach Lincoln doesn't really blame me for what I did, and while he doesn't exactly come out and say it, I think he even finds it slightly honorable that I was defending the woman helping me out with my son.

When I get home, Jack is napping and Ainsley is lying on the couch watching television. She sits up when I walk in as if I caught her doing something she wasn't supposed to be doing.

"Sorry. I was just relaxing a bit after a long morning." She smiles with a bit of timidness, and I shake my head.

"Taking care of a baby is hard work. Relax all you want."

"How did things go with your coach?" she asks.

"Fine. The team is fining me twenty-five grand, and I'm required to take anger management."

"Twenty-five grand? That's steep," she says.

"Could've been more," I mutter.

"I'm going to go shower. Will you listen for the baby? He should be up soon, but I didn't want to shower until you got back."

I nod, and she heads out as I try not to imagine her getting naked and stepping into the shower.

It's impossible.

I'm still imagining it a few minutes later when the kid starts crying. I get him out of his bed and set him on the floor in the family room while I make a bottle the way she showed me, which takes longer than it should. I don't even notice how quiet it has gotten.

When I go back to grab him, he's got this panicked look on his face, and I don't think he's breathing.

I spot a mess near him, and a little dish that held decorative dice on it on my family room table is on the floor.

It registers in the span of a nanosecond that there are only five dice on the floor.

My heart sinks into my stomach, and panic claws its way through me as I put together where the sixth one might be. He somehow reached onto the table and put one of the dice in his mouth.

"Fuck!" I yell, and I grab the kid, turn him over, and start to pound on his back. I'm not sure where in the recesses of my mind that CPR training kicks into gear, but I recall something about five blows between the shoulder blades in the class we were required to take in high school.

I may never have remembered that if the girl teaching the class wasn't as hot as she was and was standing there talking about blows. I was an immature high school kid who grew into an immature adult.

On the fourth blow, the dice pops out onto the floor, and the kid lets out a blood-curdling scream.

I turn him over in my arms and pull him to my chest as I stand, adrenaline still coursing through me as the panic gives way. The baby is crying, and I'm bouncing as I hold him and tell him he's okay, and it's the first time I feel like I've done something *right* even though the situation that landed us here was probably my own fault, too—leaving the kid unsupervised when babies put whatever shit they want to into their mouths.

Fuck.

"Is everything okay?"

I hear a voice behind me, and I whip around to find Ainsley with hair dripping onto her shoulders, wearing nothing more than a white towel around her body.

My eyes flick to the towel for a second. "He was choking on one of the dice," I say.

"And you dislodged it?" she asks. She's not as incredulous as I am about it.

I'm starting to think she really does believe in me.

"Yeah. I was making him a bottle, and he must've grabbed it off the table." I nod to the rest of the dice scattered on the floor.

"We should probably get started on babyproofing. He's been trying to crawl, and I think he's not too far off from moving all over the place."

I don't know what babyproofing means, but the way I'm hugging the kid to my chest and the relief I feel coursing through me after that whole ordeal tells me one very important thing I hadn't considered in the last week and a half since I met the boy.

I think I might be starting to fall for this kid.

Maybe it happened the moment I laid eyes on him and felt like he was mine. Maybe it's an inherent thing. Maybe it was seeing him laugh in the swing at the park, or maybe it was the panic I felt at him choking.

Whatever it is, it's a new and unfamiliar feeling that's terrifying and wonderful all at once.

Sort of like the things I feel when I'm around Ainsley.

"I told you that you got this," she says.

I nod.

"You're more capable than you let yourself think, Dex."

"I still need help," I whisper, nearly afraid to admit those words aloud.

One side of her mouth lifts into a smile. "We all do from time to time. And that's why I'm here. I'll go get some clothes on, but you totally got this, Daddy Dex."

Daddy Dex.

The words are flippant and light out of her mouth, but they do something to me I wasn't expecting.

The baby is still crying in my arms as a jittery feeling rises in my stomach. It's almost like this rush of feelings—the thrill I so often chase that causes my stomach to bounce and my chest to tighten.

Just from her calling me Daddy Dex.

It makes me want to drag her to my bed, strip her naked, and make her a slut for me.

All in due time. Hopefully.

CHAPTER 12
Ainsley Riggs

I'm Going to Be His Wife

I must be seeing things.

The way his eyes widened as they fell onto the towel wrapped around my body.

The way he stared at me, especially after I called him *Daddy Dex*…

He was just panicked after his son was choking which, honestly and only in the hindsight of everything being okay…maybe it happened so he can see that he's perfectly capable of doing the things he is so scared of.

He's starting to warm up to the idea of having his son around, and that makes me so happy. Jack is just a baby, and every baby deserves to be loved. It's why I've done everything I can to make sure he feels love after his mother was forced to leave him and while his father starts to come around.

And his father *is* starting to come around. He knew what to do to save the baby when he was choking. I ran to my room to put clothes on once we were sure everything was fine, and he managed to settle the baby down all on his own after that scary event.

I don't bother with my hair or makeup as I head back to the family room to clean up the dice and the little dish on the floor. I set all of it up high on the kitchen counter while Dex sits on the couch and holds Jack as he feeds him the bottle, and when I walk by the counter again later, the dish and the dice are gone.

I see them in the garbage can when I'm throwing something else away, and I can't help a little smile at the way he's already starting to adjust his life around having a baby in the penthouse. It's these little things now paving the way for the big things later.

Once the baby is down for the night, I find Dex in his usual spot brooding over by the window with a glass in his hand, though tonight it appears to just be water and not his usual whiskey.

"When do you want to do this marriage thing?" he grunts at me.

So it's not *exactly* the way I thought someone would propose to me, but we both get something out of this, I guess. Besides, I was proposed to with the romance and the flowers and all the things a couple of weeks ago in front of cameras, and we all know how that turned out. Maybe the dream proposal is overrated.

"How quickly do you need to work on your image?" I ask.

"Before word gets out that I have a kid with a woman who's now in prison."

I bite my bottom lip for a second. "I'm game whenever. I literally have nothing else going on." I laugh a little maniacally at that, but maybe I'm also a little nuts. I did agree to this, after all.

He chuckles and glances over at me. "Training camp starts in sixteen days."

"Do you want to do it before or after?" I ask.

"Before would be better for me."

I flinch. "So I need to pull a wedding together and babyproof this penthouse in sixteen days?"

"Less than that since it *starts* in sixteen days. You know, if you still want to go through with it." He looks over at me. "And what do you mean by babyproof?"

"You know, make it safe for a baby that will soon be mobile. Are we telling anyone about it or keeping it under wraps?" I ask.

"I'll probably admit the truth to my brother Madden. And you can tell my sister and anyone you want that you can trust. I'll have my lawyer draw up an NDA for friends and family to sign, plus our prenup and contract."

"Contract?" I ask.

"Yeah. You'll be paid for your time, of course." He returns his gaze out the window and takes a sip from the glass.

"Stop." I roll my eyes. "It's not like I'm not benefitting from it."

"Fine. Then I'll increase your pay for your work with Jack," he says, and his words have a finality to them like I shouldn't argue.

"Can you really pay a stepmother for being a nanny?"

"I can pay *my wife* for whatever I want to pay her for," he snaps, and *whoa*, hearing those words—*my wife*—out of his mouth does something to me.

Something dark and deep down low.

I can't help my little gasp, not at the words or the fact that he snapped at me, but at my body's visceral reaction to it all. An ache throbs tightly between my legs, and I have this sudden *need* pulsing through me.

I tear my gaze away from his profile as I think through his statement. I'm going to be *his wife*.

I didn't think in terms of that when I agreed to this. I didn't really think about those words when I signed up for *Speed to the Altar* either. But for some reason, they're really affecting me today.

Maybe because they're out of Dex's mouth, and it was unexpected.

"Okay. I'll get started on plans," I say.

"Or we just…I don't know. We can just get our license and get it done. No plans." He shrugs. "Just a contract."

Again, that's not exactly what I imagined for my wedding.

But I also didn't imagine the groom saying *I don't* when it came time to make our vows. I didn't imagine the princess dress and the tiara in my hair and the jewels ending in heartbreak as I ran from the groom.

So maybe this is the way to go about things with Dex. It's fake anyway, right? What difference does it make how we get there?

I finally nod. "Okay. Fine. Just a contract."

He presses his lips together and takes another sip from his glass. "Great. I'll have my lawyer draw it up, and as soon as it's done, we get married."

I press my lips together and nod as I feel a bit of sadness pull over me.

Because when I imagined my future, I never thought I'd agree to marry my best friend's hot older brother, and I really never thought I'd be agreeing to a fake marriage.

CHAPTER 13

Ainsley Riggs

City Hall

I'm not looking forward to this phone call, but somehow having Dex in the same room with me while the baby naps is giving me the vibes I need to make the call.

"Hey Ains!" Ivy answers. She plows forward before I get to talk. "I have to leave in like four minutes but saw your call come in."

Okay, good. She doesn't have a lot of time, so we'll make this quick.

"Hey, so I'm here with Dex, and, uh, we have some news."

"News? What news?" she asks. "And hi, Dex."

"Hey," he says.

And then I word vomit.

It's not the sexiest turn of phrase, but I'm a rambling idiot who spills it all in the span of about eight seconds. "So Dex's publicist has been telling him he needs to make himself look a little more wholesome, and meanwhile I literally ran into him the other day, and I'm about as wholesome as they come, and I'm breaking NDA to tell you I didn't get married on the show but was made to look like a total and complete fool, so in order help him out and so he can help me out, too, we're going to get married but it's just for show and not a real marriage and we wanted to tell you before it's public."

Silence greets me on the other end.

"Ivy?" I ask after I give it a few seconds.

"Um," she says. "I need to sit down. So wait a second, you and Dex are *getting married?*" she asks, and she's speaking slowly like she's talking to some bunnies in the yard that might get spooked if she talks too quickly or loudly.

"Yep," I say, popping the *p*.

"When?"

"Today. We're heading to City Hall soon."

"City Hall?" she repeats, and I hear all the disdain in her voice.

"Yes. City Hall. I got the romantic proposal and the magical wedding on the show, and it didn't work out, so—"

"And it's just for show, anyway," Dex adds. "But we wanted to tell you since the certificate is public record and will likely hit the media in the next few days once the clerk files it and it's live on their website."

"What about having me be your maid of honor?" Ivy asks.

"Babe, you weren't going to be my maid of honor when I was on *Speed to the Altar*," I point out. "I came to Vegas to get married, and maybe we were expecting it to be to someone else, but this is where I landed. You can be my maid of honor at my real wedding someday."

Dex grunts a little at that, and I can't help but wonder for a second if the thought makes him…jealous?

"What about payment from the show?" Ivy asks me. "Won't they pull it if you show up to the reunion married?"

"They already pulled it because I ran instead of staying to give my initial reaction to what happened at the altar."

"What happened?" she presses.

"You'll have to watch."

She lets out a frustrated breath, and Dex laughs.

"Are you going to tell Mom and Dad?" she asks her brother.

"Once it's done and before they can try to talk me out of it," he says.

"Then allow me," she says.

"I thought you only had four minutes," he counters.

"It can wait," she says. "This can't."

"Yeah, it can, Ivy. Save your breath. Anything you have to say to us isn't going to change it," Dex says.

She sighs. "How long are you staying married?"

"My lawyer drew up a contract for two years, six months," Dex says. He glances at me. "It was his idea to revisit the contract once Tawny is out of jail, but it gives me the firmer ground to prove I'm providing a stable home life just in case she decides to try anything."

I glance over at him with a furrowed brow. I thought when he kept saying until the kid turns eighteen, he was serious.

I realize how ridiculous that thought is, but we hadn't really discussed a timeline. Two years, six months is a good chunk of time.

"You guys are making a huge mistake," she warns.

"Maybe we are," I agree.

"But maybe we aren't," Dex says, his eyes meeting mine. "And it's our mistake to make."

She huffs out a breath. "Fine."

"We need you to sign an NDA," Dex says. "I'll text it over now. Please just sign it. Don't make me regret allowing Ainsley to convince me that telling you the truth was a good idea."

"Whatever," she grumbles.

"Love you, Ive," I say, shortening her name by dropping the last syllable.

"Be careful," she says in reply, and then she says, "I have to go."

She cuts the call.

"That wasn't so bad," Dex says. "Madden next?"

I'm tired since I haven't slept more than five hours at a time since I arrived here, and now my life is changing in the blink of an eye.

It's a welcome change, but it's still going to be a lot of work to fool the entire world into believing Dex and I are married. And that leaves me with an important question that I blurt out the second it enters my mind.

"We're going to have to convince the world that we're really married, so what's your answer going to be when you're asked why you'd settle for a girl like me?"

"What do you mean by that?" he asks, his brows drawn together in confusion.

I lift a shoulder. "You're Dex Bradley. You could have any woman you want. And you're marrying a plain-Jane girl eleven years your junior who doesn't even have a job?"

He stares at me as if I've grown two heads.

"What?" I ask. I tuck my hair behind my ear self-consciously.

"Plain Jane?" he repeats. He tugs at the hair I just tucked so it comes untucked. "You're anything but plain, Ainsley." His voice is low and raspy as he says the words, and need pulses between my legs again.

I blow out a breath.

I'm not sure how I'm supposed to fake this when I find myself more and more invested with every passing moment.

CHAPTER 14

Dex Bradley

I Do

I decide to hold off on calling the rest of my family until later tonight. It can wait, and the longer we put this off, the better the chances we'll decide not to go through with it.

I change into khaki shorts and a white collared shirt, and I head out to the family room. I find Madison, who is still on summer break, here to watch Jack, who's currently napping, while Ainsley and I go get married.

It sounds so wild when I say those words in my head.

Speaking of my future wife, she emerges wearing a light pink dress a few minutes later. It's simple and sweet and so very much *her.*

So why does my dick respond by shifting around as the blood rushes straight for him? I wish I knew the answer to that.

I blow out a breath, and we head down the back elevator to the parking lot, where we slip into my black Challenger. I drive us to the Clark County Marriage License Bureau downtown, and shortly after that, we're walking from the bureau down the block. I stop in front of the closest chapel.

"How about here instead of City Hall?" I ask, nodding to the chapel.

Her eyes seem to gleam at that, and she nods.

We head inside, and I immediately spot the recognition in the eyes of the woman behind the desk. She watches me carefully as we approach the desk.

"Welcome to the Best Little Chapel," she says. "Can I help you?"

My eyes flick to her nametag. "Hi, Peggy. We're here to get married."

Her eyes light up. "I'll comp the fees and give you the deluxe photo package if we can use your photo in our marketing."

I press my lips together. "That's something you'll have to talk to my publicist about."

"Let's not get all formal," she says, pushing a piece of paper across the counter to me. "This just says we can use your image and likeness in our marketing."

I narrow my eyes at her. "One photo, for one year, and you have to give me a week before you start using it."

"Deal," she says, and she reaches her hand across the counter. I shake it, and I detail everything we just said, sign the paper, and ask for a copy.

Fifteen minutes later, I'm standing beside Peggy's husband, Carl, who is serving as our officiant. Peggy sits in the front row as our witness, and a moment later, Ainsley opens the door and walks into the room to begin her walk down the aisle toward me.

She's holding onto a gaudy bouquet of fake flowers Peggy lent to her, and my heart skips a beat.

I can't piece together *why* it feels that way, but seeing this woman walk toward me tells me this is real. It's serious. We're not just fucking around. We're actually doing this.

I didn't think it through, which can be said for most things in my life, so it tracks with who I am. On top of that, it's fake…or rather, it's *pretend*. We're not faking the wedding. This is real, and it's happening, and she's going to be my wife.

In name only, of course.

But still.

And it feels unsettling watching her walk toward me as we listen to the opening notes of some love song from the early nineties that Peggy chose for us.

It feels like it shouldn't be fake.

It makes literally no sense to feel that way. While I've known who Ainsley Riggs is for eight years, I still don't really *know* her. She's best friends with my sister, sure, but my sister is thirteen years younger than me. They met when Ains was a junior and my sister was a freshman, and Ains was assigned as Ivy's *big sister* at a summer volleyball camp.

They got close and remained the best of friends, and they even attended the same college. She was often at our house when I stopped by for Bradley family dinners on Monday nights, but I can't say I ever held a one-on-one conversation with her that didn't involve something logistical like an *excuse me* for bumping into her in the kitchen or a *sorry for parking my car behind yours in the driveway* sort of situation.

I can't say that anymore. She's lived with me for almost two weeks now, and while I still don't know very much about her, I know she's an incredible caretaker with strong instincts and a killer intuition. She's fun, like the day she followed me into New York–New York and we rode the roller coaster. She's smart, like how she knows so many things about taking care of a baby. She's gorgeous, a genuine knockout, but she has no clue.

And she's about to become my wife.

Carl doesn't waste much time with pleasantries.

"We are gathered here today to join—" He pauses and glances at the paper in front of him before he continues. "Dex Bradley and Ainsley Riggs in matrimony. Marriage is a lawful promise between two people who wish to spend their lives together, and today we are celebrating this young couple's commitment."

He pauses, and we hear the click of a camera, presumably from our witness, Peggy. There are also several cameras set up around us to capture every possible angle of our quickie Vegas-style wedding.

"Do you, Dex, take Ainsley to be your lawfully wedded wife?" Carl asks me.

I pause, and I turn toward Ainsley. When our eyes connect, I say, "I do."

Ainsley seems to let go of a small breath.

"And do you, Ainsley, take Dex to be your lawfully wedded husband?"

She nods and doesn't pause. "I do."

"It's now time to exchange the rings. Dex, place your bride's ring on her finger and let it be a reminder of your promise today."

I slide the cheap gold band Peggy sold me onto Ainsley's finger.

"Ainsley, place your groom's ring on his finger and let it be a reminder of your promise today."

She slides the matching band onto my finger.

"By the power vested in me by the state of Nevada, I now pronounce you husband and wife."

We smile at each other, and I feel the tiniest bit of awkwardness as I know what comes next. We didn't discuss this part, but I'm supposed to kiss my bride. Carl didn't say it, but everyone knows it's what comes at the end of the ceremony. You seal it with a kiss.

I'm not shy when it comes to this sort of thing, but she's different. She's not one of the women clamoring to get close to me. She's unassuming and sweet.

Her eyes flick tentatively to my mouth, and I use that as my invitation.

I take a single step toward her, and I slowly lower my lips to hers.

It's barely a touch of lip to lip, and it's not enough. I slide my arm around her waist and haul her to me, and for just a second, I forget where I am. All good sense walks straight off the premises, and I'm about ready to strip her naked as thoughts of that black dress from the night of the charity event pop unbidden back into my mind.

Chapel, Dex. You're in a chapel. And you're kissing your sister's best friend.

Your wife.

Your sister's best friend.

These words are pulling at me from each direction, ready to tear me in two as I try to figure out which side is screaming louder at me.

A third voice pops uninvited into the mix. *She's caring for your kid.*

That's the one that has me pulling back. She's in a daze, and her fingertips move up to touch her lips as if she can't believe that really just happened.

I wouldn't be surprised if *that* is the photo this place wants to use of us, but in all likelihood, they'll choose one where my face can clearly be seen.

None of it matters, though.

All that matters is that I'm walking out of here with a wife.

CHAPTER 15
Ainsley Bradley

Parents

I'm afraid to ask about that kiss. He was just doing it for the photo op, I'm sure, and asking about it will only lead me to disappointment.

Still, a tiny part of me is convinced it meant more than that. I'm sure that tiny part is just nuts, but I also know what I felt. We're quiet on the drive home, and once we pull into his parking space, he pauses after he cuts the engine. He looks over at me. "Should I order in a nice dinner or something to celebrate?"

I lift a shoulder. "I don't really know what comes next, to be honest."

"Neither do I. I've never been married before."

"Same. Especially not because I'm trying to fool the media."

He laughs. "Then we pave our own way, I guess."

"I should call my parents. They don't even know filming wrapped on the show, and here I am married to someone else already." I make a face.

"I should call mine, too. My dad will demand to see the prenup and will probably yell at me for getting married without letting him see the documents first." He shrugs.

"Parents," I mutter, rolling my eyes.

"Tell me about it. The more I learn about my dad, the more I worry I'll turn out like him."

It feels like a deeper conversation for another day, and considering we just got married, I'm not sure how much more energy I have in me today to field conversations with depth.

"You're a pretty headstrong kind of guy. If you don't want to turn out like him, you won't." Mr. Bradley always struck me as a guy who puts business first, but Ivy always spoke very highly of him. She's the youngest, though, and I can see how it's possible she had a different experience as the seventh kid than the second had.

He stares out the windshield. "I'm already more like him than I care to admit."

I wonder what he means by that, and I think he might even expand on it, but then he seems to change his mind.

"We should get inside and see how Jack's doing. You know, now that we're married," he says, and his words lighten the mood in here.

I giggle. "I'm sure he's just as fine as he was when we were still single."

He chuckles, and I'm right—he's just fine with Madison, who's great with him. She turned *Sesame Street* on, and the two of them are watching Elmo sing about his world when we walk in. Jack starts to squirm when he sees Dex, and Dex walks over to him and picks him up.

He *picks the baby up*. He swings him in the air, and then he sets him back down on the floor where he was sitting on a playmat.

I've never seen Dex so lighthearted and…dare I say…happy?

He's nearly *joyful*. It's not like him, but it's a new side that's decidedly sexy.

But, then, pretty much all the sides of him are, and that's just something I'm going to have to try to get used to.

Yep…my husband is sexy as hell.

But he's my husband in name only—despite that kiss after we were officially announced as husband and wife.

This feels complicated, and I can imagine it's about to get even more complicated.

I decide to give my parents a call once Jack is down for the night.

"Hello? Ainsley, is that you?" my mom answers, and I swear she answers her phone upside down ninety percent of the time. She acts like she's in her eighties, not in her forties.

"Put it on speaker!" I yell into the phone.

"Hello? Oh, shoot, did I hang up?"

"I'm right here, Mom," I say.

"Honey! Hi! How was the show? Are you married?"

"Am I on speaker?" I ask rather than answering any of that.

"Yes," she confirms.

"Who's there with you?"

"Daddy and Henry," she says, naming my twelve-year-old brother.

"Hi, Sissy!" Henry says at the same time my dad says, "Hey, Ains!"

"Sorry, Hen, but can I talk to Mom and Dad for a minute?" I ask.

He sputters an objection but must relent because my mom says a moment later, "Okay, hon, it's just Dad and me. What's going on?"

"Are you both willing to sign nondisclosure agreements for what I'm about to tell you?" I ask.

"Ainsley, tell us what's going on," my dad says.

"I didn't get married on the show, and I need you to sign NDAs for the rest of the story."

"We'll do whatever we can to make sure our daughter is safe," my mom says.

"Okay, well, so do you remember Dex Bradley?" I ask.

"One of Ivy's brothers?" my mom asks. She always knew everything about everyone in town, likely because of her position as a fourth-grade teacher.

"Yes."

"The troublemaker or the baseball player?" she presses.

I clear my throat. One of the middle brothers, Archer, plays baseball, where the rest of the brothers opted for football. So that leaves exactly one option. "The troublemaker."

"Oh, right," she says. "The other one was Archer. He plays for Vegas now, right? The Heat?"

"Yes," I confirm.

"So what about the troublemaker?"

"Can we not call him that?" I ask, though if I were to tell her the whole truth—that I'm helping nanny for the kid his ex who had to go to jail dropped off without ever having told him that he even had a kid—it wouldn't exactly negate her nickname for him.

"Rebel? Bad boy? Pot-stirrer?"

"God, Mom, stop. Look, he took me in when he found out what happened on the show, and he's been nothing short of wonderful to me. And I just wanted to get ahead of the media when they find out and make this information public. So we, uh, well, we decided we could both benefit from being seen together in public, especially with some things that have recently happened both for him and for myself, so, uh, we sort of decided to get married."

Silence greets me on the other end of the line, and for a split second I think my mom might've messed something up with the phone since it wouldn't be the first time that's happened. "Mom? Dad? You there?"

My dad clears his throat. "We're here."

"Isn't he much older than you, sweetheart?" my mother asks.

"He's thirty-three."

"So eleven years," she says flatly.

"Yes."

"He's only ten years younger than *me*," she says. "There's less distance between him and me than there is between him and you."

"Gross, Mom."

"Oh, honey," my mom says as if she can't even take the mistake I'm making. "Is this real?"

"No," I admit. "That's sort of the whole thing and also why I need you to sign an NDA. It's just for the next two years, and nobody can know it's not real." I leave out the *and six months* bit.

"This is a mistake, baby girl. Don't do it," my mom says.

I can tell my dad is trying to calm her down when he asks, "When is the wedding?"

"It was earlier today," I admit.

My mom flies into hysterics. "You're married, and I missed it?"

"It's fine, Mom. You knew this might happen when I went onto the show, remember?"

"Yes, but I didn't think it would really happen, and it didn't, but now you're married anyway, and I didn't get to be there?" She's wailing, and my dad is shushing her, and I knew I shouldn't have done this over the phone, but I didn't have much choice.

"I know what I'm doing. It'll be fine. Someday I'll give you the big dream wedding, okay?" I don't know how, and I don't know who the groom will be. Maybe a part of why I left home to get married on a reality show was so that my parents wouldn't have the stress of having to pay for a wedding.

Dex knocks on my doorframe. "Dinner's here," he mouths to me, and I nod.

"I need to go. I'm so sorry. I know you don't love this for me, but thank you for being the kind of parents I can trust with this. I'll send over those NDAs in a bit."

"We love you, Ains," my dad says.

"Love you, too."

My mom is crying and clearly trying to muffle it, and I feel bad that I've upset her. But this is my life to live, my mistake to make.

And when I walk out into the kitchen, to be honest, it doesn't really feel like a mistake at all.

CHAPTER 16

DEX BRADLEY

Never Been Drunk

I didn't do any of it, but she looks impressed when she walks into the kitchen and sees our spread set up on the table.

"I told Milton we needed a post-wedding dinner, and this is what he sent," I say.

"You could've taken credit. I would've believed you."

I chuckle as she looks at the candlesticks glowing with a flame, the fancy plates with steak and lobster on them, and the champagne flutes filled to the brim.

I hold out a hand as I pull her chair out to help her sit, and she smiles at me as she takes her seat.

It feels like a date.

It's not. I mean, not technically. It's just dinner, but it's dinner after we eloped earlier today.

Fake or not, we're spending the next two years together, and there's something far more comforting in that than I'm ready to admit.

She holds up her glass in a toast after I sit beside her, and I touch my glass to hers.

"To the next two and a half years," I say.

She repeats me, and we each take a sip.

"Whoa," she says, and she takes another sip.

I chuckle, something I seem to be doing a lot around her. She's just so…naïve. Young. Pure. She's so unlike all the others. So unlike Tawny, who had my baby in secret and didn't bother to tell me until she needed something. So unlike the nameless host of others who came before Tawny and even after.

But Ainsley…she has the sheltered innocence thing down pat, and the more time I spend around her, the more I'm starting to like it.

She's still wearing her dress. Her hair is still in that braid thing she did for our wedding. She looks sweet and innocent because she is.

She doesn't know what good champagne—or good whiskey, for that matter—tastes like. She's never had it. She doesn't expect a single goddamn thing out of me other than to step up and accept the responsibilities and consequences that I've created, willingly and knowingly or not.

And as I glance up and our eyes connect after we each swallow that first sip of champagne, I can't help the words that plow into my brain.

That's my wife.

My wife.

It's for show. It's for the media. It's for her protection. It's for my sponsors.

But as I share this post-wedding meal with her, I can't help but wonder if it'll ever transition into something that's for *us*.

"I've never had champagne like this," she says, nodding toward her glass. "What is it?"

"Cristal," I say, nodding toward the bottle on the counter.

"It looks expensive."

I laugh. "Three-fifty for that bottle."

"You could buy, like, fifty bottles of the kind we get for New Year's Eve for that."

"You only drink champagne on New Year's Eve?" I ask.

She lifts a shoulder. "I just turned twenty-one last year."

"And you didn't drink before that?"

She twists her lips. "I told you, I don't really like how alcohol tastes."

I narrow my eyes at her, knowing full well she doesn't like it because she's been drinking the cheap shit. "Have you ever gotten drunk?"

Her hand flies to her chest, and she's nearly *proper* as she says, "No!"

"Come on, Birdie. You're twenty-two, and you've never been *drunk?*"

"Tipsy, sure. But drunk to the point of getting sloppy?" She wrinkles her nose. "It just never appealed to me, to be honest."

I wonder what else she hasn't done.

"We need to fix that. I'll get you hammered someday."

She lifts her glass. "One of these and I probably will be." She takes another sip, and then she sets her glass down. "But I can't. Jack's going to wake up at three, and again at eight, and I can't be drunk when I'm taking care of him."

"Are you always this responsible?" I ask.

"You're paying me to be this responsible, remember?"

"Touché." I cut into my steak, and it's cooked perfectly. "Still, every person in their early twenties deserves at least one night with no responsibilities. I was there for all of my siblings except Madden, and now I'll add you to the list of people I got drunk. I'll see if someone can watch the baby overnight sometime so we can hit the town."

She laughs. "Aren't you supposed to be appearing more wholesome? Getting some girl two-thirds your age wasted doesn't feel like the way to do it."

"Two-thirds my age?" I make a face at her that clearly lets her know how much I disapprove of that message.

"My mother informed me that you are closer to her age than mine," she mutters.

I bark out a laugh, and I'm about to say something totally inappropriate about a mother-daughter trio when I bring it back to the topic at hand. "Regarding the wholesome vibe, we'll dodge the media. Doesn't mean we can't have some fun. Maybe Vegas-style fun."

"I have no idea what that means."

"It means VIP lounges, bottle service, high-stakes gambling. Taking risks and not worrying about the consequences." I lift a shoulder.

She swallows the bite of lobster she just took and shakes her head. "And I'm supposed to just let *you* take care of me while you get me wasted?"

My hand flies to my chest. "You don't trust me?"

She laughs as she picks up her glass. "I trust that you'll hand me a good time."

I can most definitely give her a good time. Probably an even better time than she ever dreamed of.

I shake off the thought and cut into my steak some more, not really sure why this feels so much like a date when, to be honest, I haven't been on a *date* in the traditional sense in years. Many of them. Maybe back to the college days, back before I was playing pro football and women cared about more than just that fact.

But Ainsley is different. I know it's cliché to say the current woman holding my interest is *different*, but in this case, it's true. She's my opposite in most ways, but she's more interesting to me than anyone else I've been around in months. Years, even.

Maybe it's *because* she's so different from me.

I suddenly wonder how many men she's been with. How many men have kissed the lips I briefly got to touch today at the end of the ceremony. The lips I haven't stopped feeling against mine since it happened. I wonder how many cocks those lips have been wrapped around. How many men have fucked her until she bit her bottom lip between her teeth as she came.

It's not my business. She's just my nanny. My sister's friend. A girl helping me out.

But she's also my wife, and the side of my brain that keeps reminding me of that fact wants to know the answers to those questions regardless of whether it's my business or not.

I'm getting to the point where I want to *make it* my business.

And that's a dangerous place to be since it's completely new territory.

"What about you?" she asks.

"Huh?" I have no clue what she's talking about. I was too focused on how many dudes she's banged to remember where we left off.

"When was the first time you got drunk?"

"I was thirteen," I admit.

"Thirteen?" she practically spits.

I lift a shoulder. "Madden was fifteen, and he gave me a bottle of tequila. I didn't know you weren't supposed to chug down half the bottle at once." I shrug, and she laughs. "Speaking of getting drunk, there's another charity event next week. Want to go public as my wife and we can turn it into our fun night out?" I ask.

She gasps a little at my question. "Who will watch the baby overnight?"

I shrug. "My coach, maybe. He and his wife have little kids, and I trust him."

She contemplates that for a few seconds as if it's *her* kid to find good care for, and my chest tightens a little.

She cares that much for Jack. Already. We've barely even started down this road, and she's trying to make decisions for what's best for *my* kid as she continually assures me that I'm capable of doing it too.

She finally nods. "Okay. Let's do it."

I grin. "You won't regret it."

"That remains to be seen," she huffs, and all I can do is just laugh.

CHAPTER 17

DEX BRADLEY

The Worst Dates

After dinner, we head to the family room. It feels like the next natural step, like you have a late-night dinner after you get the kid down, and then you head to the family room and turn on a show or whatever—only the television remains off, and conversation is on instead.

"Did you ever see yourself married to someone eleven years younger than you?" she asks.

She's sitting on the couch, and I opted for the recliner. I suddenly wish I was a little closer to her.

I laugh. "I never saw myself married to anyone, period, so no. What about you? You came to Vegas to get married, right?"

"Jordan was twenty-six, and truthfully, he just wasn't ready for marriage. He shouldn't have been there."

"Want me to kick his ass?" I ask, surprised at the rage that seems to ripple through me that this guy who wasn't good enough for her hurt her.

But if he hadn't hurt her, I wouldn't be sitting here with her right now.

She chuckles. "Kind of. But honestly, I think that'll take care of itself at the reunion."

"You said that's in October, right?"

She nods. "I just got word that the show will start airing the Monday after we film the reunion."

"You okay?" I ask carefully. I take a sip from my whiskey, opting instead to save the champagne for her since she seemed to like it, but she didn't bring her glass over.

"Yeah. I'm okay. Truthfully, I had fun with Jordan. It's not like the dates with him were the worst dates I've ever been on."

I raise a brow. "You haven't talked much about him or the show. You can, you know."

"I know." She sighs, and she averts her gaze to the view out the window—a classic Dex move, if I'm being honest. "I thought I had fallen for him. It was a crazy few weeks. A whirlwind, really. It all started with a mix and mingle where we got to meet the whole cast. We did these speed dates where we picked six people we felt a connection with after two minutes. We had to rank them from one to six, and then producers matched us with three mutuals. We had talk time with those three, and whichever two the producers felt had the best chemistry got to move on. We had longer dates with each of them, and if we matched on our top pick with the other person, we got a fantasy date with that person. We always had mix-and-mingle time in between all of that, so we basically lived together and got to know each other on an expedited term."

"Like us," I mutter, and before she can respond, I ask, "So the fantasy date...that was with Jordan?"

She nods. "For me, there wasn't really anybody but Jordan from the start. We met at the mix-and-mingle thing, and I thought he was cute." She twists her lips. "He made me laugh, and we talked about everything. Or...producers made me think we did, anyway. They'd give us topics, and we'd explore them, but looking back, we never really got into core values and what we want out of life. It was more surface stuff."

"What do you want out of life?" I ask.

She chuckles, but then she sees I'm serious. She shrugs. "I don't know. I just want to be happy. To feel joy and to be a mom and to create a little life and family for myself that makes me feel excited and giddy to be alive. What about you?"

I lift a shoulder. "To play football, I guess. To have fun. To make money." I realize how shallow that sounds as soon as the words are out of my mouth—especially compared to her answer. I shake my head. "Nah, forget that. Not the money thing. You always hear it doesn't buy happiness, and I don't really think that's true. It can buy happiness. But what it can't buy is intelligence. It can't solve your problems. It can't buy logic. It can't buy personality. But it does make things a hell of a lot easier. So I guess when I really think about what I want out of life, I'm a little like you in that I just want to be happy. I like that answer. I want to feel joy every day, and I want to feel the rush that comes with taking risks and having fun."

She nods. "So maybe we're more alike than we realized. Except for the taking risks thing. I prefer to play it a little safer."

"I can see that about you. But you yelled *fuck it* on that roller coaster. I'm bringing you over to the dark side." I wiggle my brows, and her cheeks turn pink. I change the subject. "So what was your worst date ever?"

She makes a face. "Oh, let's see. Was it the time my date got drunk and puked on my shoes? The one where we were in college and his mom drove us? Or maybe it was the one where we went to a haunted house and I had a panic attack."

"Jesus. You've picked some real winners, Riggs."

She purses her lips. "It's Bradley now, thank you very much. And yes. I struck out until I struck gold."

I point to my chest as I raise my brows. "With me?"

"With what you're paying me," she jokes, and I laugh. "What about you? Worst date ever?"

I lift a shoulder and take a sip of whiskey as I avert my gaze. How do I admit that the date with her to the charity ball was the first time I've been on a *real date* in years?

The others—they were a means to an end. Someone hot or famous on my arm for show at various events that ended with sex. Not a true date in the traditional sense.

"Prom, I guess," I say.

"What happened at prom?"

"All my buddies and I were busted for drinking, and we got kicked out. My date was pissed and told my parents." I shrug.

"You drank at prom?" she asks.

"Not *at* prom. Before it."

She gives me a look.

"What? Everybody did it!"

"You were a football player who was risking potential scholarships, you idiot," she says, and then her hand flies over her mouth. "Oh my God, I'm sorry. I didn't mean to call you an idiot."

I laugh it off. "I know, and you're right. I was an idiot back then. But it's not like I grew into an adult with sense. I still chase risks, as you know."

"Like what?"

I clear my throat. "Oh, I don't know. Different shit that gives me a rush, you know?"

"Such as..."

"Drag racing down the Strip. High-stakes gambling. Riding a roller coaster with my sister's hot friend and throwing my hands in the air while I yell *fuck it* at the top of my lungs with her."

Her cheeks redden at my words. They were intended to incite a reaction.

Yeah, I called her hot. She is, okay? She's not one of the models with the huge tits and the long legs and platinum blonde hair cascading down her shoulders.

She's shorter than me by nearly a foot, and her hair is decidedly short and dark, and her tits aren't huge but appear to be perfect handfuls. And her ass…

God, I still think of her ass in those shorts that first night she was here. The curve spilling out the bottom of her shorts.

I want to ram into that ass.

Whoa.

Dex.

Pull it together.

Jesus, this girl is doing things to me that I can't seem to get under control. More than any of the blondes with the tits ever did to me.

And I think it's because she's not just hot, but she has depth to her. I want to take her to a charity event and show her off as my wife.

I want to date her. I want to see where these feelings take us.

I want to feel the rush that I seem to get from her that feels so different from the drag racing and gambling and other shit I do to try to recreate that feeling. It's stronger with her, and it's both addicting and terrifying.

Maybe the most terrifying thing I've ever done.

And that's why we can't take it any further than this. This will fade. The feelings are only there because I have a woman in my house that's taking care of not just this surprise kid, but of me, too. It's all new and different, and that's all.

I won't fuck up the balance of that with sex.

It's not worth it.

I shake off the feeling. "I should call it a night," I say. "I'm meeting some teammates for a workout and breakfast in the morning. Should be home around noon."

She nods. "Have fun. I'm going to stay out here a little while longer." She picks up the romance book she had sitting on the end table, and she's already engrossed in her book before I even get up from my chair.

I study her for just a second, and I immediately regret it when I realize my vow from only a second ago that it's not worth it was a total and complete lie.

* * *

"A certified letter came for you, Mr. Bradley," Dennis, the morning doorman, says to me as I walk back in after my morning with teammates.

It was a rowdy, fun morning, and to be honest, I can't wait to get my ass back on the field.

Six more days. Six days until training camp begins. Six days until I go back to being myself again. Six days until I get the fuck out of here and have a chance to think and breathe without this woman complicating my every thought.

Six days until I have to be away from her. Away from Jack. Away from the two people who have become such fixtures in my life in three short weeks.

I'm so goddamn conflicted, and the football field has always been where I've worked out those conflicts.

Only six of us made it this morning, but the five aside from me who came are good dudes who I consider good friends. And one of them, Deon, called me out on being quiet when I'm usually not.

He turned toward me during breakfast when the others were involved in their own conversation, and he asked, "What's going on with you?"

"Long story. I'll tell you next week," I said by way of getting him off my back.

But I'm not sure it did get him off my back, and I'm not sure I'll tell him next week, either.

I take the letter from Dennis and read the return address printed on the envelope, and I mumble a thank you before I head up to my penthouse.

I find Ainsley feeding Jack some pureed mangoes at the table, and I set the envelope down in front of her.

She glances at it, and then her eyes widen as she looks up at me.

"You open it," I say.

"Me? Why me?" she asks.

"Because I can't."

She presses her lips together, and she nods. I already know what it says. Of course he's mine. Just look at him.

But I need this confirmation anyway—at least according to my lawyer—so I wait for her to open it. I wander over to the windows as she wipes her hands on her shorts, and then I hear the rip of paper as she sticks her finger in the back and tears it open.

A few seconds that feel like hours later, her voice is quiet as she says, "He's yours."

I blow out a breath.

We both knew it, but this is confirmation. He's mine.

And before I know what I'm doing, I'm rushing over to him, pulling him out of his high chair, and squeezing him tightly against my chest in a hug.

I'm hugging my son, and now that I know beyond a shadow of a doubt that he's mine, I'm not going to let him go.

CHAPTER 18
Ainsley Bradley

Another Charity Event

Dex's publicist wasn't playing when he told Dex to attend more charity events. He got us last-minute tickets to yet another charity event this evening, and I know he's not ready to announce to the world that he has a child just yet since he hasn't even told his family, but it's going to be hard after the news he got today.

He agreed to do this event because it benefits the local children's hospital. Madison was able to babysit again, so we know Jack is in good hands.

Since this was last-minute, it's not the night he's going to get me drunk. It's not the night we're taking Jack somewhere for the night. The next one will be, though. It's where we plan to make our debut as husband and wife, too.

I'm wearing another of the gowns Milton had sent up for me. So I kept them all, okay? Dex said I could. This one is a deep navy with a sparkly belt, and I freaking *love* it. I'll wear it again, and a few others, and the ones I won't wear again are going in the donation pile. I can do good deeds and still dress the part of a football player's wife.

Speaking of which, I've been informed that several other players' wives will be in attendance tonight, and I'm excited to meet them.

"How are you feeling about the news you got today?"

He presses his lips together. "Better than I would have a couple weeks ago."

Sometimes he's so hard to read.

"Do you think you should start telling people?" I ask.

"I'll tell my family when the time feels right. I don't want him needlessly exposed to the media if he doesn't need to be. Until we're ready, it's not anyone's business but ours." His tone is resolute, and honestly…it's really freaking sexy.

We arrive at the event, and as he slips his hand into mine, I can't help but think back to that kiss on our wedding day.

I can't help but want him to kiss me again tonight.

We walk the red carpet into the event, and one side is lined with reporters and influencers yelling questions at us.

"Dex! Who's your date?" someone yells.

"This is Ainsley." He grabs my hand and pulls me inside, and my heart is racing.

How *isn't* his?

Once we're inside, my heart is still racing. As he takes me to the bar, I'm starting to see why people drink at these things. If nothing else, it calms the nerves a bit.

"Whiskey for me, vodka Sprite with three cherries for the lady," he orders, and he's being all protective, and oh God, there goes that ache between my legs getting all throbby and uncomfortable again.

I have to ignore it since the man I now recognize as Asher walks up beside us with a gorgeous redhead by his side.

"Bradley," he says cordially, and Dex turns around and shakes his hand.

"Asher, this is Ainsley," he says, introducing us.

I shake Asher's hand, and then I turn to the woman with him.

"Hi, I'm Ainsley," I say.

"Desi," she says. She flicks her neck toward Asher. "The wife." She grins, and I laugh. "It's nice to meet you."

"You too," I say, and Dex hands me my drink while Asher orders for himself and his wife.

Once she has a glass of water, she turns to me. "Nobody cares about us at these events, so I like to go bid on all the auction items while Asher isn't looking. Want to come with me?" She sticks out her elbow.

My eyes flick to Dex first, and he gives me a slight nod of his head as if to say that she's safe—a much-needed reassurance given that I know literally nobody here. I slip my arm through hers. "I'd love to."

We head toward the auction tables together, and she writes bids on several of the items while I just peruse all the things that I could never afford...except that's the thing.

I *can* now.

I'm making bank as a nanny for Jack, but it's so ingrained in me not to be wasteful, not to spend money frivolously.

I guess it was always sort of a dream to attend something like this, and as I look through gift baskets and tickets to events and signed memorabilia, I can't believe that I'm really, actually here.

And then Dex slides into place beside me, setting his hand on the small of my back, and it feels even more surreal.

How is this my life?

He guides me over to the table for dinner, and we're sitting with Asher and Desi. There are some other football players at our table as well, all guys who play on the same team as Dex with their dates, and somehow this event feels so much more relaxed than the last one.

We laugh through dinner. I chat with Desi and get to know her.

I don't admit that I'm actually married to Dex, but the news will break soon enough. Maybe I'll get a chance to know her even more when she realizes we're both football wives. Maybe we'll sit at games together and toast to touchdowns as we cheer on our husbands.

It's also possible that I'm completely delusional and nothing like that will ever happen, but I'm okay with living in fantasyland just a little while longer.

Especially since it means that I get to play the part of Dex Bradley's wife. And as we take the dance floor after dinner and sway together to a slow song, it's starting to feel more and more like a role I was born to play.

CHAPTER 19
Ainsley Bradley

One of the Safest SUVs on the Road

I drive away from Lincoln Nash's place in Dex Bradley's Challenger, and if you would've told me a month ago that this would be my life, I'd say you're bananas.

But here we are.

I feel a pull of sadness that I dropped off Jack. I miss him already.

I shouldn't be getting attached. This is a nanny and kid situation, but my heart is fully invested in this sweet baby as it starts to cling onto his father, too.

And that will only spell certain danger. There's nothing I can do to spare myself the possibility of getting hurt, yet he's taking me on a date tonight. We're married. We're living together. How am I supposed to *not* let feelings get involved?

It's easy to push them away—easy to remind myself who he is, not just Ivy's older brother, but one of the bad boys of pro football. He sleeps around, and he takes risks, and that's not somebody I want to get involved with. Or…*more* involved with, I guess, considering we're married.

And tonight we're debuting our relationship for the media. He's going to tell the press that I'm his wife.

They'll check the Nevada marriage license site and determine he's telling the truth, and then who knows what'll happen next?

I get a sort of ominous feeling about tonight. Debuting me as his wife *and* getting me drunk in the same night feels like a recipe for disaster, but he has assured me it's perfectly safe and we'll be able to avoid the press.

"Stop living in your head."

"Start having some fun."

"As my wife, you have no choice but to have some fun."

The last one made me laugh *and* warm at the same time.

When I pull the Challenger back into Dex's parking spot at his complex after dropping the baby off for the night, I'm shocked to find Dex in the space beside mine, and I'm even more shocked when I see what he's doing.

"Are you installing a car seat into that SUV?" I ask.

"That I am," he says. "Motherfucking little rat fucker," he curses at the seat, and I can't help but laugh at his colorful language now that it's just between us.

"Whose car is that?" I ask.

"Yours."

I think I choke on something. Maybe I heard him incorrectly since he's talking into the backseat. "Excuse me?"

He straightens and turns to look at me. "I'm sorry, but I don't let just anyone drive the Challenger, and while I allowed it once, I figured you should have your own car to get around town. So—" He cuts himself off to motion to the car, and this isn't real, is it?

"You bought me a car to use while I'm in town?"

"Well, you can keep it if you decide to leave town, too." He shrugs. "The title's in your name, so you're free to do whatever you want with it."

I glance at the back and spot the logo.

"You bought me a Mercedes?"

He closes the back door, apparently happy with his work on car seat installation. He lifts a shoulder. "This is supposed to be one of the safest SUVs on the road." He wipes his palms on the front of his shorts, and I can't help but rush over to tackle him with a hug.

He lets out a little *oof* as I crash into him.

"Thank you so much, Dex. This is the nicest thing anyone's ever done for me."

He slings his arm around my waist, and he pulls me into him a little. His voice is low and raspy near my ear. "My wife deserves a car of her own."

I force myself out of his arms. If I stay there another minute, I'll try to kiss him, and he won't kiss back, and things will just get awkward.

"I should go get ready for tonight," I mumble. "Thanks for the car."

It sounds ridiculous coming out of my mouth. It *is* ridiculous. Nobody has ever bought me a car before, including my parents. I worked for years running concession stands at middle school and high school events to save up enough for volleyball camp and a shitty used car, and my parents didn't have enough to help me out.

So this? This is a real gift. Something I never saw coming.

And I'm not sure how to thank him for that. My simple *thank you* doesn't seem like enough, but I've never been real good at accepting gifts or compliments from people.

I head inside and slip into another one of the gowns Milton sent up for me, and tonight I leave my hair down but add some curls. It's weird not to have to feed a baby who, according to his birth certificate, is now seven months old, but it's also a welcome reprieve. Babies are a heck of a lot of work.

I'm also bracing myself for tonight—for all sorts of things. This is the night, the one we planned for. There's the possibility that my date could get into another fight even though he behaved at the last event. Combine that with the probability that he's going to try to get me drunk and what sort of fool I'll make out of myself when he does, and I'm not quite sure what to expect tonight.

I'm excited about it even though I seemed closed to the idea when he first mentioned it. What better way to get actually hammered for the first time than with an NFL star who knows how to do it right?

I'm nervous, too. I can't pretend I'm not.

And I'm guessing that's why he has a shot glass with some liquid in it waiting on the counter for me.

I laugh when I see it, and I glance over at him. I don't miss the way his eyes flick down my body, branding every place they touch before they move back to mine.

"Wow, Ains. You look gorgeous."

"You don't look too bad yourself," I say, not allowing myself the same courtesy of studying every inch of his body the way he just did to me since there's only one way that will end—and that's with me either brokenhearted or embarrassed.

He chuckles. "This is a smooth whiskey to get you started and calm the nerves. I promise I will take care of you tonight, and if there's ever a limit you're even coming close to approaching, just say the word and it all stops."

"What word?" I ask.

"Any word. Just tell me to stop, and it ends there. But if you want more, or you want me to push you to take risks, or you want to let go and say *fuck it*, tell me that, too. Just be open and communicate. Okay?"

I nod a little tentatively, and it's like he can sense my nervousness.

He walks around the counter with his little shot glass, and he holds it up. "To just saying fuck it," he says, and I hold up my glass.

"Fuck it."

He taps his to mine as he laughs, and I tip the glass to my lips.

He shoots his down. I, on the other hand, take tiny little ladylike sips.

He laughs again as he watches me, and once I've emptied the glass, my chest warms, and I already feel a little more comfortable about tonight.

It's not going to take much to get me drunk, that's for damn sure.

"Ready?" he asks, and I nod, grab my clutch, and follow him out the front door.

Milton greets us with a nod of his head, and it seems like he's always here, but there are actually four different doormen who switch around shifts. Milton is just here during primetime hours, and he lives in the building, so we see him more often.

I also learned that he works in some capacity for Dex on the side. I don't know exactly what it entails, but he's almost like a caretaker and assistant combined into one who's always there but stays behind the scenes.

The car is waiting out front for us, and the driver tells Dex to text him when he's ready to head back. We pull up the driveway to the hotel where the event is taking place, and it's another red-carpet affair.

Nerves climb up my spine as I realize this is it. We're about to make our public debut as husband and wife.

Before Dex opens the door to get out of the car, he turns to me. "Are you ready for this?"

I wrinkle my nose. "Do I have a choice?"

"I thought the whiskey would help."

I laugh. "It wore off."

He twists his lips. "I probably should've told the rest of my family about this before we went public at an event, but honestly…I don't think any of them will be surprised."

"You didn't tell them?"

"Not all of them." He pulls his lips down toward his jaw as if to make the *whoops* face. "Well, let's do this, and then let's get you wasted."

"Let's do it," I say, and he opens the car door.

Flashbulbs explode in our faces as we hear the same noisy voices yelling at us as the last time we did this.

"Dex Bradley!"

"Dex, are you going to get into a fight again tonight?"

I roll my eyes at that one.

"Dex, over here! Dex!"

"Who's your date?"

Dex looks at me, and I mouth, "Fuck it," to him.

He grins as he turns to the entertainment reporters and influencers yelling questions at us. "This is Ainsley Bradley, my wife."

A collective gasp rises up from the group gathered, causing just a split second of stunned silence, and then more questions are fired at us.

"When did you get married?"

"Show us the ring!"

"Is this real?"

"Kiss for the cameras!"

He turns toward me, and I look over at him, and the cameras are going crazy for the two of us. I can't wait to see how we look together as we look at each other, me likely with adoration in my eyes for this hot football star who's suddenly my husband, as if any of this makes any sense at all.

He leans in, and his lips meet mine in what's only our second kiss.

This one is just for the cameras and just because someone in the crowd requested it, but I can't help feeling like this is some sort of fairy tale. Like I'm Cinderella, and this is the ball, and this swoony older single dad is the prince who rescued me as I work hard to rescue him right back.

CHAPTER 20

DEX BRADLEY

Long, Lingering Gaze

That's twice.

Two times I've kissed her.

Two times that were far too short.

Two times that were for show.

I want to kiss her for *me*. I want to kiss her not because it's expected at the end of a ceremony and not because the media is yelling at me to do it and I need to prove something to them. I want to do it because I fucking want to do it.

I shouldn't. I can't. I need to remember all the reasons why it's a horrible, terrible idea.

We walk into the event, and we grab a drink first—more whiskey for me, and she opts for a peach bellini since it's the featured cocktail and the bartender tells her it doesn't really taste like alcohol at all.

She takes her first sip and smiles with delight. "This is delicious," she says.

"Be careful," I warn. "Prosecco will likely get to work pretty fast on someone who doesn't drink much."

What the fuck?

When in the history of the world have I ever warned a woman to take it slow when it comes to drinking?

Never. The answer is exactly never.

I didn't take it slow on *any* of my younger siblings when I took it upon myself to get them drunk for the first time. It was a rite of passage. They all came to me since they knew I started with Everleigh, and they knew that as much as I can focus on having a good time, I also know how to help others have a good time in a controlled and safe way.

And, you know…puke doesn't faze me.

I don't want to get Ains *sick* drunk or *blackout* drunk tonight, though. I just want her to cut loose and have some fun.

And the more I think that, the more I want that fun to be with *me*.

Not taking her to some private VIP lounge and giving her a new experience.

Not taking her for a drag race down the Strip.

Not taking her to the members-only sex club.

Just her, me, and my place. One night of fun that I can remember every time I look at the spot where she lay naked while I took her from behind, or from the top, or while she rode me.

Fuck, man.

What the fuck am I doing?

I blow out a breath as I attempt to pull myself together.

"I'm going to go use the ladies' room before dinner starts," she says, and I'm left to my own devices by the auction items.

It's not hard to work this room alone. I know about half the people in it, and the other half seem to know me. But somehow working the room with Ainsley by my side makes it so much better.

I haven't quite worked out why that is yet, or how she manages to make it better, but I think I'm starting to figure it out.

She's been my wife for a week. She's lived with me for close to three weeks.

We've spent a lot of time around each other, and she's not really a friend yet.

And despite all that, feelings are becoming involved. Unknown feelings. Unfamiliar feelings. Uncharted feelings.

I don't like it.

But as she walks back into the room after her bathroom break and I'm chatting with retired Aces defensive back Grayson Nash about the Aces' D-line this upcoming season, I can't help but catch my breath as our eyes meet from across the room.

Whatever Grayson's talking about seems to fade away as I stare at her walking toward me. Her eye catches mine, and she glances down at herself like something's wrong—maybe she's dragging some toilet paper behind her on her shoe, or she spilled some water in the bathroom.

That's sort of the whole problem, though.

There's nothing wrong with her at all.

She's perfect.

There's a lot wrong with *our situation*, which is the main reason I haven't acted on these *feelings* that seem to be pelting me in the chest, but when it comes to her…all I see is this gorgeous woman who seems to be sacrificing everything to help me.

Her eyes flick back to mine, and I hold her gaze as she walks toward me. It's a long, lingering gaze. The kind that might dip into awkward territory for some people. But I can't seem to look away.

"It'll be nice watching another season on my couch with my wife's cookies," Grayson says, and he pats his stomach.

I think he's waiting for a laugh, but I'm in a trance with the woman walking toward me.

"Who's she?" Grayson asks, lowering his voice when he sees who I'm staring at.

I finally break my gaze at her to glance at the guy I'm supposed to be having a conversation with. I clear my throat. "She's my wife."

The words don't feel natural coming out of my mouth just yet, but the more times I say it, the more it's starting to feel real.

"I'm Grayson Nash," he says, introducing himself to Ainsley when she reaches us.

"Ainsley Ri—uh, Bradley."

"How long have you two been married?" Grayson asks.

"A week today," I admit.

"Well, congratulations to you both. Let me buy you a drink," he says.

"It's an open bar," I say, and he laughs.

"Oh, right. Well, the tip's on me."

We head over to the bar for a second drink, and as promised, Grayson tips the bartender. We're called to our seats for dinner then, and I lean in toward Ainsley as they serve the first course.

"What the fuck is this?" I ask.

She picks up a menu sitting on the table. "Truffle mushroom tartlet," she reads.

"It looks like dirt. And bugs. I'll pass."

She giggles. "As appetizing as you made that sound, I'll wait for the heirloom tomato salad coming next."

"What happened to mozzarella sticks and jalapeño poppers?"

"You're at a fancy charity ball, Dex. Remember?"

"Have you ever been to one of these?" I ask.

She gives me a funny look and shakes her head. "Not much opportunity for this type of event in the Riggs household. The fanciest dinners I had were the Monday night masterpieces at Casa de Bradley."

I chuckle. "Ivy calls them that, doesn't she?"

She nods. "What about you? Did you grow up around these things?"

"Yeah, pretty much. And I'd usually eat before I went."

She looks surprised. "You would?"

I nod. "Yeah. I'd order mozzarella sticks, jalapeño poppers, and a pizza."

She leans in as the mushroom dirt thing is taken away. "Let's order that when we get home. Except not jalapeño poppers. Breaded zucchini sticks."

I make a face of disgust. "Zucchini?"

"Jalapeños?" she counters.

"Fine. We'll get both."

She giggles, and it's that sound that's becoming music to my ears.

Fuck. What the hell is wrong with me?

We don't get much chance to talk more as the speeches from the charity officials begin. After that, there's some dancing while guests are given another bit of time to finalize their bids for the silent auction items. We follow Grayson and his wife outside to the rooftop terrace and chat with them for before they head inside to listen to the winners of the auction since they bid on some of the items, but we stay outside, drinking in the view of the Las Vegas skyline.

It's just the two of us up here along with a bartender and a server, who are murmuring in the corner. Everyone else went back inside for the auction.

We're sitting beside each other on a sleek couch in front of a fancy little gas firepit offering glowing light and a bit of heat, but Ainsley shivers beside me.

"Are you cold?" I ask.

She nods, and I move in a little closer and toss my arm around her. She snuggles into my side, and it feels…good.

I feel content. It feels like she fits. She fucking just fits in so many goddamn confusing ways.

I jump up from my seat as soon as I feel it, and she seems confused by my sudden movement. I start to pace the rooftop.

Maybe it's the whiskey, or maybe it's just *her* that's making me feel fucking intoxicated.

"Are you all right?" she asks as she lifts to a stand.

I stop in my tracks and turn to look at her. We're just a few feet apart as we face off, and no, I'm not fucking *all right*. I'm more and more confused by the second when it comes to her.

I can't seem to stop my feet as they close the gap between us. I slide my arm around her waist and haul her close—like I did at our wedding just a week ago.

But when my mouth crashes down to hers this time, it's not for a photo op or some ingrained requirement.

It's for me.

I'm taking a risk. Chasing the thrill. Doing what feels good.

And kissing Ainsley Riggs feels real fucking good.

CHAPTER 21

Ainsley Bradley

Boys and Men

I sink into him as his lips press to mine.

I've kissed plenty of boys. Just because I haven't had sex doesn't mean I haven't done other stuff. I even kissed someone new as recently as a couple of weeks ago when I almost married Jordan.

But this? This is a *man*.

Yes, I've kissed plenty of boys. But I've never kissed a man. Not like this.

His hand moves to cup my jaw, and I let myself get lost in it as he opens his mouth to mine. His arm is tugging me against his body, and I feel how hard he is everywhere as one of my hands moves to his chest while the other dives into his hair.

I'm lost in him for a few seconds that are far, far too short as I realize what's happening here.

I'm getting lost in a kiss that he's just using for a display. This is a show. It's not about getting me a little tipsy and giving in to this pull between us. There is no pull. It's simply me fantasizing about the things I cannot and will not have.

Someone somewhere must be watching, and that's what forces me to pull back from him. After I moan into him a little, naturally, because *why not* make it even more awkward and ridiculous? That's just me. That's what I do.

If he's smooth and sexy, I'm a bumbling idiot.

I don't know what to do or say as my eyes meet his heavily lidded ones.

It's for show, I remind myself.

"Another drink?" I ask brightly. Too brightly. *Awkwardly* brightly.

"Mm," he says, and he not-so-subtly adjusts himself over his pants as he gives me a strange look, then beelines for the bar.

I blow out a breath, feeling like I made the right choice by ending that before it got out of hand. But still, something deep down feels…off.

Like I shouldn't have ended it.

I didn't *want* to end it.

A moment later, we have fresh drinks in hand and head back inside to the ball. The auction winners are announced, and I guess it's time to party now as the dance floor seems to pick up.

"Want to get out of here?" Dex asks me.

"Whatever you want," I say.

He pulls out his phone, and then we head toward the front doors. A few minutes later, we're climbing into the back of the car Milton arranged for us.

"We're heading home?" I ask. "What happened to taking me out? Taking risks? Saying fuck it? Getting me wasted?"

He clears his throat and glances away from me, and I'm not sure what he's thinking. Maybe he's tired of me and wants to get rid of me so he can go back out and have some fun.

Eventually he lets out a breath, and then he says, "It didn't seem like your scene. We can have another drink at home. I was wrong to push you into getting drunk. You can just have a drink or two if that's all you want."

I tilt my head and purse my lips as I contemplate that. "Is that what you want to do?"

He presses his lips together, and then he narrows his eyes at me. "I'm not sure what I want, to be honest. But you seemed uncomfortable, and I kind of figured the easiest route to figuring out why was to get you home where we could talk."

"Talk?" I ask, a bit of incredulity in my voice. "You want to *talk*? You took me home early so we could *talk*?"

He chuckles. "Yeah, I know. I don't know what the fuck's happening to me, either. A night at home, a few drinks looking out over the view with you...I don't know. It sounds relaxing."

"What do you want to talk about?" I ask, still a bit dumbfounded.

He seems to contemplate what to say, and then he turns back into the direct guy I've come to know. Only...his direct *response* leaves me with my jaw hanging open. "I want to talk about why you ended the kiss up on the rooftop."

"Huh?"

"The kiss. You didn't like it?" he asks.

"Oh my God, Dex. No, that wasn't it at all. I was just..." I trail off as my cheeks turn bright pink.

I can't exactly admit to him that I was about to lose myself in that kiss in a way I'd never done before during a kiss in my life, so instead, I say, "I was getting caught up in the moment, and I forgot where I was for a minute. That's all." I turn away from him and look out the window, but he doesn't let me get away with that.

"What does that mean? Caught up in the moment?"

I chew my bottom lip for a few beats. "I forgot who was kissing me, okay? I forgot that this can't happen between us." My words come out as a whisper, and he's quiet beside me until I feel his fingertips under my chin, forcing me to look at him.

"Why not?" His voice is low and raspy when he asks me, and the car glides to a stop as we arrive at our destination.

Thank goodness.

I don't think I have the strength to sit back here with those eyes pinning me to my spot another second.

I practically jump out of the car, which is an absolute mistake because I'm wearing a gown, and said gown gets caught under me as I step out of the car, and I proceed to trip forward since I'm stepping on my own gown. I'm about to plow face-first into a planter when strong arms haul around my waist to save me.

Dammit.

I can't seem to escape this guy's arms tonight, and it's just reminder after reminder that *I want him.*

Well, one more peach bellini and maybe I won't be strong enough to continue telling him all the reasons why we can't be together.

I realize as soon as I think it that we never actually detailed said reasons, and as I straighten back to a stand and manage to step off the hem of my dress, I mutter a *thank you* and make my way inside.

We're on the elevator alone when he says, "I'm your best friend's older brother. I'm paying you to take care of my kid. We hardly know each other. You're ten years younger than me. You're too sweet and pure and kind for someone like me. We've got a contract. Does that cover it?"

"Eleven years," I correct, folding my arms over my chest.

"Eleven years," he repeats. "Fuck." He shakes his head a little, and then he steps closer, taking away some of the small space separating us—the space I was counting on, to be honest. "I don't give a shit about any of that. I know what I felt when I kissed you, Ains, and I didn't want it to end."

"You weren't kissing me for show?" I ask, confused at his words.

"There was nobody up there to show off to," he says quietly. "I thought you felt it, too. Maybe I misread the situation."

"I'm scared, Dex. I'm scared you're going to hurt me."

He nods. "That's valid, and I probably will. But don't you just want to say *fuck it* and give it a try anyway?"

"Give what a try?" I ask, absolute vulnerability at the top of my tone.

"This. This pull between us."

The elevator skids to a stop on Dex's floor and gives us that little pause before the doors open, and that's when I blurt, "I'm a virgin."

The doors open, and his jaw is somewhere down on the floor as he stares at me.

"You're a..." He trails off.

"Virgin," I confirm.

He's still staring at me, and we're still standing on the elevator when the doors slide shut. The elevator doesn't move, but we're still on it.

"You've never..."

"Had sex," I say. I shake my head, and then something in the air between us shifts.

It crackles and sparkles with tension.

Need.

Want.

Desire.

From both people occupying this space. Need, want, desire for the other person standing too close.

He's kissed me three times now, and I never thought it would go any further than that. Public displays of affection for public consumption.

But the way he's looking at me now tells me he wants me for more than just my mouth. He's looking at me like he wants to devour me. Like he wants to explore every untouched inch of my naked body.

I may be innocent, but I'm not naïve.

He clears his throat, and his eyes are heated. "I won't take that from you, but goddamn, Ains. I fucking want to."

"Then do it," I whisper.

"What?" he asks, the end of the word lost in the air between us.

"Do it. Take it. I want you to. There's never been anyone worthy of it. Until you."

He shakes his head and takes a step back. "No, no. Make no mistake, Birdie. I'm not worthy of it. I'm not worthy of *you*."

It's *me* closing the gap between us now. "Come on, Dexter." I raise a brow. "What's it gonna be? Are you all in? Are you gonna say *fuck it* and give me what I want?"

He takes a step back, bumping into the wall of the elevator. He closes his eyes and leans back, his neck corded and his jaw clenched at my words as he contemplates what to do here.

"You don't want it from me. Trust me," he says.

I close the final space between us, my chest against his. He's got height on me, but I'm in heels. I reach up and slide my fingertip along his jawline. "I've started to trust you, Dex. You've been letting me in. Allowing me to see parts of you that nobody else gets to see. And now I want to give you a part of me that nobody else has seen."

He stares down at me, his eyes heated and conflicted at the same time as he contemplates what to do and how to handle this.

Instead of answering, his mouth crashes down to mine. He slides his hand along my jawline as he kisses me here, *really* kisses me, his tongue tangling with mine as he pulls me in closer with his other hand, hauling me toward him around my waist.

He turns us so I'm the one against the wall now, and he has me caged in. His hips rock against mine, and I feel it, feel *him* and how much he wants to give in to this thing between us that's becoming harder and harder to ignore. He's hard and needy, all man, as my hands move to his chest and then to his arms so I have something to grip onto since my knees feel like they could give out at any second.

There's an unspoken promise between us, a vow that once we get off this elevator, something different is going to happen. Something I've never experienced before. This kiss is just a preview, but it's both of us giving our consent to moving this to the next level.

It feels like I'm flying, and that's when the *ding* of the elevator pulls me out of the trance I'm in. We *are* flying, or rather, the elevator is moving because he was too shocked by my words to get off on his floor, and now we've traveled back down to the ground floor. He reluctantly moves off me just as the doors pull open, and I'm sure my lips are swollen from his, and I look like an absolute train wreck when I spot the person standing on the other side of the elevator doors waiting to go up.

"Surprise!" she says.

"Ivy?" both Dex and I say at the same time.

Shit. What the hell is Ivy doing here?

CHAPTER 22

Dex Bradley

Surprise, Surprise

I'm in a haze after the kiss and the whole virgin comment that came from left fucking field, but somewhere in the midst of the haze, I seem to recall a text message from my sister.

She asked about her birthday and whether she could stay with me since her best friend is here. After all, my little sister only turns twenty-one once, as she reminded me.

It was a couple weeks ago, and the memory slipped by considering everything that's been going on lately.

But here she is, surprise, surprise, and my plans to take her best friend's virginity tonight are put decidedly onto the back burner.

I'm not going to fuck Ainsley with my sister right down the hall—no matter how tempted I am right now. No matter how horny I am for her. No matter how much I want her.

Maybe Ivy showing up out of the blue and us being here on this elevator to greet her at her arrival was the bucket of ice-fucking-cold water we needed to put a halt on this very bad idea.

We step off the elevator and greet her with hugs, my eyes meeting Ainsley's over my sister's shoulder.

"Did you two know I was here?" she asks. "Is that why you came down?"

"Yes! Totally!" Ainsley says, and her voice is a little higher than normal. She looks like she's about to panic, and I realize I never told her my sister was coming to Vegas.

"I didn't tell Ains you were coming," I say to Ivy. "Figured it would be a surprise. We just got back from a charity event when the doorman let me know I had a guest coming up, so we figured we'd just come back down." Okay, fine. Maybe my voice isn't higher than usual, but I'm definitely babbling, which is *not* something I tend to do.

I get back onto the elevator and press my floor, and the elevator carries us back up. This time, we step off. I remember that while Jack is at Lincoln's house for the night since I had planned to get Ainsley drunk without having to worry about being hungover first thing in the morning, there is likely still baby supplies all over, including the highchair at the kitchen table.

"Uh, there's something you should know," I say to Ivy before I slide my key into my door.

She tilts her head and looks at me with curiosity. "What?"

"I, uh…" I glance at Ainsley. "Well, *we*…"

She shakes her head furiously, and I realize she thinks I'm going to tell Ivy we were just making out on the elevator.

"I have a kid," I blurt.

Ainsley looks relieved, Ivy looks shocked, and I feel like I got hit by a truck.

My sister gasps. "What?"

"I found out the same day Ainsley left her reality show, and it all just sort of crashed together at the right time. I needed help with this six-month-old I'd just found out about, and she needed a local place to lay low, and she said she could help me." I shrug as if it all makes perfect sense. While it might to us, I realize it won't to my sister.

"You have a kid?" Ivy asks me. She turns to Ainsley. "And you—you—you are *helping* my brother with this kid?"

Ainsley nods. "I'm the nanny."

"And the wife," I say, and somehow that strikes us both as fucking hilarious because we both burst into laughter.

"The baby's nanny," she clarifies through her laughter, and she sets a hand on the wall as she doubles over with laughter. She jerks her thumb at me. "His wife."

"I'm her husband," I say between my own laughter, and Ivy just looks at us like we've both lost our minds.

"I knew that part. The kid part, though…why'd you leave it out?"

I draw in a breath as I try to pull it together. Once the laughter has calmed, I slip the key into my door and explain the situation as we walk in. "I just got the DNA test results back the other morning. I didn't want to tell anyone until I had definitive proof he was mine. We'd already arranged to have him stay with my coach tonight while we attended a charity ball." I leave out the part about getting Ainsley drunk. It seems dangerous to add that in at this point. Ivy doesn't need to know that I was just kissing her friend on the elevator, either.

"So this six-month-old kid…" Ivy says, trailing off. "Boy? Girl? Does it have a name?"

"A boy named Jack," I say.

"And does he have a mother?" she asks.

"Are you serious with that question?" I ask.

She purses her lips and rolls her eyes at me. "It was my nice way of asking where the mother is."

"No longer around," I say, dodging her real question. "She dropped him with me and signed over full custody."

"Jeez, Dex. And you've kept all this a secret?"

"Not intentionally. I was working on figuring things out. But now Ains and I have a system down, and she's been a real lifesaver."

Ivy looks between her best friend and me, and I get the feeling if I don't get the fuck out of here quickly, she'll be on to both of us.

And that's why I decide to call it a night.

I show Ivy to her guest room first, and Ainsley follows her in so they can catch up.

It's definitely not the sort of night I was planning on having, but I head to my bed alone.

I wake up alone, too. Jerking off in the shower doesn't help. I'm hot for my little sister's best friend, and a good fuck is about the only thing that's going to give me any relief at all. But as I think through the women I could call on to give me just that, I realize something important.

I don't want any of them. I just want her.

And that's a problem.

I blow out a breath as I fight it off. Five days now. Five more days until the start of my next season, and my little sister is here cockblocking me for four of those days.

On Sunday night, though…all bets are off.

CHAPTER 23

Ainsley Bradley

Drunker than I Realized

It's admittedly very fun having Ivy here, but I was expecting to wake up beside Dex this morning.

It was also admittedly nice having the morning off and sleeping in. I take a quick shower and find Dex in the kitchen.

"Where's the birthday girl?" I ask.

He shrugs. "Haven't seen her. Probably still sleeping."

"Should we talk about that kiss last night?" I ask, my voice low just in case she's up.

His eyes meet mine for a few heated seconds, and just when he opens his mouth to say something, we both hear Ivy's door open.

His jaw clamps shut, but before she walks into the room, he whispers, "I want to do it again."

My face is as red as a tomato when Ivy walks in, but I do my best to pretend everything is completely fine as I yell, "Happy birthday!"

I rush over to toss my arms around her, and she laughs.

"Happy birthday, little sis," Dex says to her, mussing her hair, and she rolls her eyes as she runs her hand over it to smooth it out.

"When do I get to meet my nephew?" Ivy asks.

"Tomorrow, probably." And then he surprises the hell out of me by saying, "I ordered breakfast about a half hour ago, so it should be here any minute. And for your birthday gift, I booked you two deluxe spa treatments for the day, the salon after, a personal stylist, and reservations at one of the hottest new restaurants in town. Go out, live it up, have some Vegas-style fun."

My jaw drops. "What?"

"I've got Jack," he says. "All day, and night, too. You two go out. I'll get him from my coach's place in a bit, and we'll have a boys' day. I only have a few days left until camp, and then I'll be out of town for two weeks. I have to get in my time while I can."

I can't tell if he's trying to get rid of me, get rid of his sister, or if he genuinely wants to spend time with his son now that he has all the facts.

The hopeful part of me wants it to be option three. The cynical part of me thinks it's option one.

But there's something else he said that's news to me.

"Wait…what?" I ask. "What's this about two weeks?"

"I didn't tell you?" he asks.

"Didn't tell me you'll be gone for two weeks? Yeah, no. That didn't make it into our conversation," I say. "Where are you going?"

"I'm sorry. I thought everyone knew. The entire Aces organization travels to California for the first two weeks of training camp."

"So you leave Monday?" I ask flatly.

"Yeah. Is that okay?" he asks.

"I mean…do I have a choice other than for it to be okay?" I know I sound a bit whiny, but so far, while I've taken on the majority of the work with the baby, I haven't taken on *all* of it. Dex is still here to help and give me time off.

But he won't be around for two entire weeks, and then his season will be underway, and I have no idea what to expect as we head into that.

"Sorry," he says again. "I really thought you knew."

I don't argue because maybe it is common knowledge that just didn't make its way to me, yet he still glances over at me. In a quiet voice, he says, "Everyone deserves a day off once in a while. And with me heading out for camp, I figured this was a good time to do it."

I press my lips together. "Thanks, Dex," I finally say. "That was really nice of you. You and Jack today…you got this."

He smiles and nods. "I know I do. I've been watching you for the last three weeks. And I ordered those peepee teepees, so I'm all set."

"Peepee teepee?" Ivy repeats.

"Long story," I say with a giggle.

"Oh, did you two see this?" Ivy asks. She flashes her phone at us and reads the headline aloud as we follow along with her. "Aces DE Dex Bradley No Longer Single."

Dex raises his brows, and his phone starts to ring before he says anything. "Excuse me."

He spends the next hour on the phone, presumably fielding calls about being married, and he has his publicist issue a statement. I guess this is what happens when we decide to go live with our news at a charity event.

He's still dealing with all that after breakfast when it's time for Ivy and me to make our way to our first appointment of the day.

A short while later, I find myself relaxing at the spa with a mask on my face next to Ivy, who just finished her facial. Up next is our ninety-minute Swedish massage, and then manis and pedis. It's been a dream of a day already, and it's been fun having Ivy here as we catch up on lost time.

But the fact that he's going to leave in a few days for two entire weeks and it's just going to be me and his baby alone in his penthouse feels like it's looming over me.

He admitted this morning he wants to kiss me again. I can still feel his lips on mine. Still feel his hips as they thrust against me. Still feel his hard cock as it pressed against my hip through his pants.

God, I want him.

And the one person I usually talk to about stuff like this can never, ever know.

Dex thought of everything, and after our massages, we head to the salon next to the spa to get our hair and makeup done for a night out. He even sent a personal shopper to greet us at the salon and get our sizes, and she returns an hour later with different clothing options for our night.

I settle on a purple sequin minidress that's slightly shorter than I usually opt for, and the birthday girl picks out an edgy corset-style top with a leather skirt.

Our styles feel different and totally Vegas at the same time, and the car from Dex's complex is waiting to take us to dinner once we're ready. When we get inside, it's packed, and our table isn't quite ready, so we head to the bar.

"Vodka Sprite, extra cherries," I say to the bartender.

"Make it two," Ivy says.

"ID," the bartender says, and we both hand over our licenses. "Happy birthday," he says to Ivy, and what better place than Vegas to spend a twenty-first birthday?

Our drinks arrive, and they're strong, and we're hungry.

They go down quickly—mainly so we can get to those cherries that sank to the bottom—and our table is ready just as we each grab a second.

By the time dinner is over nearly two hours later and our server lets us know the bill has been paid by Dex Bradley, I'm on my fourth and so is Ivy. As two women in their early twenties who rarely drink, we're both feeling it. Hard.

We head to a nightclub in the same hotel as the restaurant next since Dex told us to live it up Vegas-style, and I can't help wondering how he's doing with Jack. He hasn't called me all day, and though I've thought about texting him, I also want him to rest assured that he's capable. I don't want him to feel like I'm checking up on him.

But I sort of want to check up on him…because I miss him. I'm not sure when he became my friend in all this, but somehow, he did.

My thoughts are jumbled, and when I take my phone out to try to send him a text, I have to close one eye to focus. I'm not quite sure what it says when I hit send, but I think it says something along the lines of *hey, just checking in!*

Ivy and I hit the dance floor and proceed to start to attempt to sweat off some of the alcohol. My phone rings a few minutes later, and I see it's Dex calling.

"Hey!" I scream into the phone.

He says something, but I can't hear him.

"What?" I scream.

He says something else, but I still can't hear him.

"We're at the club you told Ivy about!" I yell. "I can't hear you!"

The call ends, and I slip it back into my crossbody and resume my dancing with Ivy.

A few minutes later, some guy starts dancing with me from behind. He didn't ask but instead is just moving along my backside. Is this how they do things here in Vegas? Because I didn't ask for this.

When I feel his boner against my ass, I turn around and glare at him, and he holds up both hands as if to say he's sorry before he walks away.

A few minutes later, a different guy starts dancing behind me, and his friend is dancing behind Ivy. We each make eyes at each other, and I'm about to turn around and glare at this guy, too, when suddenly he's down on the floor and I have no clue what the hell just happened.

But when I look up and see Dex as he shakes out his hand, I have a pretty good feeling about what it was.

Dex is here.

I force the hearts out of my eyes. He showed up, and he just slugged the guy who was coming onto me, no questions asked. He looks fine as fuck as our eyes meet, and I think I realize in the moment how incredibly powerful the feelings I have for him have become.

He's becoming someone who takes care of the people around him rather than taking care of his own needs first. Somewhere in the recesses of my mind, I know that's true.

I mean, we need to work on his reactive nature a bit, but it would appear that both times I've seen him throw a punch, he's done it *for me*.

Does that mean he's changing? Or is this just who he always was? Either way, I hope there could be a future for us.

That could be the vodka talking. I think I'm drunker than I even realized.

Reality plows into me as I realize I have no clue why he's actually here.

"What are you doing here? Where's Jack?" I ask.

"He's with Milton. Are you okay?"

My brows crash together. "I'm fine," I say, though as the guy on the floor clutches his jaw in pain, I'm suddenly not *feeling* very fine. In fact, I'm pretty sure the alcohol is ready to make an exit, and not through the standard pathways.

"Shit," I mutter, and I cover my mouth as I feel my stomach heave.

There's no time to get to the bathroom.

I don't have enough time to react. This is my first time being this drunk, and I suddenly feel like I'm stuck in place as I bend over at the waist and proceed to throw up all over the floor.

And Dex's shoes.

And possibly on the guy who was dancing with me uninvited, though I suppose I'll never know for sure.

Guess my *worst date ever* wasn't the only one to pull that move.

"Shit!" Dex says beside me, and he hauls me up into his arms and carries me out of the club. I see Ivy rushing after us behind his shoulder, but he can't seem to be moved to notice he's leaving his sister behind.

"Dex, what are you doing here?" Ivy yells at him once we're outside the club and it's quiet. She doesn't need to be yelling, and suddenly my head is pounding.

"I got Ainsley's text. I called, and it sounded like something was wrong, so I came and found you," he says. He's still holding me in his arms, and I don't really want him to let me go since I don't feel like I could function properly if he did.

I'm suddenly so sleepy.

"What did she text you that you came running?" Ivy asks.

He flashes his phone at his sister, and out of curiosity and not feeling quite as drunk now that I threw up, I ask, "Can I see?"

I read the screen.

Ainsley: *Help chekkin in!!!*

"She asked for help with three exclamation points, so here I am to help," he says.

"I meant to say, *hey, just checking in,*" I mutter.

Ivy tilts her head. "Wait a minute. Since when do you come running when someone needs help?"

We exchange a glance. I'm not sober enough to pretend like I'm not developing some strong feelings for her brother, so I let him field that question.

"Since the person who I've hired to take care of my kid asks for it," he says flatly.

There's more to it than that, obviously, but he doesn't allow any further questions. Instead, he carries me to the car waiting out front, Ivy's birthday celebration coming to an end thanks to my drunken text and her stupid, overprotective big brother and the feelings simmering between us.

CHAPTER 24

Dex Bradley

I Missed You

I set Ainsley in the back of the car and motion for Ivy to get in next, and then I take off my shoes and toss them into the nearest garbage can before I get into the car. No need to carry the reminder of what just happened.

Or the smell.

We get back to my place, and I thank Milton for helping me out in a pinch while the ladies head to their rooms.

He lets me know that Jack slept through it all, for which I'm grateful. I get Jack upstairs into his own bed again, and I make myself a drink and head over to my favorite thinking spot in front of the windows.

I figure the girls are both passed out by the time I'm a third of the way through my whiskey, and that's why I'm surprised when Ainsley sidles up beside me. Her hair is wet, and she's wearing a bathrobe, so I assume she took a shower.

"Thanks for coming tonight," she says softly once she's standing beside me. She doesn't turn to look at me, and I study her in the reflection of the glass.

"I thought something was wrong," I admit.

Her eyes meet mine in the glass. "I'm sorry." She clears her throat. "I should go lay down. I still feel drunk."

I nod, and before she turns to go, I ask, "Why'd you text me?"

"I missed you," she whispers.

She leaves, and once I hear her door click shut, I whisper, "I missed you, too."

I decide I'll handle Jack when he wakes up for his feeding at three in the morning, but he sleeps through it.

I'm up at six just in case he wakes up. He must've known it was my night because he didn't wake at all. In fact, when six rolls around, he's been asleep for eleven hours.

It's one of the first nights he didn't wake for a middle of the night bottle, and I'm wondering if some of that had to do with him adjusting to his new environment and these people who were strangers to him while the mother he knew walked away.

I hear him starting to rustle over the baby monitor about a half hour later, and I've already finished a cup of coffee and my protein shake.

I set his bottle on a warmer and head into his room before he starts to cry, and I change his diaper first. I've changed a handful of diapers now, and they're not perfect, but I'm starting to get the hang of it.

I take him out to the couch, and I feed him.

And since I missed my morning run on the treadmill, I leave a note for the girls letting them know I took Jack for a run, strap him into his jogger, and head down to run outside with my kid. We run to the nearest park, and I take him out of the stroller to put him into the swing while I catch my breath.

By the time we get back to my place, I'm a sweaty mess, and it's a little after ten. Both my sister and Ainsley are awake, and they're sprawled on the couch in a way that looks like they don't plan to leave anytime soon.

"Oh my God, is this my nephew?" Ivy asks, getting up gingerly from the couch as Ainsley sits up.

I park the stroller by the door and get Jack out, and I hand him to Ivy.

"Ivy, meet Jack. Jack, this is your Aunt Ivy."

"He has your eyes," Ivy says, staring down at my son.

My son.

It still sounds so weird.

She coos over him for a bit while I head toward the kitchen to refill my water.

"I'm gonna go shower," Ivy announces, and Ainsley helps set the baby into his bouncer as Ivy takes off toward her room.

Ainsley follows me into the kitchen, already showered and not looking any worse for the wear considering the shape she was in last night when I found her at the club.

"How are you feeling?" I ask.

"Like I got plowed over by a truck."

I laugh. "Sounds accurate."

"Why do people think this is fun?"

I lift a shoulder. "The hangover is never fun. The loss of inhibitions, the recklessness, the feeling like it's okay to do whatever the fuck you want to do…that's the addicting part."

She wrinkles her nose. "I must've had too much too fast because I don't remember any of that. I remember feeling loopy, not being able to focus on my phone, and some dude dancing against my butt."

I'm the only dude allowed to dance against your butt.

I don't say the words that rush through my mind, though I'm tempted.

"Thank you again for coming to get us. I didn't realize we needed to be saved, but you did, even though it was sort of a miscommunication on my part."

I set my water bottle on the counter and turn toward her. "I'll always come running the second you call, Ains." I surprise even myself with those words, but the bigger surprise is how much I mean them. My voice is low, and she blinks as her eyes meet mine before they flick down to my lips.

I take a step toward her, and I realize I'm sweaty from my run this morning, but I don't care. I slip my arm around her waist and pull her in closer to me, and she doesn't move to stop me.

"God, I want to kiss you," I murmur, my voice strained.

"Even after last night?" she asks, surprise in her voice.

My lips lift in a bit of a smile, and instead of answering with words, my mouth moves to hers. She moans a little as she sinks into me in that way she does, and I'm about to open my mouth to deepen this kiss when I hear a voice just around the corner.

"Dex, do you have any extra towels?"

Ainsley jumps away from me, and I casually grab my water bottle and pretend to screw on the cap like that's what we were doing this whole time.

"Should be some in the hallway linen closet," I say just as my sister rounds the corner.

"Thanks. Mine from yesterday is still wet since I took a shower before bed last night. Anyone want to do brunch once I get out?"

Ainsley raises her hand, and I nod.

"Jack and I are in. But I need to shower first."

"I can handle the baby if you want to go," Ainsley says, and Ivy looks between us as if she can't believe what she's seeing.

I'm not sure I can believe it, either. If someone would've told me a month ago that I'd be teaming up with my little sister's best friend, that I'm starting to fall for her and I want to keep kissing her in between taking turns caring for my baby, I would've laughed in their face.

But somehow, that's my reality.

Especially the *fall for* part. I'm falling for Ainsley Riggs, and there's not a damn thing I can do about it.

We head out to brunch, and it's more near misses and almost-kisses over the next few days as my sister wears out her welcome.

Look, I love my family as much as the next dude, but I love that they live in Chicago and I'm out here by myself in Vegas.

Except Archer. He's here, but we don't really talk. He's a baseball player, and we just have different schedules. That and I'm a dick who isn't great at returning calls, and he has more or less disassociated with all of us.

Sometimes I wonder if we could be closer, more like the way Madden and I are, especially since we live in the same town, but I get the feeling he feels kind of the same way about family as I do. I want them to be there when I want to be with them, but otherwise, I kind of just want to be left alone.

Though I wonder if all that is going to change now that I have a son of my own. I'm nurturing a family of my own, and I'm starting to change my outlook on the whole idea of family.

Though the moment I have that thought, it's like my father has some sort of ESP to change my mind right back.

He calls me as I'm driving away from dropping Ivy at the airport. Ainsley stayed home with Jack, and since I'm alone in the car, I pick up the call.

"Hi," I answer.

"The standard greeting is hello," he says.

"Did you call to tell me that?"

"No, I called because we're starting work on the VIP lounge. It's pretty far north on the Strip, and it's already perfect for our needs. It has a basement beneath it that we can use for our literal underground casino."

"Are you sure we should be talking about this over the phone?" I ask.

"I'm not bugged. Are you?"

"Not that I know of."

"Great. We have a few minor tweaks to the inside, but the underground will take a bit longer. The lounge will be ready to open in a few weeks, and we should have the underground ready to go within a month or two after if I can get the crews working day and night."

"I'll be in season," I remind him.

"You managed to find time to socialize in season before when it wasn't your old man asking for help," he reminds me.

I realize he still doesn't know about my kid, but with my big-mouthed sister on her way back home, I'm sure he'll know soon enough.

"Right," I say. "I need to go." I end the call even though I didn't really need to go. But I start training camp tomorrow. I have bigger things to focus on right now than my father guilting me into finding clients for his new VIP lounge. I'll find a few and do what he says, of course. I stand to make a lot from this deal.

But right now, my focus is on getting back home to Ainsley and picking up where we left off before my sister showed up with her little surprise visit.

CHAPTER 25
Ainsley Bradley

Falling

I'm nervous.

The last time we were alone, he kissed me on an elevator. We haven't been truly alone since that moment with the threat of an extra houseguest looming around the corner at any given moment.

Ivy's on her way home now, though, and my *husband* will be back any minute.

We still have a few hours before Jack goes to bed, and I have no idea what might happen between us after that.

Will he kiss me again? Will it lead to more? Will we have sex? Will I wake up in the morning and no longer be a virgin?

It's weird that I still *am* one. So many of my friends started having sex in high school, but maybe it was their horror stories that made me want to wait it out. I never had a real boyfriend in high school, and the few guys I dated in college weren't worth it. And now it's built up into this huge thing that it really doesn't need to be.

So I've never had sex. Is it really that big of a deal?

And maybe I'm worried about all this for nothing. In my previous relationships, we experimented with hand jobs and fingering. I've given blow jobs, but I've never actually been on the receiving end of oral sex. See what I mean about the guys not being worth it?

Maybe we'll start there.

Or maybe I'm delusional.

Either way, he's leaving tomorrow, and he's going to be gone for two weeks.

And then what?

We haven't talked about it. We haven't talked about much of anything in the last few days since Ivy's been around.

When he finally walks through the front door, he closes it and leans on it for a few beats as he eyes me in the kitchen, where I'm creating my signature dish for him. It's not as romantic as his steak and lobster dinner the night of our wedding, but I'm putting in an extreme amount of effort to make chicken tortilla soup. It's an old family recipe that requires a lot of chopping, and I've had Jack in his highchair next to me watching my every move as we have *Bluey* blaring from the family room television across from us.

"It smells fantastic in here," Dex says, and he kicks off from his spot by the door as he walks through the penthouse toward me.

"I decided to surprise you with dinner," I say. And fingers crossed I cook everything properly so he doesn't wind up sick for his first day of training camp.

"That was really nice of you," he says, and he moves in behind me sort of like that second dude at the club who got punched did. But this time, it's welcome despite the fact that I never actually invited it.

He sets his hands on my hips, and he presses his lips to my neck. "Finally alone," he murmurs.

"Ba ba ba!" Jack babbles, reminding us that we are not, in fact, alone after all.

Dex chuckles. "Little cockblock," he mutters for just me to hear, and I turn to swat his arm with a giggle. He doesn't move out of the way, instead rocking the front of his body against the back of mine.

I think the idea that blossomed on the elevator last Tuesday night is still very much alive between the two of us.

I set down the knife I'm chopping tomatoes with and turn around, and he lets his hands skim my hips as I move, never moving them until I'm firmly in place with my chest against his. He takes the moment to wrap his arms around me then, and his lips drop down to mine.

"Ba da ba da ba!" Jack says.

Dex pulls back with a sigh, and he looks up at the ceiling, his neck corded as he clenches his jaw. He clears his throat, and his eyes are hot on mine when he says, "I've been waiting four and a half days to get you alone. I guess I can wait another hour or two."

I lean up and press my lips to his for a quick kiss. "We can try to get him down early tonight."

He chuckles. "I'll start packing now for camp so I don't need to do it later. Then I can give you all my focus."

"I can't wait," I say softly.

"Are you sure about this?" he asks. He nips another kiss to my lips.

I nod probably a little too enthusiastically. "I'm sure. Are you?"

"I've been counting the seconds, Ains. I'm sure."

My heart skips a beat at that, and he lets me go and moves out of my orbit.

"Can I help in here at all?" he asks. He swipes a tomato off my cutting board.

"If you want to keep all your fingers, you'll stay away from my knife," I warn.

He laughs and holds both hands up. "Okay, okay," he says, and he heads off toward his bedroom to pack.

The soup is a hit. In fact, Dex's exact words are, "Can you add this to the weekly menu and make a double batch so there's extra next time?"

The words are enough to make me giddy that he liked something I created for him.

I do manage to get Jack down about fifteen minutes earlier than usual, and when I emerge from his bedroom, there's a vodka Sprite with three cherries in it sitting on the counter for me. Dex is by the window, as usual, and I grab the drink from the counter and take a sip before I set it back down. I wander over and step into place beside him.

"Have you ever thought about putting a couch over here?" I ask.

"I do my best thinking when I'm on my feet," he admits. "I do it on purpose since I can't sit and make split-second decisions when I'm on the field."

"Are you excited to go to camp?" I ask.

"Yes and no."

"Why no?"

He glances over at me, and he shrugs. I get the sense that this is harder for him to talk about than he wants to admit.

But then, to my complete and utter shock, he starts talking anyway.

"That poor kid was left here with strangers, and he's always just so...I don't know. Happy, I guess. Despite everything. And now his only other biological parent is leaving him for two weeks, and I didn't realize I never told you I'm leaving, and now you're forced into this situation—"

"Hey," I interrupt, reaching out to touch his shoulder. I leave my hand there to rest. "Hey. It's okay. You're not forcing me into anything I don't want to do."

He seems torn, and I watch as he tips his glass to his lips, chugs what's left in there, and turns to slam his glass on the end table not far from where he stands. He moves back toward me.

"You needed a job, and you had no clue what you were getting into," he says, and he grits his teeth together as if he's ashamed of that fact.

"Sometimes I think the best parts of life are going in blind. Not knowing what the outcome is going to be. Remember that first charity event we attended together and how I followed you all the way to the roller coaster? I think about that night all the time."

His head whips toward me. "So do I, Birdie. It's the night I started to fall—" This time he cuts himself off.

"The night you started…what?" I ask softly. Carefully. Nervously.

He glances at me, and then he moves his gaze back out the window. Eventually, he blows out a heavy breath. "Fuck it. The night I started to fall for you." He closes his eyes as he braces for the impact of those words.

I don't know what to say. He started *to fall* for me?

I knew I was starting to feel a certain way about him, but I had no clue he was feeling a certain way about me, too. I figured it was just that sexual connection. All the kissing. The admission that I'm a virgin. He wants the forbidden, the untouched, the innocent.

But he's falling.

And I'm falling.

"You're the first person I've spent time with in a long time who didn't care about the fame or the money or the status," he says, averting his gaze back out the window. "You jumped in headfirst to help me with a situation you knew nothing about, and you've been so fucking important in helping me navigate all this." He clenches his jaw, and I study his profile as I watch his jaw move back and forth.

He's clearly struggling with what to say. How to handle this. How to handle *me*. How to move forward. *If* he should move forward.

"You helped me, too, Dex," I say softly. "It's not like I'm not benefitting from being here."

He finally glances over at me. "You could've walked away at any time over the last few weeks, and you didn't. Instead, you went all in. You fucking married me. And now you're going to stay here with my son while I head off to training camp for two weeks." He shakes his head in wonder. "It takes a special person to put up with me. I know I'm not easy. But I want to be better. For him. For you." He says the last two words on a whisper, and then he moves in toward me, closing the space as I turn toward him, too. He walks toward me, and I walk backward until I bump into the window.

I'm out of room, and he cages me in against the window.

"What if I want a little of the bad boy, too?" I ask softly.

He moves so one arm rests above my head and the other hand rests lazily on my hip. "You're about to get all of him. If you still want him." His face is inches from mine, and he waits for my consent before he moves a muscle.

"I'm falling for you, too, Dex. Of course I still want you. All of you." The words are barely out when his lips crash to mine. His fingers flex on my hip, and his tongue moves around my mouth in a skilled, practiced way that leads me to wonder how it would feel on other parts of my body.

I arch into him, in part because I'm up against the window and in part because my body seems to be moving reflexively, seeking the hardness his body has to offer. The ache that has pulsed between my legs for weeks is throbbing now, waiting for this man to do something about it, something no one else has ever done.

But first, he kisses me. We've built slowly to this point, taking our time with each other, getting to know one another in small bursts of conversation here or charity events there, and while it feels very slow in some ways, in other ways it feels like record speed as we race toward some invisible line that we're about to cross.

We're both in jeans, and in a perfect world I'd be in a dress waiting for him to slip his fingers under it. Instead, his hand gripping my hip moves up toward my breast as his lips break from mine and trail down my neck. I lean back, my head bumping against the glass as I arch my chest out and give him more room along my neck. The scruff lining his jaw burns and tickles at the same time, and it's an addictive sensation I want to keep feeling over and over—here on my neck, across my nipples, down my abdomen, between my thighs.

We'll get there. Maybe. Probably. Likely not tonight since our time is limited. Literally. He has to leave in nine hours, and he should probably get some rest tonight so he's focused tomorrow.

But that doesn't seem to be a thought in his mind as he takes his time kissing my neck and massaging my breast. His lips trail down to dip into the V-neck of my shirt, but it's not deep enough for him to get a taste of my cleavage. Instead, he lets go of me and reaches for the bottom of my shirt. He pulls it off and tosses it to the ground, and his fingertips come up to my tits as his mouth crashes back to mine again.

He finds each of my nipples and teases them through the cotton fabric of my rather plain bra, but he doesn't seem to care that I'm not wearing lacy, silky lingerie for this occasion.

Instead, he seems totally focused on my body, on my mouth, on us in this moment.

I buck my hips toward him, suddenly needing some relief down low, and he thrusts his hips toward me in response. I moan when I feel his hard cock hit me right where I need it to, just with far too many clothes separating us.

He seems to lose some of his control at my moan, and he bucks his hips toward me again. I reach for his shirt and lift it over his head, and as I toss it to the floor, he uses one hand to somehow unhook the back of my bra.

It's impressive work, really.

I shimmy out of it and toss it to the floor, and his hands are immediately back on my breasts, his fingers pinching my nipples as he tests how much pressure he can exert to get a moan out of me. I want a moment of silence for his abs, but his body is pressed to mine, so I dig my nails into his shoulders instead— more intensely the harder he pinches my nipple, and less so when he goes lighter.

His mouth moves from mine and trails down to take one of my nipples in his mouth, and it sends a shot of need straight through to my pussy.

I let out a loud grunt, and he increases the pressure from his mouth. My God, that feels good, and I feel like I could fall apart just from a little nipple play.

But not yet.

Not before I feel him inside me.

Not before I give him my virginity.

I let out a shaky breath as I realize what's about to happen, and excitement seems to course through my veins.

I'm about to lose my virginity to Dex Bradley.

This is the stuff dreams are made of.

CHAPTER 26

DEX BRADLEY

Enough Foreplay

I could do this all night.

Her tits are absolute perfection. I've dreamed of what they look like since I first saw her in that black dress at the charity event where I hit Jensen Bybee, when I was waiting for one of them to fall out on the roller coaster and it never did.

And now one is in my mouth as the other is in my hand, and fuck, they're everything I dreamed they'd be.

I may be an ass man, but I can still appreciate some good tits. And these right here are some *good* tits. The best that have ever been in my mouth.

Jesus.

I'm further gone than I realized.

It's probably enough against-the-window foreplay. I think I'm ready to take this somewhere more comfortable.

But I also can't seem to make myself move from right here. I've always kept foreplay brief to get to the main event, but for the first time…I don't *want* to rush to the main event.

I want to take my time.

I want to worship her body. I want to watch her fall apart with my fingers and my tongue first, and then I want to fuck her until she falls apart from my cock. First I'll take her pussy, and another time, I'll take her ass.

Once we do this, she's mine.

I've never told a woman I'm falling for her, and maybe that's what makes this so different. I thought it was because she's a virgin, but hearing her tell me that she's falling for me too made me realize it has nothing to do with her virginity and everything to do with the fact that there are actual real, deep feelings here between us.

And *that* is a new experience for *me*. I'm no virgin, but she's still managing to give me something new.

I lift her up so she's straddling my waist, and her tits are still at the perfect level for me to keep sucking on as I carry her through the penthouse, stopping every so often to kiss her, to hold her against the wall, to take her tits in my mouth. She holds my head against her tit as I suck hard on her nipple, and she cries out when I let it go with a loud pop.

"God, Dex, that feels so good," she moans.

"Your tits are pure perfection." I take her other nipple between my lips, and I move my tongue back and forth over it until it's a hard, tight bud for me.

I thrust my hips up toward her, and I know I'm going to fuck her like this someday, but not for her first time. She has to get used to me, my size—to all of it—before I get too creative with her.

I let go of her tits and carry her into my bedroom. I was going to detour to the couch, but the condoms and lube are in my nightstand, and this way we can just go to bed afterward.

I set her gently on the ground, and I reach down to flick the button of her jeans. At the same time, she reaches down and rubs my cock over my jeans, and I thrust my hips at her hand, showing her just how fucking hard she makes me.

I dip my fingers into the front of her jeans, bypass her panties, and head right for her cunt. I slide my fingers through her, and she parts her legs for me, closing her eyes as the rubbing of my cock momentarily stops and she loses focus.

"Oh, God," she moans as I push my finger in. It glides right in because she's as wet as the fucking ocean floor down there.

I can't help my hiss as I ease my finger back. "Fuck, that's a wet cunt," I murmur.

Her only response is to shove her hips down onto my hand, as if telling me to finger her harder.

I want to, but her jeans are restricting me. I get them out of the way by peeling them down her legs along with her panties, and I back up a second to appreciate the beauty that is a fully naked Ainsley Riggs in my bedroom.

"You're so fucking gorgeous," I murmur, and I move to guide her to the bed.

She stops me, and she yanks on my jeans button. She pushes them down my legs, leaving my boxers in place for now, and I let her take the lead. If she's not quite ready for my cock, I won't release him yet.

She grabs hold of my cock over my boxers, however, and starts to pump, giving me a hand job.

"Fuck, Ains, that feels so good," I mutter. I shove my hips toward her hand to encourage her to keep going, but it's *too* good. I'm going to lose it before I get the chance to push inside her, and I refuse to let this night end too early.

I pull back out of her reach, and this time I grab her into my arms and set her on the bed. I pull my boxers off so we're both naked, and her eyes go wide as she takes in my naked body.

"Holy shit, Dex. That's…uh, you're…um—wow."

I chuckle as I move around the side of the bed and grab a condom and the lube just in case she needs it, and then I climb over her. I hover there, and our eyes meet. Her lips are parted, and she looks gorgeous as she looks up at me with nervous, still trusting eyes.

I reach down with one hand to slip my fingers back inside of her, and she leans her neck back as her eyes close. Her hips sway in time with the way I'm fingering her, and soft moans fall from her mouth, the kind of moans I'll be thinking about next week when I'm trying to fall asleep at camp and can't because I can't stop thinking of her.

Fuck, I want to be inside her. I know I need to take this slow for her sake, but I'm only a man. I'm not sure I have the strength to wait another second.

"I'm ready, Dex," she moans, and that's my cue.

I grab the condom, and I kneel on either side of her thighs. I hand the condom over to her because, fuck, if having a woman roll a condom on me isn't the goddamn hottest thing to watch, and she looks at me with furrowed brows.

"Roll it on me," I say.

"I don't know how."

"Open the pack, pinch the tip, and roll," I instruct, and she starts by tearing the package open and setting the wrapper beside us. She follows my instructions, and she strokes my cock a few times once she's done.

"Is it going to hurt?" she asks quietly.

I grab the bottle of lube. "You're real fucking wet, but if you're worried about it, I can use some lube." Since this is her first time, I'll be extra careful. I want her to enjoy it, not dread it. And first times *can* be enjoyable. Ask me how I know.

"Is it going to fit?" she asks next.

I nod slowly. "Yeah, baby. It'll fit."

I get some lube and squirt it on my hand, and I palm myself with it to get my cock nice and slick for her.

"God, that's hot," she murmurs.

I glance down at her and see her watching me stroke myself, and I can't help but think maybe there will come a day when she can watch me get myself off and then I can watch her get herself off.

But that day isn't today.

I stop fisting my own cock and move so I'm hovering over her again.

"Are you ready?" I ask quietly even though she already said she is.

She nods, a bit of fear in her eyes. "Go slow," she begs.

I keep my eyes on her as I nod, and then I reach down between us and swipe my cock through her slit.

"Oh," she moans, closing her eyes.

I push just the tip in, and her eyes fly open. "Dex!"

"Yeah, baby?" I murmur as the sweet feel of her cunt grips all around me. I push in just a centimeter more.

"Oh God! You're so big!"

Have sweeter words ever been spoken? I'll take compliments on my size any day of the week.

"There's more. You okay?" I ask.

"Yes! Give it to me!" She's an untamed animal now, wild and needy, and I'm ready to be the one who gives her exactly what she needs.

She said she's done other stuff aside from sex, and with the amount of lube combined with how fucking wet she is, I know she can take it all.

Still, I keep it slow despite her demands for more, inching in a little at a time. It takes every single ounce of my self-control since it's in my nature to take what I need. It's in everyone's nature. We're selfish beings intent on getting our needs met, and for the first time, I'm putting someone else's needs first. For the first time, I care about someone else's needs above my own.

It's a heady realization to make as I push another inch into this woman who has taken me both by surprise and by storm.

"Fuck, Ains, you're so fucking tight," I mutter.

"It's for you," she cries, and I feel like it's true, like she saved this for me.

She didn't. She couldn't have. It's not like she ever knew this moment would exist between us when I picked up and left for Vegas, leaving Chicago behind along with the rest of my siblings and their networks. She couldn't have had any clue that this would be in our future.

Yet here we are, fate finding us anyway.

I push in a little more, and fuck, I want to jam it home.

I keep it slow and steady, and I feel her pussy contract around me. I'm starting to sweat both from taking it so slow and from the body heat we're producing together.

"Mm, you like that," I murmur.

"God, yes! I love it! I need it, Dex. I need more."

I give her more, pushing in until I'm buried inside of her, and I still—or I try to, anyway. My dick has other plans, and I twitch inside her.

She moans, and I slide out. "Oh!" she cries.

I push back into her, and her eyes roll back. "Oh, God, yes! Do that again!"

I push forward, still being careful and gentle with her, and she wraps her legs around my waist.

Fuck. I'm not going to last long.

She's wet, and she wants it, and she asked for the bad boy.

I start to move, and her moans get louder and more intense.

"You like it when I fuck this pussy, don't you?" I grunt.

"I love it!"

Well, I love it, too.

I don't say that in the moment, and maybe I'll regret that later, but I can't. I'm seconds from coming, and I need to hold off. I need to let her come first.

Sandpaper.

It's my go-to when I don't want to come yet. I have no idea why, but the idea of sandpaper is about the most boring thing I can think of in the moment.

I start picking up the pace, allowing my mind to wander as I pump in and out of her.

Why does sandpaper come in coarse and medium and then variations of fine? There's the regular sort of fine, very fine, extra fine, super fine, and ultra fine. Couldn't whoever named sandpaper come up with better words? Synonyms, perhaps? Delicate or smooth. And why isn't microfine one of the options? Furthermore, why isn't there a very coarse, extra coarse, super coarse, or ultra coarse option?

Her pussy contracts around me, and even though it's a tight vise, I can read the signals. I push sandpaper out of my head and focus on the task at hand.

"Yes, Dex. Oh, God, yes, this feels so good! Oh my God, Dex!" She's losing all control, and it's hot as fuck to witness. I watch her as she bites her bottom lip and squeezes her eyes shut.

As I thrust into her over and over, picking up speed as I feel my own climax start to climb through me, her moans get louder and louder as she starts to scream my name. That's it. Her pussy clenches tightly to me, and that sends me into my own release.

I grunt as pleasure roars along my spine, and I let out a low growl as I start to come, too. I freefall into the type of release I've needed for weeks now, and I bask in the feel of her body surrounding mine as I bury my face in her neck. I bite her skin lightly as I finish, and I hold inside her for a few extra beats.

We're both panting now, desperate to catch our breath as we cling to one another. Her legs are still wrapped around me as if she doesn't want to let me go, and I don't want her to. I don't want to slip out of her. I don't want this moment to be over between us. I don't want to wait two weeks until we can do this again.

I don't want to leave her in the morning.

But what we want doesn't always line up with reality.

Eventually she relaxes and drops her legs, and I pull out of her.

I press another kiss to her mouth before I climb off her and head to the bathroom to take care of the condom, and when I return, I bring a warm, wet washcloth with me.

She's exactly where I left her, her breathing more even now. I press the washcloth gently to her pussy, and she moans.

"Is that what I've been missing out on all this time?" she whispers.

I laugh and wiggle my brows in jest. "I can't speak for anyone else, but probably not."

She sits up, and I stop what I'm doing with the washcloth. "Dex, that was—"

"Incredible?" I supply.

She nods. "I thought my first time would hurt. It didn't."

"Because I know what I'm doing."

"Clearly." She clears her throat. "I'm just, uh—I need to go clean up."

I nod, and I hand her the washcloth. She heads to the bathroom, and I take a minute to collect myself and my thoughts. I have no idea how I'm going to say goodbye to her in the morning.

I guess because I've never had to worry about goodbyes. When it was over, I left.

But suddenly, I do.

CHAPTER 27

Ainsley Bradley

Doing This All Backward

I glance at myself in the mirror, and I can't help but think I actually *look* different.

An hour ago, I was still a virgin. Now I'm not.

And holy hell, it was freaking amazing.

Dex knew exactly what he was doing. He knew exactly how to handle me, and I truly never realized what I was missing since the others I'd messed around with didn't know what they were doing at all, and my own fingers are hardly a match for the way Dex can use his body.

Damn.

I'll be dreaming of him and how good he felt for the rest of time.

How many people get to say they lost their virginity to someone they were really, truly falling for? We have an actual shot at a future. Maybe. God, I don't know. I'm so confused. But after the last few weeks, and after what just happened…I hope we can find a way.

We're doing this all backward. We got married, and then we started to fall, and then we had sex, and I went and fell even more.

And there's a child on top of the equation. I'm a nanny, a stepmother, and a wife, fake or not, and yet we just slept together.

I don't think we can come back from this and survive as separate entities now that we've been together in this way.

I don't want him to go in the morning. I feel like there's still so much I don't know about him. He's let himself be vulnerable with me, but there's still so much more to Dex Bradley left to uncover. I can't wait to peel each part back bit by bit, but I can't do that when he's in another state working day and night to prepare for his upcoming season with his team.

I'll be here when he gets back. I guess we just…hit the pause button until then and pray that nothing changes in the meantime.

I draw in a breath and head back out to Dex, and he's lying in bed. I don't want to make any assumptions, so I ask the question that's on my mind. "Should I head back to my room, or…?" I trail off, letting the question hang there.

"Get your cute little ass back in my bed," he demands, and I can't help the relief that darts through me.

This is different. I've only been in his bedroom once since I've lived here, and it was when I didn't know the layout of his penthouse and I had no idea where I was going back on that first day when Jack's mother was here saying goodbye.

I couldn't have known the roller coaster I was about to get on—both literally at the New York–New York and figuratively with Dex. Less than a month ago, I thought my heart was broken by some idiot on a reality television show.

Now look where I am.

I can't wait to tape the reunion show. I can't wait to show up and throw my new relationship—my marriage to a pro football star—right in Jordan's face.

I'm sure the accusations will fly. But I'll be going home to Dex, and the two of us know the truth. That's all that really matters to me.

I slide into bed beside Dex, and he immediately pulls me into his arms. And that's where I sleep, my body exhausted from the workout he just gave me, until his alarm blares at us far too early.

I get up with him even though I don't really have to get up until Jack does. He said goodbye to his son last night, but he sneaks into his room anyway before it's time to leave. He presses a kiss to his own hand, and then he gently lays his hand on his son's back.

I melt. I freaking melt. He's becoming so sweet with Jack, and it's such a one-eighty from the day I ran into him.

It makes me feel like we can do this. There's an actual, real possibility of a future here, and I am beyond excited to see what could happen.

But then it's time for him to leave.

He drops his duffel by the door and turns to face me. He blows out a breath. "I don't want to go." His words are simple, and I get the feeling that he's never felt that way before. Football always came first, but now he has someone waiting at home for him. Well, two someones.

"You have to," I say softly. "I know what football means to you, and even though the next two weeks will be hard, Jack and I will be here waiting when you get back."

He presses his lips together and nods, and then he hooks an arm around my waist and pulls me closer into him. "Last night meant a lot to me, Birdie," he says quietly.

"It meant the world to me."

He leans down and presses a gentle kiss to my lips. When he pulls back, he holds me close for a few extra beats, hugging me and breathing me in. And then he grabs his duffel and heads out the door without another word.

I sigh as I lean back against his door. I wish we had more time, but he'll be back.

It's only two weeks.

We can do this.

It just sucks that we have to do this right now, right after we admitted our feelings and we're at the precipice of something new and exciting.

Jack wakes up a little earlier than usual, and thus begins my first moments as a single mom. While I'm being paid to be his nanny, I'm also legally his stepmother now, and with no other parent in the picture for the foreseeable future, I'm it.

And that's a bit of a scary thought.

CHAPTER 28

Dex Bradley

Phone Calls

It's my first night at training camp, and I'm about to call Ainsley when my phone starts to ring.

It's my mother.

My mother rarely calls. If ever.

"Mom?" I answer. I'm in a hotel room that I'm sharing with Nick Ryan, another defensive end, at the vineyard where we travel for the first two weeks of training camp. My roommate is currently in the shower. I might not have picked up this call if he were out here in the room.

"What's this about a grandson?" she demands.

Freaking Ivy. That little brat.

I'm not shocked she spilled the news, but I'm sort of shocked it took my mom this long to call me. Ivy's flight must've gotten in late.

I blow out a breath. "Ivy has a big mouth."

"Maybe yours is too small," she hisses.

I laugh. I can't help it. I often laugh when I'm in trouble, which usually gets me into even more trouble.

"Can we have this conversation later? I just got back from my first day of training camp, and I don't have the energy for this."

"No. We will have this conversation right now."

"Fine. What do you want to know?"

"When can I meet him?" she asks.

"He's at my place now. Head on over and introduce yourself."

"Who's he with?"

"Ivy didn't tell you that part? Her best friend Ainsley. She's nannying for me." And she's the best lay I've ever had, so don't get on my case about her.

I leave that part out, obviously. I'll leave it out for my sister as well until Ainsley is ready to say something.

"I'm disappointed you didn't feel you could let your family in on this part of your life. He is part of the legacy, you know," she scolds.

"Now you sound like Dad," I mutter, but I don't really address her sentiment. "I get back in two weeks. We can arrange a meeting then."

I can picture her pursing her lips, but it's not having its desired effect due to the abundance of Botox and fillers.

"Fine. We'd like to welcome Ainsley to the family, too. Do well at camp," she says, and we end the call.

We don't end with an *I love you,* as some parents do with their adult children. We never have, even when I wasn't an adult.

It just drives home exactly how powerful my feelings for Ainsley are since I've rarely said or heard those words my entire life.

Not to mention how powerful my feelings for my son are. I feel the love for him, too, like my heart is expanding from the shriveled black rock it was before into something new and different that's allowing in not just one person, but two in very different ways.

Day two at camp is more intense than day one, which was really more about getting our bearings at the vineyard and having some meetings.

Today we're installing new plays, and it's just as important for me to be out there defending against plays as it is for the offense to be out there learning how to run them. Our defensive coordinator, Andy Glen, always asks for our feedback so he can bring it to the offensive coordinator and our head coach when they discuss new plays.

I show Coach Andy where the mistakes or gaps are on offense, and he makes me feel like a valued part of the team.

My position coach runs us through some drills before we're dismissed for lunch, and we're back at it all afternoon in the sweltering afternoon sun until dinnertime, when we finally have a little piece of freedom.

I video call Ainsley after dinner, hoping to get a glimpse of Jack even though she sent me pictures of him throughout the day. I can't have my phone on me while I'm out on the field, but I do check it when we get breaks, and seeing their smiling faces gives me the energy I need to get through the next set of plays.

So when she answers and the camera is pointed at the two of them, I can't help my wide smile.

"How was your day, Daddy?" she asks.

"You know I love it when you call me that," I say, thankful that Nick is once again in the shower. The dude takes long showers, and truthfully I don't care to know what he's doing in there, but I'm grateful for the quiet time to myself.

She giggles, and Jack babbles.

"What's on your neck?" I ask.

Her hand immediately moves to the spot I was indicating, and her cheeks redden a little. "That's from you," she whispers.

My brows dip together. "From me?"

"Yeah. You…kind of bit me a little when you were, well, you know." She clears her throat. "Finishing."

"I bit you?" I remember some gentle kissing, maybe baring my teeth a little, but it looks like she has a bruise.

"Yeah." She squirms a little. "And it was hot."

I can't help my laugh. "We can talk more about that later, and we will, but first I want to know how your day was."

She launches into a story about everything the two of them did together, and honestly…this feels like the best part of my day. It's mundane, and the details don't really matter, but it's listening to her talk and seeing the two of them that's making me feel that little slice of home that's always missing at camp.

"How about you? How was your day?" she asks.

"Fine." I give her some details about what we did, and then I say, "My mother called right when I got back to my room last night asking about her grandchild."

"Ivy," she hisses.

"Ivy," I agree.

We both laugh.

Jack starts to fuss, and she says she better go. I feel good after talking to her, but then I always do.

The next conversation I have takes me down a notch.

I see my brother Ford is calling, and I pick up expecting to shoot the shit with him about camp in our respective cities, but that's not what I get.

"How's Tampa Bay?" I answer.

"Did you hear about Coach Murph?"

My blood runs cold for a second. "No. What happened?"

"He was in an accident last night. They're not sure he's going to make it."

"Fuck," I mutter. Coach Murph was the high school varsity coach starting my junior year. Madden had already graduated, and he took over the program and revolutionized it. He was only at the school seven years, but he led the team to a state championship every year. He went on to coach college, where he still coaches today.

He was more than a coach to us. He pushed us to work smarter, to find our motivation, and to cultivate bonds with our teammates. He steered me in a smarter direction when I started getting into some heavy shit my junior year, and I wouldn't be the player I am today if not for him.

I might not be here at all if not for him.

But I'm not sure what I'm supposed to do with this information Ford is feeding me. I'm at training camp. Murph would want us working our asses off, getting to know the team dynamic, and securing our starting position for the season. He wouldn't want us to worry about him. He'd want us to put our focus on the game.

His words at every practice come back to me.

Show up or make excuses.

He always told us those were our two choices.

But what does that mean now? Do I show up for him, or do I show up for my team?

"Where is he?" I ask.

"Northwestern Memorial," he says, naming a hospital in Chicago.

"Are you doing anything?"

"I'm not sure. I want to say goodbye, but I'm sure the other hundreds of players he coached over the years would all feel the same," he says.

I hadn't thought of that. "What if he doesn't make it?" I ask quietly. "Would you leave camp to attend the funeral?"

"If I need to."

"You had him four years. I only had him two," I say. It sounds like an excuse. The truth is that I only needed him one year for him to change my entire life.

Ford knows that, too. "Excuse."

"I know." I let out a heavy sigh. "He was there for us when we needed him. What if he needs us now?"

"He has a team of doctors doing everything they can. He doesn't need us, but his family might. They might need to see how we're all pulling for him."

"Yeah," I mutter. "Thanks for letting me know. If you hear anything…"

"Yeah. I know. You too."

I hang up with Ford, and Nick emerges from his shower a few minutes later.

"You want to go grab some food?" he asks.

I shake my head. "I need a few minutes. I have some calls to make."

"Everything okay?"

I lift a shoulder. "Don't know. One of my high school coaches was in an accident, and it's not looking good."

"Shit, man. I'm sorry. Anything I can do?"

"That's what I'm wondering myself." And I feel like I know just the person to call.

CHAPTER 29

Ainsley Bradley

Babe

"**H**ey! I wasn't expecting such a quick turnaround, but I'm not complaining," I answer when I see Dex calling. I just got Jack out of the bathtub, and he's currently bouncing in his play bouncer while he listens to the sounds of "Baby Shark."

"My brother Ford just called. He said Coach Murph was in a bad accident last night and might not make it."

"Oh, God, Dex. I'm so sorry." I don't know who Coach Murph is, but I don't choose this moment to say that. He tells me anyway.

"I can't think of another coach who made a bigger impact on my life. He started my junior year of high school and was only there for seven years, but I was starting to get into some hard shit my junior year, and he quite literally saved my life."

"How?" I ask as I make Jack's bedtime bottle.

"I was at a party where other kids were shooting up heroin. I had a needle in my hand and was ready to shoot it when he walked through the doors, took the needle out of my hand, asked me what the fuck I was doing, and took me back to his place. It turned out the heroin was laced with something, and another kid died that night." His voice is quiet and broken as he talks. "It could have been me."

I'm frankly shocked that he was into that sort of thing when he was younger, but the truth is that we all make mistakes. He was lucky he had someone in his life to stop him.

"But it wasn't, Dex. You were always meant to be here." I glance over at his son, and that's all the proof I need.

"I just…I don't know what to do." He's clearly conflicted.

"What can you do, babe?" I ask.

He's quiet, and I think it's because he's contemplating my question. Instead, he says, "Babe?"

My cheeks burn. "It slipped out. Let's move past it."

"What if I liked it?" His voice turns a little warmer, and in truth, the fact that he called me to talk to me about this makes me feel like I'm in an important position here.

"Then I'll do it again. Now answer the question."

He gets serious again. "I don't have any idea."

"What would he want you to do?" I ask.

"His catchphrase was always *show up or make excuses*. I think he'd want me to continue showing up at camp."

"I'm sure he would," I say. If he's half the coach Dex claims he is, he'd always put his athletes and their success first. "But it wouldn't hurt to make some kind of show of support for him or his family."

"Like what?" he asks.

"Oh, I don't know. Off the top of my head, you could call his family—his parents or his wife. His kids if he has any. You could make a monetary contribution to his care. You could do something as simple as send a card letting the family know you care about him and your thoughts are with them during this difficult time."

"Where do I even get a card?" he asks. "Or their address?"

"Dex. Show up or make excuses."

He's silent on the other end, and for a moment I worry I overstepped with those words. But then he shocks me by saying, "You're right. Can you help me?"

"Absolutely."

He fills me in on what he needs, and it feels good to help him out.

The next day, I mail a card to the family with Dex's information on it.

A week later, he gets the call he was dreading. And once again, I'm the first person he calls after he finds out what happened from Ford.

"Coach Murph passed away," he says, and his voice is quiet. So quiet that I can't even tell if he's been crying, but a soft sniffle gives him away.

"I'm so, so sorry, Dex. What can I do?" I ask.

"Nothing," he mumbles.

"Do you know any of the arrangements yet? I can book you a flight to the funeral. Jack and I can meet you there if you want us—"

"I'm at camp for four more days," he says, interrupting me with a pointed tone. "I can't just leave."

"Surely if you told your coach why—"

He interrupts me again. "I can't."

I want to ask him if that's showing up or an excuse, but I also want to be sensitive to what he's dealing with. I don't throw those words at him. Maybe the way he sees it, he's showing up for his teammates.

But I also know he'll regret it if he doesn't pay his final respects. I know from personal experience.

"Can I tell you a story?" I ask carefully.

He grunts some reply, so I dive right in.

"I didn't go to my grandmother's funeral. She was my dad's mom, and we only saw her a few times a year, but we had a special bond. My parents needed someone to watch my younger siblings, and rather than pay a babysitter, they asked me to do it. I was thirteen and felt like I didn't have much choice. Because I helped them out, I missed saying goodbye. It's a moment I'll never get back, Dex. I could talk to her up in heaven, sure, but it's not the same as those final respects. It's not the same as being with the other people who loved her so much and sharing in both grief and memories."

He sighs. "You're telling me to step up and do the right thing without saying those words."

"I'm telling you that you don't want to live with regrets, Dex."

"The funeral is Friday morning in Chicago."

"I can get you there on the latest flight Thursday and an afternoon flight back to California on Friday," I say.

He's quiet a minute as he contemplates it, and then he says, "Meet me there. With Jack."

"Of course," I whisper, and tears fill my eyes that he'd want me there for it.

"I'll see if we can stay the night at Madden's place. He plays for San Diego now, but he kept his place in the city," he says. "He won't have a crib or anything, though."

"We'll make it work," I say. I can pack a travel bassinet and everything we need.

Truth be told, I've never traveled with a baby before.

"His birth certificate is in the safe in my office. The key is in the middle desk drawer," he says, and it feels heavy that he's trusting me with this sort of thing.

"I promise I'll take care of everything," I say.

"Thanks, Birdie," he says quietly, and his little use of his special nickname for me gives me butterflies.

"Of course." We end the call, and I set to work.

CHAPTER 30

Dex Bradley

Wife and Kid

Coach Nash gave me clearance to leave for twenty-four hours to attend the funeral, but I won't be gone that long. Actually, he told me my place on the team is secure and I could take an extra day or two if I need it.

"I need to show up for my team." Those were my words to him, and he looked…*proud* of me.

It's rare to have anyone look at me with pride. Sure, I make killer sacks and great plays, and fans cheer me on. But my parents have never looked at me with pride. I was always the troublemaker, the one causing them early onset gray hairs—according to my mother, anyway.

My mother, who I'll probably have to see in the next twenty-four hours. It's only a small part of why I told Ainsley to meet me there.

Ford is coming in, too, and more than likely my parents will attend the funeral. Any chance to put in an appearance, I suppose—especially with an elite crowd of football players and coaches, both pro and college, in attendance. My father will see it as an opportunity for business, and my mother will see it as an opportunity to socialize.

I just see it for what it is: a funeral celebrating the life of one of the greatest men I know.

I need to call Madden to ask if I can stay at his place, but something seems to stop me short.

It takes me a while to piece together what it is, and it's once the day is quiet as I lie down to fall asleep that it hits me.

My father's words about my older brother.

"Madden actually kept his mouth shut?"

He knew about the underground casinos, and he didn't tell me. I don't know if he told anybody, but he took it upon himself to keep the secret from me.

It gives me little motivation to share my secrets with him. If he can't trust me, maybe the feeling is mutual.

With everything going on, from discovering my child to running into Ainsley to falling for her and my kid, it's been a whirlwind of a month. I haven't had time to think through the fact that my brother never said a word to me about a deep, dark family secret.

It's only now I'm putting that together.

Maybe we were never as close as I always thought we were. He's got a girl now, and his focus is there. I guess I'm starting to get that.

I don't bother calling him. Instead, I book a hotel near the airport, and I find myself boarding a plane from California to Chicago on Thursday evening. It's been nearly two weeks of hard work, and the chance to just sit and do nothing for a few hours isn't the worst thing I can think of.

When I land, I find Ainsley waiting at my gate for me with my son. The baby is in his carrier snapped into his stroller, and Ainsley is standing as she watches eagerly for passengers to deplane. I'm one of the first, and she stands by the stroller as she waits for me to stride over to her.

I take her into my arms, and I lower my lips to hers for a brief, airport-friendly kiss.

I lean my forehead to hers. "God, I missed you." I don't think I realized exactly how much or how strongly until I got to pull her back into my arms again.

"I missed you, too."

We take off for the hotel, and it turns out that Ford is staying at the same hotel—something we didn't actually talk about, but it tracks since it's close to the airport and not far from where the funeral will be held in the morning.

He's checking in just ahead of us, and it's then that I realize I haven't told him about the baby…or my wife.

I slap him on the shoulder the way brothers do, and he turns with a grimace.

He grabs me into a bro-style hug, and we slap each other on the back as he says, "Bro, watch the shoulder, man. I took a hellish hit yesterday at camp." He pulls his sleeve up to reveal a dark black and blue mark, and I laugh.

"Shouldn't have shown me that," I tease, and I lightly tap him there again. When we were kids, we were fucking ruthless. If one of us had a bruise, it became the mission of the other one to continue punching it as many times as we could.

Maybe we haven't really grown out of that.

He chuckles, and I glance back at Ainsley.

"You remember Ainsley Riggs, right?" I ask Ford. He's a little closer to her age at just seven years her senior, so he might've been around the house with Ivy a little more than I was.

"Hey, good to see you," he says. He moves to give her a hug, and I bury the pang of jealousy I feel. It's just two acquaintances reconnecting.

That's what we were, too, though.

I brush it off.

"Oh, is this your baby?" Ford asks Ainsley.

She looks at me.

"He's mine, actually," I say, and Ford whips around to face me.

"What?"

"Yeah," I say. "Didn't the family gossip make its way through the mill yet? I have a kid."

"You're a dad?" Ford asks.

"That I am."

"Daddy Dex," Ainsley says brightly.

We both turn to look at her—me with heat in my eyes and Ford with absolute confusion in his.

Ford clears his throat. "How do you fit into this?" he asks her.

"She's my wife," I answer.

"Your *wife?*" Ford says. Actually, it's more of a sputter, really. Followed by a cough.

"Jack's stepmom and primary caretaker, too," I add.

"What about the kid's mother?" he asks.

"Long story." One I don't particularly want to get into in front of the hotel receptionist.

"Dude, I think we need to get a drink," he says.

I laugh. "Yeah. Probably long overdue."

The receptionist gets his attention, and I quietly turn to Ainsley. "I really want to spend time with you two, but would it be okay with you if I grabbed a drink with my brother while you went up to the room?"

"Of course. You don't even have to ask," she says. "In fact, just go now. I'll get us checked in and text you the room number."

"You wouldn't mind?" I ask. She shakes her head, and I lean in and press my lips to hers. "You're the best."

Ford catches me kissing her, and he looks incredibly confused.

I can't help my laugh as I slap him on the shoulder—on purpose, of course. "Let's hit the bar, yeah?"

"You fucker," he mutters as he grabs his shoulder in pain.

We head toward the bar and find a table near the back that offers a little bit of privacy. Once we both have a glass of whiskey, he finally looks at me and winces a little.

"So when did you get married?"

"A little under a month ago," I say.

He squints at me a little. "Why?"

"It's complicated. You want the whole story?"

He sips his whiskey. "Why the fuck not?"

I chuckle. "Well, this woman I slept with a while back showed up with a kid on July first. I ran into Ains the same day, quite literally, and she agreed to nanny for me. One thing led to another. I was warned I needed to look a bit more wholesome, and she was escaping this reality show nightmare, and we both stood to gain a lot with a marriage contract."

"Ah. So it's fake. Convenient." He nods as if that makes sense.

"Yeah, it started that way, and then before I left for camp, we had this night, and—"

He holds up a hand to interrupt me. "You had a night? You sound like a chick now."

I roll my eyes. "I fucked her good and hard. Is that better?"

"How hard we talking?"

"Fuck off. The point is that it started with a contract, but I'm not sure the end of the contract spells the end of our marriage. At least not the way I was so sure that's what it meant only a few weeks ago. Things feel like they're changing. I like having her at my place. And the kid…" I trail off as I try to put into words what it feels like to suddenly be an actual father. I blow out a breath. "He's incredible."

"How old is he?"

"Eight months tomorrow."

He whistles quietly, and I briefly think about asking if he knows about the casinos, but then I realize my dad didn't want

Madden telling anyone in the family about them, and he probably doesn't want me talking about them, either.

I can't help but wonder what other secrets we're all keeping from each other.

Hell, I did my best to keep my kid and my wife a secret from them until one of my siblings crashed the premises, and I had to admit the truth.

We're admittedly not a very close-knit group, but having a kid of my own and a woman I'm falling for—on top of being here for a funeral that reminds me how short life can be—is making me want to change all that.

I just wonder if it's far too late to make that change.

CHAPTER 31

Ainsley Bradley

I Hear You Married My Son

He gets up to the room a little before midnight. I'm still awake since it's only ten back home, and it's weird to think Vegas has become home while Chicago no longer is.

First it was home living out of that hotel while I filmed the show, and then it became home because of Dex.

Who would've thought?

Things seem perfect right now, which is a scary thought indeed since right when they feel perfect is when they tend to fall apart.

"How was your drink?" I ask.

"It was nice catching up with my brother," he says. He glances out the window. "God, I don't miss this city."

I laugh. "Why not?"

"Smog and traffic out the window here versus palm trees and mountains there." He shrugs. "And this place feels…I don't know. Claustrophobic. Like my family is all nearby, ready to swoop in and fuck it all up."

I pat the bed, a king since we're playing husband and wife, and he sits next to me. "Do you really feel that way?"

He shrugs and glances at Jack, who's asleep in his travel bassinet a few feet away from us. "Do you?"

"It's not like I'm running to my parents' house to let them know I'm in town."

"Why aren't you?" he asks. "You could've stayed a few days longer."

"I know, and I thought about that. But you'll be back in Vegas on Sunday, and I want to be there waiting for you." I lift a shoulder. "That feels like home now, you know?"

"Yeah. It *is* home."

"Are you okay?" I ask softly.

"I don't know. It feels like everyone in my family is keeping secrets from each other."

"How?" I press.

He doesn't answer, which only serves to make me feel like he's keeping secrets from me. And maybe he is. We're *married*, and we've gotten closer, but that doesn't mean I'm privy to the things he isn't ready to share.

I wish he was, though. I wish he'd share everything with me.

And it's just another stark reminder that for as much as he's let me in, there's still a hell of a lot I don't know about Dex Bradley.

He holds me in his arms through the night, and as we head to the funeral the next morning, I can't help but wonder if I'll learn more about him today. He'll know some of the people at this funeral—some he probably hasn't seen since he graduated high school fifteen years ago, and others he probably left in the past.

I didn't know him when *he* was in high school, but when I was in high school, he was already a famous football player. I didn't know when I befriended Ivy that her brothers were superstars, but I met them on a few different occasions. It never fazed me one way or the other, but I suppose it's pretty cool to have a best friend whose brothers play professional sports. To me they're just Ivy's much older brothers.

Dex was twenty-seven when I first met Ivy. He was so much older that the thought didn't even cross my mind to have a crush on him. Ivy was a happy surprise that came along six years after what the Bradley family thought was the last of the siblings with Liam. Apparently Mr. and Mrs. Bradley were busy little bunnies.

It's drizzling, not uncommon for the unpredictable Chicago weather, and the car carries Dex, Jack, myself, and Ford. We head to the church where the funeral is being held, and it's already standing room only when we arrive a full twenty minutes early.

Apparently Coach Murph, or Kenneth Murphy, was a beloved member of his community.

We listen as different people speak to his kind spirit and how much he'll be missed, and the officiant invites guests for a final viewing at the end of the service.

The rows file out with family first to say their goodbyes, and when it's finally our turn to walk up, Dex glances over at me. He looks almost nervous, and then he grabs my hand in his.

It's a small gesture, but it's one of comfort as he prepares to say his final goodbye to a man who meant a lot to him. And that small gesture speaks loudly to me. I'm here to comfort him. To be by his side in this difficult moment. Isn't that what marriage is all about?

It's starting to feel more and more real all the time.

We head to a luncheon at a nearby restaurant, and that's when we finally run into Mr. and Mrs. Bradley.

They don't hug their sons, who have stayed close by each other for the duration of the funeral so far, and they both glance at me.

"Ainsley," Mrs. Bradley says formally to me by way of greeting.

"Mrs. Bradley, it's lovely to see you."

"I hear you married my son," she says.

Well, that's awkward.

"Yes, I did." I offer a smile.

"Welcome to the family, I suppose. Is this my grandchild?" She nods to the carrier in my hands, and we both look down at the sleeping Jack.

I nod. "Yes." I offer a smile. "Would you like to hold him later when he wakes?" I ask softly.

Her eyes meet mine, and I think I almost see them soften for just a second. "I'd like that."

Dex mingles, and I follow him around as he introduces me to everyone here as his wife. It's strange meeting important people from his past and essentially lying to them. Sure, I'm his wife— but he doesn't specify that our marriage came with a contract and an end date. He doesn't tell anyone that I'm really just his nanny. But maybe I'm more than that to him now—now that we slept together. Now that I'm here for him at this funeral. Now that I've made arrangements to show him that I care about him and believe in him and will push him to step up and make the kinds of decisions he won't regret later.

I'm not trying to change him, yet I think he's starting to change anyway.

And I am, too. The old me never would've hopped on a flight with a baby to meet my best friend's older brother in Chicago. I guess I'm becoming a new version of myself who likes to feel the rush of butterflies when my husband's eyes meet mine.

Maybe I'm not the nerdy little girl who liked to play volleyball and didn't mind a good crossword puzzle. Truth be told, I still like a good crossword puzzle.

I'm still wholesome, sweet, sunshiny Ainsley, but now I've got a little of the Bradley bad boy in me. Quite literally since he was inside me two weeks ago tonight.

When Jack starts to stir in his carrier, I find Mrs. Bradley before he fully wakes. She's talking to a woman who possibly uses the same Botox person she uses given the sheer amount in both of their faces, and she turns toward me with a look like I'm a bit of a nuisance.

"What is it?" she asks.

"The baby is waking if you'd like to hold him." I offer a shy smile.

"Oh, yes, of course. Excuse me, Karen," she says to the woman. "This is my first grandchild and my first time holding him."

"You can feed him if you'd like," I say. "It's time for his bottle."

"That's okay," she says.

She twists her lips, and I wonder for the briefest of moments how many times she bottle fed her seven children. From what Ivy has indicated, her nanny was around more often than her own mother was.

My parents might've put me up to babysitting when I didn't always want to, but they still always made us feel loved and cared for. I guess nobody's life is perfect, but if I had to pick between having all the money and advantages the Bradleys have but being raised by a nanny or scraping together and working hard to earn my own money to pay for gas but having loving, caring parents…I think I'd still pick my own history.

And lucky Jack here will hopefully get to have both.

I get him out of his carrier and hand him over, and it feels like a photo op. Literally. Mr. Bradley shows up as if out of nowhere, snaps a few photos, and then she hands the baby back to me.

It's all very strange, but I feel better with the baby in my own arms anyway.

I spot Dex talking to a group of men, and I excuse myself to a table so I can sit and feed the baby. He may be my husband, and we may have some confusion about where our relationship is actually headed, but I'm still being paid to be a nanny to this little boy, so I settle in to do my job.

Happily.

Gladly.

It's a joy and a privilege to take care of this happy boy, and I think, not for the first time, how wrong I was to go into freaking *communications* instead of education.

I'm in my own little world when a woman slides into the chair across from me.

"So you're the one who landed Dex Bradley?" She looks me up and down, and the look of disdain in her eyes makes it very clear that she doesn't think I'm worthy.

I press my lips together in a fake smile. "That's me."

She leans in a little closer to me. "Come on. Tell the truth. Is it for the press? His image? What is it?"

The truth is that there are probably dozens, maybe even hundreds, of women just like her. Women who were with him once upon a time. Women who were hoping to be the one who landed him.

But it was me. Or, at least for our purposes, it was me. It wasn't *really* me, though, and that thought pulses a dart of sadness through me.

Did he just tell me he was falling for me to get me to sleep with him? I have no idea. The heat between us tells me otherwise, but I'm letting insecurities creep in now that I'm faced with a woman who might've *also* slept with him. Who I'd have that in common with when we did the deed wasn't a consideration that ever crossed my mind. But now that I'm faced with her, it sure as hell is.

"I'm the image consultant in the family, and Dex isn't one of my clients," a voice behind me says, interrupting me before I get the chance to respond.

I turn around and find Everleigh, the oldest Bradley sister, standing there. She's got her arms crossed over her chest and she looks like she means business…until her eyes fall onto the baby.

"Oh my God! Is this my nephew?" she asks, turning her attention away from whoever that woman was.

I nod. "Want to hold him?"

"I'd love to." I hand him over, and she takes over the bottle, too. "Oh, he's just so precious," she murmurs, staring down at him. "God, my brother's a *father*. It's hard to believe."

He's thirty-three. At this point in his life, it shouldn't really be that hard to believe. But given Dex's history, I get it.

I look around the room for him, and when I finally spot him, he's talking with his father, but he's looking at me.

And I'm starting to wonder whether we're rewriting history.

CHAPTER 32

Dex Bradley

Your Side Project

I glance across the room at her. I've had my eye on both her and my son the entire time I've been here, and when I see that Everleigh is with her, I know she's fine. I didn't like leaving her alone, but she walked away to feed the baby, and then my dad pulled me aside.

"Not here, Dad," I mutter.

"We're opening the front room this weekend. I'll have someone bring you the details and the keys. I have some big whales coming your way, and I need you there every Tuesday night to host."

"Fuck that," I say.

"What did you just say?" he says.

"You heard me. I'm in season now, Dad. I can't just hang at your side project on my one day off. I have shit to do."

"Be that as it may, this is now one of the items on your list. You agreed to it. You signed a contract."

"You know as well as I do there's nothing you can do to enforce that contract," I hiss at him.

"So you no longer want thirty-five percent of the profits? It goes both ways."

I know this man, and I also know he will do whatever it takes to shave those profits down as low as he can so I only get a portion of what was promised to me.

That's just how he works. It's how he's always operated, and I don't have to like it, but I did know that going into our agreement.

"I'll do what I can, but if I have events going on, I can't duck out on my responsibilities to run your side gig." I give him a pointed look.

"You won't be saying that when it's the *main* gig. I've hired some of the best in the business to handle things. It'll be fine. You put in your weekly appearance, and you stay on the payroll." He throws my own pointed look back in my face.

I realize as my eyes meet Ainsley's across the room that I don't want any part of this deal anymore. The money is nice, sure. But aside from that, I can't really put my finger on why I agreed to it. Family loyalty, I guess. Working hard to make him proud when I should know by now that's an impossible feat— or an uphill climb at the very least.

"I don't want her to know," I say.

"Who?"

"My wife."

He rolls his eyes. "Everyone knows that's a sham, son. Stop playing into it. You look ridiculous."

"What if it's not?" I ask.

"Isn't it?"

I don't answer, and I suppose not answering is an answer in itself. It might've started that way, but it's certainly not where we are now.

And the more I look across the room at her, the more regretful I feel that we don't get more time together.

I have to get back to California. I'll be back in Vegas in a couple of days, but seeing her and not having enough time to *be* with her tells me how deep my feelings have started to run for her.

When it's time to head to the airport, she goes with me. She bids my sister goodbye, mostly because Everleigh has been holding Jack since Ainsley handed him over, and I don't bother saying goodbye to my parents. Ford has to catch a flight back, too, and the four of us share the same car to the airport that we took to the funeral this morning.

"Good seeing you, man," Ford says to me when we arrive at the airport. "Wish it was under different circumstances."

"I'll see you in Vegas in a couple of months," I say back, and we high-five but hold on as we turn it into a hug. He hugs Ainsley next, and then he goes in to clear security while we get the baby carrier out of the back of the car and gather up everything we need to head back home.

"Thanks for meeting me here," I say once we're all checked in for our flights and we're waiting in line for security. "I know it wasn't easy traveling with the baby."

"It wasn't hard," she says, glancing down at Jack. "I actually quite enjoy taking care of him."

"You're good with him. You told me once you wanted to be a teacher, right? I think you would've made a good one."

Her eyes get a little misty at that. "Thank you, Dex. That's really sweet of you to say." She looks like she wants to say something more, but she twists her lips instead and doesn't add anything.

I can't help but wonder what that was about, but it's our turn at security, so we each fumble through our wallets for our licenses and Jack's birth certificate before we're waved through. She's quite early for her flight, but I need to go board mine, so she walks to my gate with me.

"I'll see you in a few days," I say softly, and I lean down and press my lips to hers. I glance at the carrier next, where Jack is awake and smacking the little toy Ainsley attached to the top of the handle. "And you, little man. See you on Sunday." I lean down and press my lips to his forehead, and I think it might be the first time I've kissed him in front of Ainsley.

I've kissed his head before, but only when we've been alone. I'm not sure why showing affection feels strange to me, but then I think of the fact that I didn't even say goodbye to my parents today, and I guess I can understand why.

"We'll miss you," Ainsley says as I start to walk away, and I backtrack for one more kiss before I have to go get on the plane.

"I'll miss you, too," I say as I disappear into the jetway, my heart squeezing a little as I realize I'm leaving a piece of it behind me here…a piece they'll carry home and have waiting for me when I return.

CHAPTER 33
Ainsley Bradley

Rock

I t's late Sunday, and the baby is already down when the front door opens and Dex walks through the door.

I didn't know what time he'd be home, but I've been waiting all day.

My instinct is to rush over to him, but I also don't know if we're there. I don't want to be the desperate girl who…

Oh, screw it.

I follow my instinct, and I race into his arms. He laughs even with the *oof* that escapes him at my impact, and my mouth crashes to his. I hear the thud of his duffel as he drops it on the floor beside us and kisses me intensely for a few beats.

He pulls back. "That's one hell of a greeting," he says. We kiss between sentences. "Maybe I should go away more often."

"Don't you dare," I say, and he laughs.

"I'll have to with my schedule, but it'll only be for a few nights at a time." Another kiss.

"I can probably manage that." More kissing.

He pulls away. "I brought you something."

I step back and clap my hands together. "A souvenir?"

"Not exactly," he says, and he reaches into his pocket. He pulls out a ring, and my jaw drops as he grabs my hand and slides it on. "I was thinking when we were in Chicago how people kept asking to see the ring. You should be wearing one if you're my wife, so I picked this one up. I hope you like it."

He sounds nearly shy at the end, and it's very sweet.

I glance down at the rock, and make no mistake, that's what this is. It's a freaking *rock*. It feels heavy on my hand, and it must be four carats at least. It's a radiant cut with double pavé bands, and I've never seen a more gorgeous ring in my entire life.

"Like it?" I repeat. "I freaking love it, Dex. You shouldn't have, but I'm glad you did."

He chuckles, and I toss my arms around his neck.

"Thank you."

He leans down to kiss me. "You're welcome." He hooks his arm around my waist and pulls me in, and there's no more studying the ring as instead we make time to study each other.

We didn't have enough time in Chicago to have sex again, especially not with Jack sleeping a few feet away from us, but now he's back and we have time again.

Sort of.

He has to be at the practice facility at eight tomorrow, which means in less than twelve hours, we'll be apart again. I'm sure he's exhausted after a trying couple of weeks, and I'm sure he's eager to get back to his own bed after sleeping in a hotel for so long.

But he's not rushing me. Instead, as his mouth opens to mine and his tongue starts to move in my mouth, I feel like he's taking his time. He's moving slowly, intentionally, and there's something really sexy about it.

I slide my fingers into his dark hair, and the strands are soft between my fingers. He deepens our kiss, still keeping a slow, tender pace as we move in closer to each other, our bodies pressed together in delicious anticipation of what's to come.

He sweeps me up into his arms and carries me over to the couch, and he wastes no time in getting us situated before he's hovering over me, slamming his hips to mine in a preview of what's to come. His lips move from mine and across my cheek toward my ear. "I've been dreaming of your cunt for two weeks," he murmurs.

He licks the shell of my ear before he slowly moves down my body. He grips my pants and pulls them off with my panties in one fell swoop, and I'm left breathless by his agile, quick movements. He reaches under the shirt I'm still wearing to find one of my breasts, and he hisses when he feels my naked breast there, not covered by a bra.

He thumbs one nipple until it's a hard peak, and then he moves his attention to the other as he continues to kiss his way down my body and toward my pelvis. He moves to the side to kiss my naked hipbone, and then he continues his downward trek as he moves his hand from my nipple, creating a trail down my skin that leaves me shivering until he slides a finger directly into my pussy.

I cry out, my hips jerking off the couch at the feel of his welcome intrusion, and he starts to move his fingers in and out.

"I've wanted to taste this cunt since that night we went on the roller coaster," he says, and he moves his fingers out to dip his tongue in.

"Ah!" I yell, my hips jerking out of control so my thighs basically slap his face.

"Mm," he groans, his hum vibrating warmly through my entire being. He pushes his tongue in and out, and he grunts a hot little, "Fuck," when he slides his tongue out toward my clit. "Fuck, you taste so good." He sucks on my clit, and nothing has ever felt like this.

I cry out some moaning, incoherent sounds as I try to get a grip, but what he's doing to my pussy is causing everything else to short-circuit. My brain can't seem to focus on anything except for the pleasure he's delivering, and my *God*, is he delivering. His tongue dips back down inside me, and he thumbs my clit at the same time.

"Tell me what you want," he demands.

"You," I cry.

"What do you want me to do? You have to ask for it, baby. You deserve everything you want. Don't be shy."

"My clit!" I cry, and I thought I'd feel weird asking for what I want, but I don't. He's telling me to do it, and he's right. I deserve what I want. He's teaching me to ask for it. "I want your tongue on my clit and your finger inside."

He does exactly as I ask, and my orgasm hits me out of nowhere. It's this rush of pleasure that I can't even begin to define that plows into me with an excruciating, blazing force. My legs clench together as my entire body tightens while this release pumps through me, throb after intense throb, and he somehow follows the jerking of my hips, his tongue still moving in and out of me even though my knees are pressing against his head. I scream his name as I fly through it, not really sure where I'm going or what I'm doing, as it feels like all I can see are stars peppering the darkness with my eyes squeezed shut and my body writhing along with the motion.

When the pulses start to slow, I gradually force my knees to relax their grip on his ears, and he sits back on his knees. He wipes his mouth with the back of his hand, and he raises a brow as his lip curls into a sexy smile.

"Fuck, Ains. That was the hottest goddamn thing I've ever seen."

My cheeks flush. Hell, I think my entire body might flush.

It might've been the hottest thing he's ever seen, but it was the hottest thing I've ever *experienced*, too.

And we're only getting started.

He reaches into his back pocket and produces a condom, but I sit up and set my hand on his arm to stop him. His brows push together in confusion as he angles his head to look at me.

I raise a brow and nod toward his dick, and he seems to get what I'm saying.

"Take off your pants," I say.

He chuckles. He shakes his head a little lazily. "You want them off? You take them off."

I'm not sure why his words are *so* incredibly steamy, but they are. It's a clear demand for dominance after he just told me to ask for what I want, and I am willing to bend to his every word. I love when he tells me what to do. He's experienced at this, and I'm not. And if he wants me to take off his pants? Hell yeah, I'll do it.

I'll freaking pull them down with my teeth if he asked me to. That's how good that last orgasm he gave me was.

I flick the button of his jeans and start to yank them down, but he's not moving from his position where he's on his knees over my legs, still sitting back on his legs.

I force my legs out from under him, and I move so I'm kneeling in front of him. I can't push his pants down if he doesn't move, so instead, I pull the zipper down, reach in, and stroke his cock under his boxers for a few seconds.

He tilts his head as he watches me, completely in control of the situation despite the fact that I literally have him by the balls at the moment.

I pull his cock out, and I glance up at him, curious about his reaction. He hasn't really moved at all. I see the heat in his eyes, though, and it's a dead giveaway that he wants this. Wants *me*. He's just watching me to see what move I'll make next, and there's something really hot about having all the power in this moment.

I get off the couch and move to the floor, his cock still in my hand, and I push on his hip to indicate he should move. He finally does, unfolding his legs from beneath him, and he sits on the couch with his feet on either side of me on the floor. This is a much better angle to work with, and I sit up a little higher, bend over him, and lick the tip of his cock. I look up at him, and he's looking down at me, and a searing moment passes between us before I keep my eyes on him as I suck his cock into my mouth.

"Ohhhh fuck," he moans, and his hand moves over my head, where he gently presses the back as if to tell me to take him deeper.

I do, breaking our eye contact so I can take him all the way to the back of my throat until his cock is choking me and cutting off my air supply. It's not in a panicked kind of way but rather in a hot-as-hell kind of way. I know I'm still fully in control even though he's trying to control from over me, and just as he pushes the back of my head, he thrusts his hips.

He lets out possibly the sexiest little growly moan I've ever heard when he does it, and the fact that I'm turning him on as much as I am gives me the sort of power trip I wasn't expecting to feel in this moment.

It's hot. It's sexy.

It's achingly beautiful, so achingly that my own body starts to throb for him.

I'm new at a lot of this. It's not like it's the first time I've had a cock in my mouth. I'm not totally innocent. But I'm inexperienced compared to him, not that I particularly want in this moment to think about the sheer number of women he's been with. Still, the way he's reacting to what I'm doing to him makes me feel like I'm the queen of the world. Like I'm the only one who matters. Like whoever came before me couldn't possibly have given him what I can.

Maybe he makes every woman feel that way, or maybe I really am special. I can fool myself into thinking I am, anyway.

I bob my head up and down his shaft, and he occasionally pushes my head down further. He holds me there for a few beats, and sometimes he takes over and thrusts into my mouth, taking what he needs from me.

It's all working well. Too well.

"Fuck, Ains," he grunts. "I'm about to come."

I appreciate the warning but don't move from my spot, and hot streams of his cum jet to the back of my throat as I finish him off. And once he's finished and the quaking of his body starts to slow, he pulls me up into his arms and cradles me there a few quiet moments.

He's so different than I expected. He comes off as this bad boy football star without a care in the world, and that's not at all who he is.

He's sweet and kind. He's scared, and yet he's not running from the things that scare him. He's facing them and tackling them head-on.

And he's doing it all while holding my hand in his.

CHAPTER 34
Ainsley Bradley

I'm a Slut

We went to bed last night after all the oral sex. He has to be at his practice facility this morning by eight, so I decided to get up early to spend a little time with him before he has to go.

"There's Daddy Dex," I say when he walks into the kitchen while I'm making him breakfast. It's a little after seven, and I'm still getting out the supplies to make a nice, hearty breakfast. The baby is still asleep, so I don't know why those words come out of my mouth.

Apparently he likes them.

He stalks across the kitchen toward me, and his voice is low and intimidating when he asks, "Are you on birth control?"

I shake my head. "Why?"

"Because I want to fuck my wife in my kitchen, and I don't have a condom on me. Let's get it sorted."

My heart thunders at his words. Hell yeah, I'll take care of it. Today, if I can.

"Call me that again," he says.

I clear my throat, and my voice is tentative when I say, "Good morning, Daddy Dex."

"Get your ass in that bedroom, get naked, and wait for me on the bed so I can treat you like the good little slut you are for me."

Oh my God. Nobody has ever spoken to me like that before, but suddenly it's all I want. I want to be his good little slut. He likes when I call him Daddy Dex? Well, I like when he calls me his little slut.

Who would ever have thought that would sound so hot? It should sound degrading. But we both know I don't sleep around, and he used a very important prepositional phrase in that sentence: *for me.*

I'm a slut *for him.* Nobody else. And I prove that when I rush to the bedroom and strip off my clothes as requested.

I shiver as the chill in the air makes my nipples harden. I rub my fingertip along the peaks, and it sends a shot of need straight through me. I want his rough hands on my breasts again. I want them all over my body, touching and caressing and giving me everything I need.

I'm so wet I feel like I'm dripping. I'm ready. I'm needy. I'm waiting.

In fact, I feel like I've been waiting a lifetime for him to come in when he finally does.

"There's my good girl," he says, and his lips curl into a smile as he stares down at me. Rather than take his time since we both know we don't have much, he grabs a condom from his nightstand, yanks his cock over his athletic shorts, and rolls it on.

He moves toward me, and he runs his hand along my breasts and across each of my nipples. "Your tits are perfection," he murmurs, and his hand dips along my torso and down toward my hip. He slips a finger in me, and he hisses at the feel of that dripping wet pussy just waiting for him.

"Fucking hell, Ainsley. This is the wettest pussy I've ever felt."

"It's what you do to me," I murmur.

He pulls his fingers out of me and moves quickly so he's hovering over me, but he doesn't slide inside me just yet. Instead, he flips us so I'm on top of him. He helps me lift up a little, and then he aligns his cock with my body and pushes in. My body stretches for him, as if my pussy seems to remember this intruder and is happy to let him in again. Holy hell, I'm happy, too.

I sit down on him, and *God,* that angle feels like pure heaven. I cry out at how good it feels, and he sets his hands under my ass to move my body over his.

Once I get the feel of the motion down, I set my hands on his chest and really start to move. I'm gyrating wildly over him, moving in ways I had no idea I even could. His eyes are hooded and locked on mine as we do this for only the second time. His fingertips inch over on my ass until I'm almost certain he's going to push a finger in, but he doesn't. For now, anyway. It's not something we've talked about yet, but I also don't know if that's something you bring up over dinner. *Can I stick my finger in your ass next time we're doing it? Oh, and could you pass the green beans?*

I sort of *want* him to do it, though. Every experience with him feels new to me, and if that's something he's into, then I want to try it.

I want to try it all.

With him.

He continues lifting me over him, and eventually he lets go since he can see I've found my rhythm here. He reaches down between us with one of his hands and he rubs my clit, and he bands an arm around my waist to pull me down over him. I have to stretch a little, but he's able to shift to get my nipple in his mouth, and he sucks on it as I continue to gyrate over him.

There are too many sensations plowing into me at once. My body doesn't seem to know how to handle all of it as I tip over the edge.

I claw at his chest as I try to hold on through the roaring wave that crashes over me. I cry out his name with a series of moans that carry me through the crest of the wave. My body pulses over his, pulse after powerful pulse, and a growl rips from his chest as he starts to come, too. He keeps sucking on my nipple as he rides the wave, his body contracting beneath mine as my own climax starts to pull away from me and his reaches its peak. He moves his hand that was on my clit to grab my other breast, and he squeezes it as he comes—*hard*—into me.

"Fuck, Ains," he grunts as he finishes, and then he lets go of his grip on my breast as he relaxes back. I collapse over him, and he tosses one arm around me, keeping me in place as I rest on his chest, our bodies still connected in this intense, perfect way.

And speaking of perfect, it's damn near perfect timing as we hear the first signs that the baby down the hall is waking up.

I push off of him, and I feel the intense loss as his cock drops out of me. I move off the bed to start gathering my clothes, and I head to the bathroom to use it and get dressed before I go get the baby. When I'm out of the bathroom, though, Dex is sitting on the bed, fully dressed and waiting for me.

"Come here," he demands quietly, and I walk over. He pulls me down on his lap, and I straddle his waist as I sit on him. He reaches up and takes my face between his palms, and he kisses me gently. "I just wanted to say that I think I'm past the falling stage. I love you."

My eyes soften as they meet his, and I see all the sincerity in them that I need to see to know that this is real. "I love you too, Dex."

They're not the words I was expecting to hear—or to say—this morning, but somehow they're perfect.

Somehow *he* is perfect. And when I ran out of that wedding when Jordan told me he didn't, I had no idea that I was running right into what would turn into *this*.

CHAPTER 35

DEX BRADLEY

Not Very Traditional

Ainsley: *Did you know Daddy Dex autocorrects to Daddy's ex? Or Daddy Sex?*

Me: *I'll be your sex daddy if you'll be my slut.*

I stare at the words as I send them. Never in my wildest dreams did I ever imagine that I'd be sending a text like that to Ivy's best friend, but here we are.

I head to morning practice and leave my phone in my locker. When I get out, I have a text from my father.

Thomas Bradley: *Don't forget about tomorrow. Did you get the keys?*

Me: *Yes, my doorman had them. I won't forget.*

I don't want to go. I want to go home and spend the little free time I have with Ainsley and Jack. I want to continue to build upon the foundation we've set down.

But I don't have much choice. My father likes to put me into positions where I'm forced to put the family first. The goddamn legacy.

I shove my phone back in my locker, and I think about how I still haven't spoken to Madden about all this. And that's why I decide I'll call him on my way home from practice. It's late enough that I should catch him after practice.

I haven't left the parking lot yet as I dial his number, and in fact I decide to sit right there in the parking lot to have this conversation.

"What the fuck do you want?" he answers, his standard greeting that comes off like a dickface but is actually kind of the way we tease one another.

"Just calling to check in on my favorite much older brother. How's training camp going at your advanced age?"

He chuckles. "Knock it off with that. You're only a couple years behind."

"Yeah, and it's been hell on these old knees. I can't bend down like I used to." And a big portion of my job happens to be bending down.

"I hear that, man. What's going on?"

I'm not one to beat around the bush, so I ask, "Why didn't you tell me about Dad's casinos?"

He's quiet on the other end. "How'd you find out?"

"When Dad asked me to run one for him in Vegas."

He lets out a low whistle. "That man has some balls, dude."

"Yeah, no kidding."

"What did you say?" he asks.

"What choice did I have?"

"So it was a yes, then," he says flatly.

"It was a yes with negotiations."

"Still a yes."

"Yeah. So how do I get out of it?" I ask.

He's quiet for a beat, and he sounds surprised when he asks, "Why do you want out?"

I clear my throat. "You've heard about the kid by now, I assume."

"Jack? Yeah. I heard."

"It's him," I say. "Well, and also…it's not just him. The woman I hired to nanny for him, we got married, and I'm falling in—"

"Wait, Ivy's friend, right? Can you explain why you married her? You know, just between the two of us."

"It was a contract," I say. "She just got out of a reality show thing, and I needed to look a little more wholesome. You know, that whole thing. So we agreed to get married since it had benefits for both of us. But then I went and caught feelings."

"Damn. You? Feelings?"

"I know. I didn't think I was capable."

He chuckles. "But she's caring for your kid, right?"

"Yes."

"Is it a good idea to get involved with the person who cares most for your son besides you?" he asks.

"Isn't that traditionally how these things go?" I point out. Mom. Dad. Kid. It's a pretty simple equation.

"Yes, when it's two people who love each other and create a new life from that love. Not when it's someone who doesn't do relationships. You can't fuck up the balance when that poor kid already lost his mom."

Maybe the equation is traditionally simple, but I've never been very traditional.

Throughout this entire journey with her, she's held me to a higher standard. One I'm certain I can't measure up to. Yet I keep measuring up for her, *showing* up for her, and I like who I am when I'm with her.

But my brother makes a solid point here.

I don't do relationships. I never have, and this is my first. First tries don't normally pan out the way people hope they will. It's why it's called a *first* try. The assumption is that there will be more.

I'm at a point where I want to say that I don't *want* to try with anybody else. But that doesn't mean that this will automatically work. While I'm doing my best to meet the standard she sets for me, I have a history. I have patterns. I have a father pushing me in one direction. I have a career pulling me in another. And I can't escape any of that.

The last thing I want to do is hurt either Jack or Ainsley in all of this.

But it does feel like Madden reminded me on this phone call about who the fuck I am.

He may not have told me to get out, but I can read between the lines. It's a solid reminder that I may never be good enough for someone like Ainsley.

* * *

The next night, I head to the VIP lounge, which is already open and in full swing. I look around the place, and I'm actually pretty impressed with what my father has come up with here.

High-limit tables, top-shelf bars, private rooms, velvet and marble…it's all very high-class and all very much my father's doing.

I don't want to be here, but he demanded it. I can stand up to basically anyone else in the world, but somehow he still has power over me. I'm not sure how he does it.

"Mm, Dex Bradley," a blonde woman says, sidling up beside me and grabbing my arm between hers to pull it against her tits in some attempt to give my arm a hug, perhaps.

She looks familiar, but I can't place her.

"Jessica May," she says, and it dawns on me. She's a model for one of those famous lingerie lines.

"Right, of course," I say, not sure how she got in here, but also not really caring.

Except I should care, of course.

We don't just have the *eye in the sky* kinds of cameras here. No, no. My father wanted me here tonight because *the media* is here.

Would've been nice if he would've clued me in on that, but he didn't.

I could've brought Ainsley with me. Instead, I've got a model trying to smother my arm with her tits and cameras all around me decidedly working hard to demolish the *wholesome* family man image I'm just starting to build.

Excellent.

Thanks, Dad.

The rest of the night doesn't go much better. More models, more of the rich and famous, more money exchanging hands, more alcohol, more photos.

It's nearly three in the morning by the time I get home, and Ainsley is asleep in my bed. I should've been there with her when she fell asleep on my chest, and instead I smell like dingy cigarette smoke because what pairs with gambling and drinking? Smoking, naturally.

I blow out a breath and take a quick shower, and I slip into bed beside my wife…into the place I wish I'd been all night as I try to come up with how the fuck I can get out of going back to that lounge again next week.

CHAPTER 36
Ainsley Bradley

An Appearance

He said he'd get Tuesdays off during the season, but I guess training camp is different. He said he'd be out late, and I guess I assumed he'd be with his teammates. And that's why I'm so surprised by this morning's headlines.

NFL Player Dex Bradley Entertains at New Vegas Lounge.

Okay, fine. So he had an appearance he didn't tell me about.

But that doesn't explain the photo accompanying the article of a woman with enormous breasts smashing them up against *my husband*. You know, that sham of a marriage we have. Just for show. All pretend.

Still, he told me he loves me. That means something to me.

On the other hand, he has a history with this kind of thing. A well-documented history. And I'm just the naïve little girl eleven years his junior whose lack of experience might've drawn him in but perhaps has turned boring to him already.

"Does my little slut want to be a good girl for me again?" His voice interrupts me as I read the article.

I turn toward him, steam possibly coming out of my ears, and I flash the photo at him. "What's this?"

He sighs, and he takes a step back. He closes his eyes. "It's nothing."

"Doesn't seem like nothing. Also doesn't appear you're trying very hard to get away." I press my lips together.

"Wait a second," he says, and I glance up at him with pursed lips. "Is my wife *jealous?*"

"This isn't the time for teasing, Dex. What's going on?"

"I had to put in an appearance. That's all."

I purse my lips but don't say anything.

"Tuesdays are appearance days in season. I told you that."

"Yeah, but I thought you meant like at charity events or at a nightclub. Not at some fancy luxury lounge with models humping your arm." I fold my arms over my chest.

"My wife *is* jealous," he says, diverting the subject. "And honestly, it's kind of sexy." He moves in to kiss me, and I'm so damn hot for him that I momentarily forget that I'm angry. Only…what's there to be angry about, really?

He's a football star. He had an appearance. I'm not going to be the kind of wife—real or fake—that's going to harp on him every time he gets in late.

Especially when he breaks our kiss and says his next words low and deep close to my ear. "I would've rather been here with you."

His mouth moves back to mine, and fifteen minutes later, I'm sanitizing the countertop and blushing as I think about what he just did to me on top of it.

He comes out with Jack a few minutes later, and he says, "I've been thinking. I want to get Jack's last name changed from Jeffries to Bradley."

My chest warms. Of course he does. Of course he's falling into the role of daddy—all jokes aside. He's turning into this swoon-worthy dad, and I'm totally here for it.

But there are other things at play I'm decidedly *not* here for. For example, another week comes and goes, and the exact same thing happens the next Tuesday.

Only this time, I'm still awake at three in the morning when he walks in, and I'm seething a little that he did this again.

Why didn't he just invite me? He's done that at other events, so why not this one?

"Hey," he says, and I purse my lips and glare. He moves over to kiss me, and he stinks of cigarettes. I wrinkle my nose, and he sighs. "Come on, Ains. Don't be like that."

"Then just be honest with me, Dex."

"I *am* being honest." His eyes are pleading with me, and regardless of whether I feel like he's leaving something out of the story, I can't help but believe him.

"Where were you?"

He diverts his gaze from me. "The same lounge as last week."

"What is this lounge you keep going to?" I ask. His court date is the day after tomorrow—or tomorrow, actually, given that it's three in the morning—for punching that asshole at the charity event, and I'm possibly a bit snippier than absolutely necessary, but I'm tired of feeling like he's avoiding me.

He blows out a heavy breath. "My father decided to open a VIP lounge here in Vegas, and he asked me to stop by and entertain the clients. Schmooze a little. That's all it is."

"Why didn't you just tell me that?"

"Because I don't have to answer to you," he snaps, and then he stops himself. "I'm sorry. I didn't mean that. I'm just stressed and overwhelmed with everything right now. My dad…he's always coming up with these grand plans that somehow involve his kids, and none of us ever know how to say no to him until he drives us as far away as he possibly can." His voice is low and full of regret as he says the words, and I wonder exactly what he means by that. Before I can ask, he adds, "He wants me to put in an appearance every Tuesday. I didn't know he'd have the media there documenting my arrival every week, but he has. He wants to blow this lounge up into something huge. He wants to be the next MGM Entertainment or whatever, and he's using my status to attract clients. That's all."

I get the sense he's leaving something out of the story, but I don't press him—mainly because he told me the truth, I think, and because having him go there and do this thing without telling me not once but *twice* makes me feel like he's already backing away.

All of this is yet *another* reminder that there's a lot about Dex I still don't know, and it makes me wonder not for the first time whether he'll ever really let me in to see all the parts of who he is.

I know he's busy. So busy that his team of lawyers ended up making a plea deal with Jensen Bybee so he doesn't have to waste his time with court appearances for a silly misdemeanor. We talked about how once the season starts, he won't be around as much. I get that. But nerves still pulse in me that this has nothing to do with football.

I already lost everything once—back when Jordan said he didn't after I said I did. I didn't know at the time how very little Jordan really mattered to me, but it felt like my life was shattered. The second he said the words until the moment I quite literally ran into Dex, I was completely devastated. I had no idea how I was going to pick myself up.

And then this man saved me. He gave me a job. He gave me a place to stay. He married me so I'd have something to throw in their faces at the reunion.

It didn't matter with Jordan, but it *does* matter with Dex and Jack. I love them both, and I can't lose them.

But when the third Tuesday comes and goes and he doesn't get in until three in the morning again, I can't help but wonder whether he's as sincerely in love with me as I am with him. He can't even bother to keep me updated about his schedule. He still hasn't invited me to the VIP lounge with him. It seems like he's spending *all* his free time there—which is short to begin with anyway now that preseason games have started.

I keep trying to blame this very strange sudden divide between us on the season, but I can't help feeling like it has nothing to do with football and everything to do with him suddenly not wanting to be around Jack and me.

It's probably just my insecurities, but I feel like I haven't even seen him enough to talk to him about any of it—and when we finally *do* get some alone time, we certainly aren't using it to *talk*. Which is good. Amazing, even.

But for the vast majority of the time, I'm alone with Jack. I'm raising him, and I'm being paid handsomely to do so.

Still, a little thought keeps creeping in as I think about how little I actually get to see my husband, and I can't help but wonder whether this is really the life I want.

CHAPTER 37

DEX BRADLEY

Drifting

I hate this place.

It feels like everything I've worked so hard for is slowly drifting away from me because of this stupid VIP lounge, and I don't know how to pull it all back in.

Ainsley has been standoffish since I admitted half the truth about the lounges to her, and I think she can sense I'm leaving something out.

But I can't exactly tell her about the fact that in another couple of weeks, my dad is opening an underground, illegal operation where we're going to be raking in the cash.

It's dangerous for her to know that. It's dangerous for *me* to know that, too, and truthfully, I'm angry with my father for putting me in this position. I went my entire life not knowing about his illegal activities. Why did he have to tell me *now*?

Oh, right. Because now he can benefit from my help.

I hate it.

It feels like a huge betrayal only to be used by a person who should never do that to his children, and somehow, I have a feeling he's going to involve us all by the time he's done. I wonder if he's got Ford on something illegal in Tampa, though I think Ford would lean on the line of legalities. He's the traditionalist of this family, my opposite in most ways, and I think he'd have a moral issue with running something illegal. It would appear I inherited my father's moral compass since that's not the part I have a problem with.

I'm trying my best to protect Ainsley and Jack, and even though I just want to walk away from the casinos, I can't. It's not just the promise of a huge payday lurking around the corner, a promise big enough that it has the potential to set us up for life after I retire from football. It's for the entire Bradley family, and while my parents have done little to earn my respect or my loyalty, I do feel a sense of that loyalty for my brothers and sisters.

I'm paving the way for the future, and when I think of the future, I'm thinking of both Jack and Ainsley in there, too. What I *don't* see in my future, though, are my father's illegal operations.

But I also feel like I've hardly seen Ainsley lately, and I know one of my major flaws tends to be avoidance. I avoid problems that I can't throw money at. It's how I was raised, and it's part of why I can't get out of this deal with my father. I tried. He wouldn't let me, and now it feels like I have to choose between the only family and legacy I've ever known or the life I never wanted.

I never wanted it until I got a taste of it, and now it's all I want. But what if I pick that life—what if I choose to walk away from my own family—and it doesn't work out with Ainsley? It's a heavy debate to carry the weight of, but since I've never done this relationship thing, I have no way of knowing.

And it's not just that.

I keep thinking of abandonment. My parents abandoned us in favor of nannies.

Just like I'm doing to my own son.

Fuck. I feel like I'm handling everything the wrong way, and maybe Madden was right. I shouldn't get involved with someone who's caring for my child. I don't know anyone else who would love Jack the way Ainsley does, and maybe it was a mistake to get involved with her.

Or maybe it's everything I never knew I needed.

I run harder on my treadmill as if that'll give me the answer.

It doesn't.

I go harder at practice as if that'll give me the answer.

It doesn't.

I flatten a backup quarterback in a preseason game as if that'll give me the answer.

It doesn't.

No amount of pushing my body to its limits helps. Nothing gives me the rush I'm looking for.

Nothing makes me feel the way Ainsley does.

And that's why on a Sunday after our final preseason game—one in which we emerge victorious—the second I walk in the front door, I finally say the words I've been holding onto for weeks. "We need to talk."

"I was going to congratulate you on the win first," she says.

I chuckle. "Thanks."

"What do you want to talk about?" she asks. She stands from where she was seated on the couch, and I indicate she should sit.

I sit next to her. "It feels like we're drifting, and I don't want that for us."

"I don't either," she admits.

"So how do we fix it?"

"I don't know for sure, but open communication would probably be a good start."

I press my lips together. Isn't that always the sage advice successful couples give to make a relationship last? Open communication? "Right. So I'm communicating that I feel us drifting, and I don't want to drift from you."

"I figured it was just the start of the season."

"That's part of it." I clear my throat, and I open my mouth to admit how it feels like everything is spinning away from me when she interrupts me.

"That and your father's lounge. And it's okay, Dex. I'm right here. For the next two years at least. Right?"

Right. The contract. Our sham of a marriage.

So maybe it's time to give her some attention—to help her feel like this is less of a sham since it's starting to feel more and more real to me.

"I hope it's longer than that," I say softly.

Her eyes dart to mine. "So do I."

I lean over to press my lips to hers to seal in those words, but the heat between us burns too hot. My mouth opens, and so does hers, and suddenly I'm on top of her, humping her with our clothes still on.

She moans beneath me as she wraps her legs around me, and then she breaks the kiss to whisper, "I got on the pill last week."

That's my green light.

I pull her shirt over her head and start by giving some attention to her perfect, gorgeous tits. I suck her nipples into my mouth until they form those sexy as fuck tight little peaks, and then I shift off her to get the rest of our clothes out of the way. Once we're both naked, I move to hover over her once again.

My eyes are on hers, and my voice is a low rasp when I ask, "Are you sure about this?" I reach between us and fist my cock, bumping the head against her clit.

She closes her eyes and leans her head back as she moans, "Oh yes, Dex. God, yes, I'm sure."

I pump my cock against her clit a few more times, and I let go of my cock to slip a finger into her.

She's sure.

She's ready.

She's wet as fuck.

I hiss out some incoherent appreciation of just how wet she is, and then I fist my cock again and move down to slide into her.

Her pussy clenches onto my bare cock as I move in and out of her, and it feels somehow sexier and more emotional with nothing between us at all. It's intense as I open my eyes and look into hers, and a moment seems to pass between us that I've never had before.

I can't say I've *never* fucked a woman without a condom before. Jack exists, so obviously that's not true.

But I've never been in love with someone I've fucked before, and doing this very intimate deed with Ainsley Riggs pushes me to a place I've never been before. I'm no virgin, but she's still managing to give me these thrilling new experiences.

It's too good, from hearing her sexy moans to feeling the way her cunt greedily pulls me in, to tasting her lips and seeing her bite her lip as she leans her head back at the pleasure of it all.

I pump into her, and my body barely gives me any warning at all before I hit the edge. My balls tighten as my release plows into me, and I start to come inside her. It's a long, shuddering, hot release that seems to go on forever, and as my cum fills her up, she's pushed into her own climax.

Her pussy contracts around me as the sweet relief hits her, and I ride out the rest of my orgasm as she flies into hers. I'm depleted, but I continue pounding into her anyway because I don't want to be done. I focus on the sensations as she comes around my cock, the only thought in my mind the fact that my cum now lives inside of her, that I'm the only man on the planet who has that designation.

And it leaves me feeling proud, a little emotional, and still incredibly horny as I realize the thrills I've been chasing my entire life have landed right here beneath me.

CHAPTER 38

Ainsley Bradley

Open Communication

When he pulls out of me, his cum oozes out behind him, a new sensation I haven't experienced yet. I'm still coming down from the high of that orgasm when he moves. I'm expecting him to get up so we can both go clean up, but instead he moves to the side of me. He reaches down and slips his finger into me, and he hisses as he feels how extra wet I am now that I have his cum paired with my own.

He rubs slow, lazy circles around my clit, spreading his cum out as he leans over and sucks my nipple back into his mouth, and then he pushes his finger inside of me, as if he's trying to push all that cum back in.

Holy hell. It's hotter than I expected it to be. It's like he's marking me as his, as if there was ever any question. He's leaving a part of himself behind for my body to absorb so he's literally a part of me. I've never thought of it that way until this very moment, but somehow it's sweet and sexy in a sort of caveman kind of way.

I like it more than I thought I might. In fact, I kind of love it. I kind of love that we share this new intimacy.

I want it to be something that's just between the two of us, but there's a reminder sleeping in a room down the hall that he's had sex with other women. Probably a lot of them, truthfully. And at least one other time, he didn't use a condom.

I was living with him when he had a physical a few weeks ago, so we didn't really need to have the awkward chat about whether it's safe to do this or not. He may be a bad boy, but deep down, I know he cares about me, and I know he'd never put me in harm's way.

So I revel in what we just did as he pumps his finger into me, as he sucks my nipple, as he pushes me into my second orgasm in a matter of minutes.

It's stronger. More intense.

There's nothing fake about this, that's for damn sure.

My legs squeeze together, clamping shut over his fingers, but he rides it out with me, his finger continuing to pump as my hips jerk all over the place, his mouth firmly latched onto my nipple until my quakes start to slow.

I must fall asleep after that. Two intense orgasms in a row, and I'm freaking spent.

I wake in his bed, and a glance at the clock tells me it's been an hour. I use the bathroom, slip into my pajamas, and sleep soundly until morning, when I'm awakened by the sounds of a baby crying through the monitor.

I'm about to leap out of bed when I hear the door to Jack's room open, and then I hear Dex.

"Shh, Jack. Shh. Let's let Ains sleep, okay? I kept her up past her bedtime, and she's wrecked."

I can't help the smile playing at my lips as I listen to Dex. I think I might swoon a little as I listen to him *narrate* what he's doing—just like I always do.

"I'll pick you up and then we can find you some clothes for today, okay, little buddy? Let's check the dresser drawers."

I try to picture him holding the baby. He's gotten better about it, and he may even have Jack on one hip with one arm tied up as he uses his other hand to open and close the dresser drawers.

"How about a green shirt and black shorts? Green is my favorite color, but don't tell anyone. It's supposed to be red since I play for the Aces. Don't want anyone thinking I'm secretly throwing games to the Packers or the Jets now, do we?"

I giggle. So his favorite color is green. Duly noted.

I listen to him as he changes the diaper and then the clothes, and Jack listens to his daddy, too. The crying stopped long ago, and it might be the single cutest thing I've ever witnessed—and it was all over a baby monitor.

I get up once I hear them leave Jack's room, and I use the restroom and brush my teeth before I head out to join them. I find Dex on the couch feeding Jack a bottle.

"Good morning," he says, and I smile as I look at him and the baby and think about the sweet little life we've created here.

If only that feeling could last a little longer.

The next night, he's back at his VIP lounge until three in the morning again. And the morning after that, more pictures emerge of him rubbing...*elbows* with big-name celebrities, mostly women and all with rather large...*assets.*

I'm not jealous. I'm not jealous. I'm not jealous.

I'm not jealous my husband has gorgeous women pressed up against him for the entire world to see.

Oh, hell. Who am I trying to fool? Of course I'm jealous. He's out doing what he calls "work," and I'm home alone with the baby. That's my work since he's paying me to do it, but it's starting to feel strange to act like his wife on one hand and be a nanny on the other. Either I'm a stepmother or a nanny, but I'm riding this strange line where I'm both.

And I don't know what to do about it. I don't know if there's anything I *can* do other than ride it out. I signed a contract, and this is what I agreed to. I guess I need to figure out my end goal.

Do I want to go to this lounge with him—a lounge he hasn't actually invited me to—and act like his wife? Yes. I'd love to.

But I also love being with Jack. I love raising him, and hearing his sweet baby giggles, and taking care of him. And talking about any of this with Dex—that whole open communication thing we talked about—feels like I'd just be complaining even if that's not the place it's coming from.

What if Dex and I are meant to make it the distance? Will he always just assume I'll be the one to shoulder the majority of the responsibilities with Jack since that's how it started for us?

That's not what I want out of a husband. I want to split responsibilities. I realize that's harder when he's in season, but I'd love more of hearing him tell Jack to let me sleep in through the baby monitor and less of the apologies every Wednesday morning before he heads out the door to another day of practice.

I finally get the nerve to bring it up on a Monday afternoon.

It's the week before the first regular game of the season, an away game for the Vegas Aces, and he has both Monday and Tuesday off this week with a little bit of homework. He's studying something on his iPad when I walk into the family room after I get Jack down for his nap.

"Can we talk?" I ask.

He doesn't respond right away, instead looking down at his tablet, but he glances up a moment later. "What's going on?"

"I've been struggling with some things, and in the interest of open communication, I wanted to talk to you about them."

His brows pinch together. "Is everything okay?"

I nod. "Yeah, it's just…I don't like seeing the pictures every Wednesday morning of you with these other women at your lounge when we're supposed to be married."

"Then don't look at them." He says it simply, but to me, it's anything but simple. He lifts a shoulder.

"You look like you want to be with them."

"I don't," he says, and I want to believe him. "It's just part of running this thing for my dad. They're big spenders, and I'm trying to get them to spend. That's all. You know who I'm coming home to."

"Yeah, but *they* don't," I point out.

"So?"

"So if the whole point of this fake marriage was so I have my big revenge when I head to the reunion in a couple weeks, what good is it when my husband is constantly being photographed with other women?" I ask.

He presses his lips together. "So what do you want?"

"I want to come with you to the lounge. Let it be me you're photographed with."

I spot something that flashes in his eyes, but it comes and goes so quickly that I can't quite put my finger on what it was.

"What about Jack?" he asks.

"You always manage to find someone to watch him when we need it. What if it was a charity event instead of the lounge? Wouldn't you find a way then?"

"Yeah," he mutters.

"There's more I want to say. I know I'm just the nanny, but sometimes the line between stepmother and nanny gets blurred, and I'm worried if we make it out of this contract that you'll always expect me to pick up the slack."

His brows crash together, and this time it's in anger. "*Just* the nanny? Are you fucking kidding me?"

I shrug.

"First of all, how can you think that after everything we've shared? And second, what do you mean *if* we make it out? And third, what the fuck do you mean by slack?" He's yelling, and I guess I pressed a button I hadn't meant to press.

It's his insecurities mingling with mine.

"I'm just trying to communicate what I'm feeling," I say softly.

He blows out a frustrated breath. "I'm sorry. I know you are. And I'm feeling pulled in ten different directions. I don't mean to take it out on you. I just thought our arrangement was working."

"It was—back when it was an arrangement. But we've crossed lines, and I just want to be clear where my place is in all of that," I say.

He presses his lips together again and nods. "Give me some time to think about it, okay?"

I nod because what choice do I really have? But the truth is that I don't really want to give him time to think about it. Now I'm worried he'll overthink it, and I'll end up in a worse place than where we started.

CHAPTER 39

Dex Bradley

The Lounge

I t's the worst possible timing for her to bring up coming with me to the lounge.

The *illegal* underground lounge is opening for the first time this weekend. My father expects me to be the liaison who invites the whales down there on Tuesday when I'm there. I can't have Ainsley tailing me while I'm doing that.

She's the only woman I want. It probably looks to the general public as if I'm slipping back into old habits, but I'm not. The only woman who means a single damn thing to me is at home raising my kid.

She's right.

Most of the time, I'm treating her like a nanny, but she's my wife.

What a strange situation we find ourselves in. How do I differentiate between the two when I'm paying her to do a job? How do I make sure I'm putting in equal time when I simply can't do that because I'm not home?

The lines are blurring, and I'm starting to fear she's retreating.

I'm worried she'll get sick of this and leave me and Jack, and then what the fuck will I do?

On the other hand, what if she stays because of Jack but *not* because of me? Wouldn't that be even worse?

There has to be a solution out there, something I'm not thinking of.

Because I don't even have a goddamn second to think for myself anymore. If I'm not at practice, I'm at the lounge. I get a few hours here and there with Ainsley, but mostly she's left alone with my kid.

This isn't the life she was expecting when she came to Vegas, but she got tossed headfirst into it anyway.

She takes the baby out for a walk in the jogger, and I use the opportunity to call my father.

"Are you ready for tomorrow night?" That's how he answers the call.

I blow out a breath. "I have a problem. I can't be involved in the underground shit tomorrow night."

"It's your first night. Figure out a solution."

"It's not that simple," I say.

"What's going on?"

"My wife. She wants to know why I haven't invited her to the lounge. If you weren't so goddamn loud about it, trying to attract big clients, I might've gotten away with brushing her off."

"Find a way," he hisses.

"I can't. It's my marriage on the line. She wants to see the lounge, and I have to bring her there tomorrow night or she'll suspect something's up."

"Then bring her, sit her at a table, and let her learn how to play while you invite the clients with the most money downstairs."

"Fine." I end the call without a goodbye.

When she returns from her walk, I'm in the kitchen preparing lunch for all three of us. Or, rather, I'm taking the soup and salad spread I had delivered out of the packaging and warming a bottle.

"What's all this?" she asks.

"Lunch. Welcome back from your walk."

She narrows her eyes at me, and then she gets Jack out of his carrier. "I'd invite you to come with next time, but then I might not get lunch, so forget it."

I chuckle, and I nod toward the table. She buckles Jack into his highchair while I arrange the food on the table, and I help Jack with his bottle. At eight months, he's getting decently good at holding it for himself now when we sit him in his chair, and I also spread some puffs on his tray since he's getting good at attempting to eat them. Or knock them on the floor, depending on his mood. Mostly he knocks them on the floor.

"I'd like to invite you to come with me to the lounge tomorrow night," I say.

She raises both brows in what appears to be complete shock. "Are you sure?"

No. "Yes."

"What about Jack?"

"I thought about Madison, but she's back in school now, and it'll be a late night. One of my buddies on the team has a baby, and he said Jack could crash there for a night."

One of the Aces' tight ends has a son who just turned one in June, and he can't stop raving about how great his wife is with the baby. I texted him to ask, and he said yes.

"What buddy?" she asks.

"Asher."

"Oh, yes. I love Desi, and Jack and Jake will be cute together," she says.

"Yeah. I was thinking he could spend the day there so you could have a day off, and then maybe we can grab him together and go out to dinner on Wednesday night after practice?"

"That sounds great."

I nod. "I also thought about what you said about the stepmom versus nanny blur, and I realize I'm paying you to nanny, but I want you in whatever role you feel most comfortable in." I hold up a hand. "This is your place now, too. I think we both want that to be true for more than the terms of our contract."

She nods, and she tilts her head as her eyes seem to get a little misty.

"I hired you as a nanny knowing I wouldn't be around as much when I'm in season, and I'm sorry if I didn't make that clear," I say. "We should set clearer boundaries, and if we need to schedule time off each day for you to do the things you want, then let's do it."

"I'd like that. And I knew you'd be busier. I just miss having you around, that's all."

"I miss being around, too. For both of you." I turn to look at Jack, who's in the process of emptying his tray by sweeping his hands back and forth across it so the puffs go flying, and he giggles his little baby giggle as he does it.

He lightens up the mood in here, but I'm glad we had this talk even though I'm nervous about what tomorrow night will bring.

* * *

We drop off Jack together on the way to the lounge, and the women disappear into the kitchen with the boys while Asher glances at me. "Where you off to tonight?"

"My dad's running a VIP lounge, and he wants me to make an appearance. You interested?"

He shakes his head. "Nah, thanks. I gave up gambling a long time ago."

I recall him being suspended for a season for betting on the outcome of games, but I'm the last person who would judge anyone for the decisions they make, considering I've had enough of my own interesting choices over the years.

When we get to the lounge, Ainsley takes in every inch of opulence the place offers, and cameras snap in our faces as we enter.

"Wow," she breathes beside me. She's wearing a glittery blue gown, and she looks gorgeous. I'm certain I don't deserve her.

I'm surprised my father has people taking photos given the fact that we're escorting some of the wealthier players downstairs this evening, but the underground portion has been open since Friday, and so far, it's Vegas's newest best-kept VIP secret.

I just need to keep Ainsley in the dark, too, and I'll be golden.

I hate keeping things from her, but I have to. It's for her own good.

I wish I didn't know about it, either.

But I do, and I plan to make a shit ton of money out of the deal.

"This is gorgeous, Dex. So luxurious. Not at all what it looks like in the photos." The place isn't a typical dark casino. This lounge is the essence of luxury, and it's all white and gold, from the leather chairs to the white marble floors with gold veins.

We take a few photos, and I introduce her to some of the workers, including the men my father has chosen to run this place. I'm not running it—I'm simply a celebrity host who stops in on occasion to drum up business.

These guys are the real brains behind the operation, I guess.

We get some drinks and mingle a bit as I introduce Ainsley as my wife, and I know it's getting to the time where I need to start moving some of the guests downstairs.

"Why don't you play some Texas Hold'em while I entertain a few of my dad's clients?" I suggest.

She looks a little annoyed that I'm ditching her, but I don't really have much choice here. Riding a line for my own safety is one thing. Involving her is another thing entirely.

I recall my father telling me that the feds were on his tail when he first presented this idea to me months ago. I can't help but wonder who, aside from the FBI, might be tailing him. Who has he pissed off, and am I safe from them or not now that he's got me involved?

I won't do the same thing to Ainsley and Jack that my father did to me.

CHAPTER 40
Ainsley Bradley

Two Baseball Players

I'm fuming as I sit at the table, unsure as to whether I'm supposed to bet or fold—especially because I'm not playing with my own money.

I'm still learning this game, and Dex just threw money at me before he ditched me. I have no clue where he went, and frankly, I'm not sure why he invited me along if his plan was to just leave me at a table.

I could ask the guy beside me what to do, but I'm playing against him, so that idea is out.

I end up folding only to discover that I would've won.

I leave the table and head toward the cashier's cage to exchange the chips for money, and then I wander around looking for Dex. The place isn't huge—not like one of the grand casinos on the Strip, anyway. It's elegant and luxurious, clearly meant for people with much more money than I have.

What a waste. These people could be giving their money to charity. Hell, Dex's dad could've done that with the money he spent on the marble floors or the white leather chairs.

Instead, he pumped it into this place, and now Dex is here all the time supporting the waste. Getting these rich people to waste even more with the hopes that they'll double it or triple it or walk home with more money than they ever could've dreamed only to waste it on something else equally as stupid tomorrow.

Maybe I just need a drink. I need to loosen up a little.

It's just hard when I think about how I grew up. Two teachers' salaries with barely enough to scrape by. Having to work for everything I ever had.

I'm not saying these people don't work hard, and I'm also not saying that I've never wasted my money frivolously. But not like this. The amount of excess here is appalling, and it's making me uncomfortable.

I don't belong here. And if Dex does, maybe I don't belong with Dex, either.

It's a strange realization to have in the middle of his father's VIP lounge, but there it is. We come from two different worlds, and maybe it would just be easier if I went back to being *just* the nanny. He might've swept me off my feet, rescued me from my hardships, and made over my entire life in that rags-to-riches kind of way, but that doesn't mean my story has the same ending as Cinderella's despite the sparkly blue dress I'm wearing.

Two hours pass before I find him again. He walks through a door that seems to lead to some sort of back room.

"What's back there?" I ask.

"Staff break room." He says it in a strange way as his eyes dart to the side.

I almost don't believe him, but I don't call him out. I can't see any reason he'd have to lie to me.

"Can we go home?" I ask.

He nods. "Let me just say some goodbyes." He doesn't invite me to come with him, so I claim one of the white leather chairs as he walks away from me.

"You're Bradley's wife?" a male voice says beside me a moment later.

I glance up and find myself face-to-face with Danny Brewer, the first baseman for the Vegas Heat. He's married to Alexis Bodega, and I'm a huge fan of her music.

"I am," I say softly.

He sits in the chair next to me. "I play ball with his brother."

"Archer?" I ask.

He nods.

"I haven't seen him in years. I'm actually best friends with Ivy, Dex's youngest sister." I realize maybe I'm saying too much. I don't know Danny Brewer from anybody else, and it would likely be in my best interest to keep my mouth shut.

Another man walks up beside Danny, and he slaps him on the back. It's clear they're good friends, maybe even teammates, but I don't recognize him. The only reason I know Danny is because of Alexis Bodega.

"Do you know AJ Winters?" Danny asks me, and he slaps AJ on the back as he introduces us.

I shake my head. "Ainsley Ri—, uh…Bradley."

AJ reaches out a hand to shake mine. "Nice to meet you." His eyes flick down my dress, and he offers me a grin. He's definitely handsome, and it feels almost like some sort of invitation, but I only have eyes for one man.

And speak of the devil…

"The fuck's going on here?" a voice booms behind AJ.

I pull my hand from AJ's, and both men turn around to see my husband as he's about to rage on someone.

"We were just introducing ourselves to your wife," Danny says smoothly.

"You're goddamn right she's my wife," he says, and he moves between them to slip his arm around my shoulders.

He hasn't paid me one ounce of attention tonight until some handsome men started chatting me up. Duly noted. Apparently any man getting too close to me is grounds for him to lose his mind.

I roll my eyes. "He's a total caveman."

"Well, you managed to get a ring on his finger, so you must have some pretty persuasive skills yourself," AJ teases.

Dex glares at him, I laugh a little uncomfortably, and Danny steps in to save another awkward moment.

"We were just about to head over to some Hold'em. See you later."

The two baseball players walk away, and Dex glances over at me. "What did they say to you?"

"Nothing. They were just introducing themselves. They were perfectly pleasant, and why do you care, anyway? You couldn't be bothered with me even though you invited me here tonight."

"Because you didn't give me any other choice," he hisses.

I fold my arms over my chest. "What are you talking about?"

He grabs my elbow and steers me toward the exit. "Let's not talk about this here."

We get into the car waiting out front for us, and we're both quietly seething as we stare out our own windows while the car navigates back toward Dex's building.

Tonight didn't go well. At all.

I'm afraid of what that might mean for the two of us going forward.

CHAPTER 41

Ainsley Bradley

Two New Friends

Neither of us says a word the entire ride home, up the elevator, or in the hallway. I wait until he locks the door and turns around to face me before I unload.

"You didn't want to talk at the lounge, but we're home now." I fold my arms over my chest.

He rubs the side of his face as if this conversation is already taxing to him. "What do you want me to say, Ains?" He sounds tired.

"Why'd you bring me with you if you were only going to ditch me?" I demand.

"You asked me to bring you. I had work to do. I'm sorry, but part of my job is entertaining clients, and not every aspect of my life involves you."

"It doesn't have to," I practically yell. "But if you want to really give this a chance, we need to be honest with each other. And to be honest, I was pissed you left me at that table."

"Then you shouldn't have come," he yells back at me.

"I didn't know you'd just leave me to fend for myself and play a game I have no business playing!"

"What did you think was going to happen?" he demands.

The truth is…I don't know. Not that. "I guess between the opulence and wastefulness and then being left alone, I just felt out of place."

"Maybe you *were* out of place."

"Are you kidding me?" I yell.

"The whole point of it is to be a VIP experience. It's a place for the rich and famous to spend their money so I can line my pockets with it. Or so my father can, anyway." He spits the last part as if the words taste sour leaving his mouth, but I can't focus on that.

All I can seem to focus on is the fact that he just agreed that I was out of place.

I wanted him to deny it. To reject the very thought that I didn't belong there. We're partners now, and I should be by his side.

Instead, his words manage to spike my anger and leave a hole in my chest that makes me feel cheap and unworthy at the same time.

And that's no way to feel as someone's wife.

"Sorry I made you drag me along," I hiss.

"Ains, don't be like that," he says, his tone switching to a bit of begging now.

"I'll sleep in my old room tonight. We can talk tomorrow." I stomp off toward the guest room that was mine when I first moved in, and those are the last words we speak for the night.

Don't go to bed angry, right?

Well, I am.

I sleep like shit ahead of a rare day off, and I'm not really sure what to do with myself once I wake up. Dex is already at practice, and Jack is still with Desi and Jake. I take a long shower, make myself some breakfast, watch some trash television, and call Ivy to check in. I text each of my parents since they're teaching right now. It's not even eleven, and I'm actually sort of bored.

I wonder what sorts of things I could do out here in my spare time. Maybe volunteer at a school or something. I think about all the money being thrown around last night. I wonder what sorts of local charities might benefit from that money. Schools come to mind again. Funds to treat overworked teachers with care packages or gift cards or classroom supplies so they don't have to spend their own money on it.

I decide to take a quick drive to the Strip. For as long as I've been here in Vegas, I haven't really spent any time exploring. Maybe today's my day.

I park at the MGM Grand near the south end of the Strip, and I start walking. I stop in shops, wander through casinos, and quietly enjoy my alone time.

I stop in a cute little bakery for a late lunch, where I order a chicken salad sandwich. I study the cookies in the display, and some are little football cookies, while others have the Vegas Aces logo on them. I grab a dozen to bring home to Dex even though I'm still mad at him after last night. Maybe I'll throw them at him.

It's not terribly crowded in here since it's a little after two o'clock now, and a woman walks by and asks me if I'd like a free cookie for dessert.

I nod way too enthusiastically. "I'd love one."

She grabs one with some tongs and sets it on my tray. "Are you local?" She nods to the Vegas Aces box of cookies I bought.

I lift a shoulder. "Sort of. I recently moved here and actually just got married." I laugh a little at how ridiculous it sounds, but it's my truth.

"Congratulations! That's so exciting!"

"And my husband is actually a player on the Aces, so I had to get him these cook—"

"Oh. My. God! My husband used to play for the Aces, too!" She turns toward the counter. "Grayson!" she yells.

A minute later, Grayson Nash appears from the back room. He walks to the woman and leans down to press a kiss to her cheek, and I remember meeting him chatting with Dex at that first charity event we attended together.

"Yes, Cookie?"

Cookie, the woman who gave me the cookie—is that her real name?—grins up at Grayson. "She said she's married to a player!"

"Who?" he asks.

"Dex Bradley."

Grayson's jaw drops. "Dex Bradley got *married?*"

I hold up my hand with my giant rock on it. "To me."

"Congratulations!" the woman says again. "I'm Ava, by the way. This is my bakery, and this is probably too aggressive, but if you need a local friend who knows what it's like to be a football wife, you can hit me up anytime."

"I'd love a local friend," I say. "I actually started as Dex's nanny, and now we're married, and I feel like I'm home taking care of the baby all day. I love it, but it would be nice to have some adult conversations once in a while that didn't involve Bluey."

"Wait. Dex has a kid?" Grayson asks.

I nod. "An eight-month-old named Jack. Oh my God, I just realized—he's actually at your brother's house right now!"

"Lincoln?" Grayson asks.

I shake my head. "Asher. Desi's taking care of him today since Dex and I went out last night."

"What a small world!" he says.

"That will grow by one in about five months," Ava says, and she rubs her stomach. She's wearing an apron, so I can't see a baby bump, but she's got that glow about her.

"Oh wow! Congratulations!"

Ava and I exchange numbers, and it feels good. It feels like I'm finding my way. Like eventually I may even fit in here.

It changes my entire mood.

I'm still angry at Dex, but I'm also working my way toward being forgiving. As long as he apologizes.

When Dex gets home, I don't move from the couch. Instead, I wait for him to go first.

"I don't want to fight with you," he says.

"I don't, either."

"I'm sorry."

"Me too." It's good enough for now. "I got you something." I get up and grab the box of cookies, and I'm excited to tell him about my new friend.

He reaches for me and hauls me by the waist into him. "Thanks, Ains." He drops a kiss to my lips.

It's time to get Jack, and Dex drives, darting in and out of traffic as usual. I distract myself by talking about my day. "Speaking of the Nash family, I ran into Grayson today. His wife and I are basically best friends now."

"Is that where the cookies came from?" he asks.

I nod.

"Best bakery in town," he says.

We chat some more before we arrive at Asher's, and I get to catch up again with Desi. She's as sweet as Ava, and I let her know if she and Asher ever need a break for a night, Jake is welcome to stay with us.

That's *two* local friends in one day. I'm riding a high as we get back into the car.

I just wish the high could last a little bit longer.

Jack is strapped in the back as we make our way to some steakhouse Dex likes, and he's driving like a maniac.

"Can you slow down a little?" I ask.

He side-eyes me, and I shut my trap.

He glances in his rearview mirror, and he changes lanes again. And again. And again.

"Dex, what the hell are you doing?" I ask. "The baby is in the back."

He looks in his mirror again just as the car in front of us slams on the brakes.

He swerves into the next lane, and I look out my window to see a car coming straight for us. I hear the screeching tires and brace for the impact of metal crushing metal, but the other car must stop in time because it never happens.

"Oh my God, Dex! Will you slow down? You could've gotten all three of us killed!" I'm yelling at him. Now the baby is crying, and this isn't how I wanted this night to start.

"I thought I was being followed, okay?"

"Why would someone be following you?"

"Forget it, okay?" He swerves again, clearly learning nothing from what just happened.

"I want to get out of the car."

"Stop it," he says, rolling his eyes. Jack is still crying in the backseat.

"Slow the hell down! And who is following you?"

"The black car behind us. He's changed lanes every time I have."

"Why?" I demand again.

"Forget it. Just leave like everyone else does. You're better off without me," he mutters.

"Dex, what the hell is going on? Where is this coming from?"

"I'm helping my father run an underground casino, okay?" he yells at me.

My jaw slackens. Of all the things I thought he might say in that moment, that wasn't one of them. "What?"

"The FBI might be following me because of it," he says, his voice quieter now. "Or maybe someone's trying to get to my dad through me. Someone with a grudge, someone who lost it all because of him."

My gut reaction is absolute and total *fury*. He's the one who brought up open communication and then withheld what he was actually doing on Tuesday nights. Is he fucking kidding me with this? He's running an *illegal* underground casino, and someone with a grudge may be following him? Me? Us?

"You're putting the baby and me in danger by doing this," I say, my voice controlled and quiet. Almost eerily so. I don't feel controlled or quiet. I feel rage building inside of me.

"It's why I didn't tell you," he says. He reaches over and places a hand on my thigh, and I bat it away.

"Ains, come on," he begs.

I shake my head and fold my arms over my chest. "Take me home."

"We have reservations."

"So call and cancel. I don't want to go to dinner. I want to go home."

He blows out a breath, but he starts heading in the direction of home anyway.

I think about this situation for the rest of the ride home. I think about what to do. How to protect Jack. How to protect *myself*.

I don't see any other choice. There's too much wrong between us for this to ever work. We're from two different worlds. Two different decades. Two different timelines, and ours wasn't one that was ever meant to merge together.

So once we're back home, once flared tempers have calmed, and once Jack is in his highchair with some puffs, my eyes meet Dex's across the kitchen. "I can't do this with you. I can't get invested in you and your baby knowing you're not telling me the whole truth."

"What are you saying?" he demands.

"I'm saying I'll take care of the baby until you can find another nanny."

"We have a contract," he hisses.

I press my lips together. He's not giving me much choice, but he probably also doesn't have the time to find a new nanny now that his first game of the season is Sunday in New York. "Fine. Then I'll stay until the end of our term. But that's all it is now. A contract. This? Us? We're done." I slide the ring off my finger and set it on the counter.

He stares at it for a long beat, and then he spins on his heel, heads toward the door, and slams it shut behind him, the sound echoing and reverberating in my chest as my heart smashes into a million pieces.

Maybe I made two friends today.

But it appears I might've lost one, too.

CHAPTER 42
Ainsley Bradley

Coax

The thing about having a driver for your building that will take you anywhere you want is that he signed an NDA long ago.

"Take me to Coax," I say.

It started as a secret sex club owned by the manager of the Vegas Heat, Troy Bodine, and a few others. Over the years, it's become Vegas's worst-kept VIP secret.

I'm sure it'll be all over the news that I went to a sex club when I'm married. It won't be great for the wholesome image I'm supposed to be working on, but fuck it. I'm not going to the club to have sex.

I just need to get away for a little while, and it's a place where I know I can find my friends but also where I know my father has zero influence and zero people on his ass—and therefore, zero people on *my* ass. The place has a study with a bar and the most comfortable chairs I've ever sat in, and between that and the view by the pool outside, it's where I feel called when I need to relax away from the bright lights of the Strip.

Or away from the devastating words at my penthouse.

I needed to get the fuck out. Her taking the ring off was a step over the line for me. It felt too final. A nail in the coffin.

Sure, we've been arguing the last few days. But I thought it was a blip. I have a fiery temper. Nobody was ever in danger when I was driving. She's sensitive, I'm aggressive. Opposites attract and all that shit.

It was more than an attraction.

I fell in fucking love with her, and she just ended it.

She didn't care that I was keeping secrets *to protect her*. All she cared about is that I kept the damn secret.

It's not even *my* secret. It's my father's. But I'm sure as shit the one being punished for it.

The goddamn club is a full thirty-minute drive from my place, and it's too quiet. So quiet that the silence feels like it's screaming at me.

I could call Madden and admit he was right.

I don't feel like it. I don't feel like talking to anyone. I just want to sit in a corner with some whiskey and drink until I stop feeling the pain.

I should've known from the start that this would happen.

If anyone ever wondered why I've spent my life alone, this is it. I never wanted to get involved emotionally with a woman because I never wanted to endure this part of it. I like to keep things light. Simple. Fun. Have a good time, and move on to the next good time.

This? This is stupid. This pain in my chest is stupid. This feeling like I let someone else down wouldn't fucking be there if I hadn't let her in.

I never wanted to be like my dad—lying, keeping secrets, abandoning the very people who should come first in my life. But the more life I live, the more I'm starting to fear that I'm turning out exactly like him.

Even going to the club is a stupid idea. I have practice in the morning. We have two more days to prepare for our first matchup against the Giants. We leave Saturday morning for the game.

And I'm heading toward a sex club as I mourn the loss of my sham of a marriage that was pretty fucking real to me. She'll stay because I reminded her of the contract, but she doesn't want to be there. Is that really any better than her just going on her own terms? I'm not convinced it is.

The ride to Coax feels eternal, but we eventually arrive, and I sit in the backseat an extra moment before getting out.

"Would you like me to wait, sir?" the driver asks.

"Please." I want to leave when I want to leave. I don't want to wait a half hour for him to show up.

I head inside. I don't need to show my membership card. I'm waved right in, and I pass through a room set up like a nightclub to get to the lounge. I beeline for the bar, get my first glass of whiskey, and find a chair. I look around me once I'm settled in. The action doesn't happen in this room, but I can see the negotiations taking place.

There are a few guys from the team here. They shouldn't be here any more than I should be. We have practice in the morning.

I spot other familiar faces. People from television or movies. The Heat is out of town tonight, but usually a few players end up here, especially since the team manager sold his stake years ago to keep his name out of the local gossip columns.

I see women flirting with men. I see men drooling over big tits.

It's all so...

So...

So pointless.

I never felt that way before. I'd come here, get my rocks off, and head home. It was a good enough time. Usually fun. Always something I could take or leave.

But as I watch those negotiations taking place now, it feels like another lifetime ago.

I don't feel like I fit in here anymore.

Some dudes bring their significant others here, sure. It's their thing to be watched through the windows upstairs.

The thought of another man seeing Ainsley without any clothes on makes me want to punch my fist through a wall. I'd *never* bring her here.

It's probably why I ended up here right now, to be honest.

What now? What's next for me?

It's too soon to know. I'm not stupid enough to think I need an answer to that right now.

But it's hard to think past the pain I'm feeling right now. I can't stop seeing her sliding that ring off her finger and setting it on the counter.

Maybe it's why my instinct was to show up here. Replace that image with something else. Tits, perhaps. There's a room upstairs that's basically a high-end strip club. I could go there and watch the women.

I don't feel like it.

I take another sip of whiskey, and another, and another. I chug down the contents of the glass, and I return to the bar for another.

"Dex Bradley," a sultry voice says beside me. "You come here lookin' for me?" I glance over to see Tiffany. She's a dancer on the Strip who I've fucked around with a few times when I've come here.

"No," I answer.

She laughs. "Always did love your honesty. I heard you got married. Is your wifey here?"

I shake my head. The bartender passes my glass across the counter, and I sip it gratefully the second it's in my hand. "She's not."

"Shame. Would love to watch you with her." She wiggles her eyebrows.

"Not going to happen." My voice comes out a bit more aggressive than I mean for it to. Tiffany doesn't know I'm going through something, and it's really not fair to take it out on her.

I shouldn't be here.

But I can't go home, either.

And so I chug the rest of my whiskey, return to the car, and tell the driver my next destination.

CHAPTER 43

Ainsley Bradley

The Ring

I stare at the ring on the counter. I slid onto one of the stools there at the kitchen counter once he left, and I haven't stopped staring at it since.

I'm trying to piece together what just happened.

We're over. Really and truly. I didn't mean for it to come out the way it did. I don't want to end things with Dex. But I can't live like this, either.

When I pictured life with my husband, I never pictured him lying to me—for protection or otherwise. I always assumed I'd end up with someone who'd come to me with his problems so we could work them out together. I pictured a true partnership.

But that's not what we have, and it hasn't been since the start. It's why we never could've really made it out of the contract with a solid foundation for the rest of our lives. It's always been a power struggle since I was just the hired help.

We didn't expect to fall the way we did. We didn't expect this to be anything more than what we both signed up for. It all started with that one little kiss at the altar after we said "I do," and it snowballed from there. If I could go back in time and warn myself about what was going to happen, I would.

I'm a smart girl. I knew better than to get involved with someone like Dex Bradley. He's a bad boy. A player. He doesn't do relationships. We're not just from two different decades. We're from two completely different lifestyles. There's too much that sets us apart, gaps too wide to navigate our way across.

Not to mention he's my best friend's brother.

Speaking of which, I still haven't admitted any of this to Ivy. It's not like I can call up my best friend and cry over the fact that I just ended things with the only man I've ever truly loved. The only man who's ever loved me. My first in so many ways. My *only* in so many ways, too.

I get up and make myself a drink—vodka and Sprite, heavy on the Sprite, with three cherries. I slip back onto my stool to continue my staring contest with the ring.

The vodka isn't helping. I take three sips, eat the cherries, and push the glass away.

I don't have a solid solution for us. I can't seem to find a path forward out of this other than finding some way to start over completely. Tear up the contract. Figure out how to get him out of this illegal casino thing with his father. Start a life of our own.

But he won't do that.

He's loyal, and I guess I can understand that. It's hard for him being in the public eye and knowing who to trust. But when it's your own father using you, that makes it a little harder to see the truth.

Like when my parents used me as their babysitter. I was a teenager, and I didn't really want to do it, but I did it out of obligation.

This is different, and I realize that. For one thing, what he's doing is illegal.

Still, I'm sure Dex had his reasons for doing it.

But it doesn't really matter.

We were never destined to find our happily ever after together. I may have the rags-to-riches Cinderella story with my new life in a Vegas penthouse, but Dex is no prince, and the happily ever after that I thought was within my reach just slipped away.

So now what? I continue to nanny for Jack, continue to love that baby more and more every day, and continue to live with Dex and pretend I'm not head over heels for him until the term of our contract runs out?

I can't live in this penthouse with the man I'm in love with for two more years and not get to play the part of his wife, not get to lie in bed beside him each night, not get to jump off the couch and greet him at the door with a kiss every time he walks through it.

How do I go back now that I've experienced a taste of that life?

I want to convince myself this is temporary, that we'll find our way back.

But taking that ring off somehow felt pretty damn permanent. It was the symbolic end of what we shared, even if the contract is still in place for a while longer.

I have this sudden, intense feeling of homesickness. It's just a side effect of what went down tonight, I'm sure. But I want to go home. I want to see my brothers and sisters. I need to get away from this penthouse and Dex, and maybe I even need a break from Jack, too, since he represents the whole reason I'm here to begin with.

That poor baby.

It's not his fault his parents can't get their shit together.

And ultimately, that's what's going to keep me here. Jack Dexter Bradley.

I start to cry as I feel suddenly very stuck. I stare at that damn ring as despair fills me.

Maybe I'm homesick and want to go back to Chicago for a while, and maybe I will. But I can't find it in me to abandon Jack when he's already been abandoned by the only mother he ever knew. I can't just walk out of his life and hope Dex finds a suitable nanny to replace me when I've somehow moved into the role of his stepmother over the last couple of months.

And as I continue to stare at the ring, lost in thought about Jack and Dex and our situation, I can't help but start to wonder…

Where the hell did Dex go when he stormed out that door, and when will he be home?

CHAPTER 44

DEX BRADLEY

Lime Green Lambo

My dad's lounge isn't the only game in town, and I find myself at another VIP lounge that I frequented before my own opened up.

It's where my buddies typically hang out, though none of my teammates are here tonight. They're all probably in bed like good little boys while I'm out chasing thrills I can't seem to find.

I play some Hold'em, lose a bit of cash, and grab some more whiskey. I'm almost ready to call it a night, but I'm not sure where to go. I don't want to go home. It's too early. She might still be awake, and I don't want to face her. I *can't* face her.

Not when she ended it. Not when that goddamn ring that belongs on her finger will still be sitting on the counter.

I just need a night.

So I get some more whiskey.

I'm half-drunk, maybe more, on a barstool when Cole Dawson, one of my incredibly successful buddies who owns a tech company, sidles up beside me and claims the stool beside mine.

"Heard you've got your own place now. What are you doing here?" he asks.

"Drumming up business," I deadpan. I swallow what's left in my glass.

He laughs. "You wanna race tonight?"

I turn and narrow my eyes at him. "You want to lose again?"

He winces as he recalls the last time we drag raced down the Vegas Strip. I kicked his ass.

"If I win, you come to my new lounge and spend some time there," I say, and we both know that I mean money, not actual time.

"And if I win?" he counters.

"You do it anyway, but I give you an off-the-books personal line of credit."

He laughs and sticks out his hand. "Deal."

We shake.

"I don't have a car here," I say as I remember I was driven here.

"We can get you one."

"Get two, and I get to pick," I demand since I know Cole, and I suspect he'd give me the slower car if he knew the difference.

He laughs. "Fine. Deal." He sends a text, and we make our way outside to figure out the logistics of how this is going to go down.

I shouldn't get behind the wheel. I know that. But Cole will blow a shitload of money at my lounge if I can get him there, and I know I can beat his ass into the ground with a race.

I feel that old surge of adrenaline starting to kick in.

It's a Wednesday night, so the Strip isn't overly crowded, but it's still a long wait for Cole's guys to bring the cars around for us.

They finally do, and we're on a side street. It took goddamn long enough that I'm pretty sure I'm sober now.

I choose the lime green Lamborghini, while Cole is left with the cherry red McLaren. I walk around to the driver's side, and I'm halfway to seated in the luxurious driver's seat when I feel a hand grip onto the collar of my shirt and pull me out of the car.

I turn with rage on the offender, ready to go the fuck off that someone thinks they can manhandle me that way, when I find myself face-to-face with Coach Lincoln Nash.

And he looks well and truly livid.

I am so fucked.

"What the fuck do you think you're doing?" he demands.

"Racing," I say calmly.

"Not the fuck tonight," he growls, and he yanks me away from the car like I'm some goddamn child. But what can I do? This is my head coach. If I fight back, I'll be suspended or worse.

I might be anyway.

I have no choice but to let him embarrass me in front of Cole, and for the first time, a rational thought enters my brain.

And it's in the voice of fucking Ainsley.

It's a good thing Lincoln showed up when he did.

Once Lincoln drags me into the front seat of his car, he starts driving before he starts yelling.

"The fuck you think you were doing out there, Bradley?" he asks. He doesn't wait for my reply as he continues laying into me. "You're acting like a child. Did you even consider what could happen if you got behind that wheel?"

No, I didn't. I can't say that, obviously. I'm already in pretty big trouble here, though he's right. It could've been worse. *Much* worse.

"Minimum three games for a DUI from the league, not to mention the legal ramifications for reckless endangerment paired with a DUI. Stupid, Dex. Just plain fucking stupid."

"You're right. I shouldn't have—"

"You're goddamn right you shouldn't have," he interrupts. "You've got a game to play this weekend in New York, and we need you. I thought you were settling down. Thought you were pulling your shit together. You have a kid now, and you're still acting like this? I'm disappointed, Dex. I thought you were better than this."

He thought wrong.

I haven't grown. I haven't changed. I've pawned my kid off on Ainsley, and the second things got tough, I reverted back to exactly who I was. Who I am. Who I'll always be.

Silence spans across the car before I finally ask, "Where are you taking me?"

"Back to my place," he mutters. "You can *quietly* sleep it off there and be at practice in the morning. On fucking time, or you'll get stadium stairs. And if you wake my kids after I let you into my home, stadium stairs. You know what? Fuck it. You're getting stadium stairs tomorrow either way, but you'll get an extra set if you wake up my kids."

Stadium stairs are the literal worst punishment. They're exactly what they sound like they are. I have to run up the stairs of one section and down the stairs of another, making my way around the entire lower bowl of our stadium.

Football stadiums are huge. It's a lot of fucking stairs. And it's not at our practice facility, which means I have to go do it on my own time.

And I'm going to be doing it hungover. I'm definitely not as sober as I thought I was, which is why I pass out as soon as Lincoln shows me his guest room.

CHAPTER 45

DEX BRADLEY

Picture-Perfect Family

Light peeks through a crack in the blinds and angles across my eyes in the morning, and I squint as I try to open them.

I feel like I got hit by a fucking truck. Pain slices through my head when I try to lift it.

Fuck.

I'm not in my twenties anymore.

My twenties.

Ainsley is. She's in her *early* twenties.

Why is she always right there at the center of my thoughts? Front and center.

I force myself up, and it takes me a second to remember where I am.

Oh, right.

Lincoln's house.

Because he stopped me from doing something stupid last night.

He saved me a hell of a lot of trouble—a headache twenty times the size of the one I'm dealing with now.

I take a shower in the bathroom connected to my guest room, and I head downstairs, where I find Lincoln and his family eating breakfast.

They're this picture-perfect family, one you see on TV or in the movies. The wife is dressed and ready for her workday in her heels as she brings glasses of orange juice to the table for her three kids, including an eleven-year-old boy, a three-year-old girl, and a baby boy close to Jack's age. The husband is laughing with the eleven-year-old, and when the wife leans across the table to place a glass down, I catch the husband checking out her ass. She bends down to kiss his lips, and a surge of jealousy rises through me.

We were just starting out, but I had that. For a mere moment in time, I had that.

And now it's gone.

"Come join us," Lincoln says to me, and I sit in an empty chair.

"Pancakes or cereal?" Jolene asks.

Both sound like they'll come right up. "No, thank you."

"Kids, this is Dex. He's a player on my team. Dex, this is Jonah, Josephine, and Joey." He points out each kid.

"Lots of Jo-names," I remark.

"Jolene's tradition. I wanted Brady, but she gave me a hard no."

She rolls her eyes. "Who are you kidding? You wanted to name Joey *Gronk*. Can you imagine? A sweet little boy named *Gronk*?"

"Could bode well for his future," I say, and I gratefully chug the glass of orange juice Jolene hands me that I didn't ask for.

Jolene walks the older boy to the bus stop, and then she grabs the younger two to take them to their preschool. When it's just Lincoln and me after he says his goodbyes, he asks, "You okay this morning?"

I nod. "Thanks for what you did for me last night. I was about to make a really stupid decision. How'd you know?"

"Your driver told your doorman, and he called me."

Milton. Of course. He's always looking out for me, and that's why I've always thought of him as a father figure. Meanwhile, my *real* father is the entire reason my relationship just ended. Well, sort of. I guess my secrets regarding my father had a little something to do with it, too, and I'll shoulder that part of the blame.

"I can see you're hurting this morning, so I won't make you do stadium stairs today. But I do want to talk to you about what's going on. Can you explain to me why you thought getting drunk and then getting behind a wheel was a good idea last night?"

"I wasn't thinking clearly." I clear my throat. "I felt like I was okay to drive."

"You weren't." His tone is pointed.

"You're right. And I like to think if I'd have gotten behind the wheel, I would've been smart enough not to hit the gas." I like to *think* that. I have no idea if it's true or not. I haven't always been known to make the smartest decisions, but drag racing down the Strip is probably a stupid decision stone-cold sober, too.

He sighs. "Well, I'm glad I was there to stop you, and the worst thing you're dealing with today is a headache. Get your ass to practice, and get your life together, man. Okay? You have a kid in the equation, so it's time to grow the fuck up."

"I know. And my wife…she ended things with me last night. That's why I was out doing stupid shit last night." If there's anyone I can be honest with about this, it's Coach.

"Jesus, Dex. I'm sorry. I didn't know. But that doesn't change anything I said. The things you were about to do last night are *never* okay under any circumstances, regardless of how much you're hurting. I get having a few drinks to numb the pain. Trust me. But to go out and put other lives in danger? That's never okay."

"I know. You're right."

"So what are you going to do about it?"

I draw in a deep breath as I contemplate that. I'm not really sure I have an answer, but I'm alone now, and I need to turn it around. I need to be the role model I never had in a father. I need to pull it together for my son. I glance at Lincoln, and I tell him that. "I'm going to step up for my son."

He slaps my shoulder. "That's what I wanted to hear."

"I'm going to get my shit together."

He nods. "If you need a place to stay while you figure things out…" He trails off, but the invitation is clear.

"I appreciate the offer," I say with a nod. I can't stay at the penthouse, but I also can't stay here with my coach. He's an authority figure, and I don't want to be under his constant supervision.

There are other options, though.

Namely, Coach's brother.

Once I get to the practice facility, I find Asher by his locker as he laces up his shoes.

"Can I talk to you?" I ask.

He finishes his task, and then he looks up at me. "What's going on?"

"Can Jack and I stay with you for a few days?"

His brows dip. "What happened?"

"Ainsley and I are fighting. I just want to give her some space. Maybe a few days off while we figure this out."

"Let me check with Des, but I don't see why that would be a problem. She's in her momming era and would probably love having an extra boy around who can make faces at Jake."

"I realize it's a lot to ask her to take on watching Jack, so don't feel obliga—"

He holds up a hand to interrupt me. "She'll love it. I'll text her now."

"Thanks, man," I say. "You're a good friend."

"Don't you forget it." His eyes are on his phone as he texts his wife, and it feels like I'm finally taking control of this situation…even if it means I'm pulling further away from Ainsley first.

CHAPTER 46

Ainsley Bradley

Playdate

Desi Nash: *Hey, you around to come over here for a playdate today?*

Dex never came home last night.

I have no idea where he was all night. No idea if he was with another woman, or if he was out making stupid decisions, or any one of a million other horrible things that have run through my mind today, but there aren't any headlines with his name in them this morning, so at least he was discreet with whatever he did.

I don't have any other plans, and I need to get out of this penthouse before I go crazy…even though my senses are tingling at the timing of Desi's invitation.

Me: *Yes, and we'd love to.*

Desi: *Great! Jake is usually up from his morning nap by 11 and goes back down by 3. Does that window work for you?*

Me: *Sure! Jack gets up around 11:30, so we'll come by around noon. I can bring lunch!*

Desi: *You don't have to do that! I have an entire salad bar in my fridge from meal prepping. We can just dig into that.*

Me: *Sounds perfect. See you at noon!*

I project an enthusiasm with my exclamation points that I don't really feel in my heart.

I'm excited for a playdate, sure. But it's for *his* kid with the wife of one of *his* friends.

My entire life in this town is so entwined with who he is that it's barely been twelve hours since I took off that ring, and I'm already struggling to figure out where the hell I might land in all of this.

How do I even stay here in this town where so much of who I am is wrapped up in him? And furthermore, how do I film the reunion show in three weeks when the whole point of Dex even bringing up a fake marriage was so I'd have something to throw in Jordan's face?

I guess we need to have a conversation about what this means going forward. We're supposed to attend a charity event in a couple weeks, for example. Are we still going to that?

It shouldn't be this hard. I shouldn't be this sad.

None of this feels right, to be honest. We haven't been together long enough for me to feel this broken. And yet, somehow…I do.

Jack is up, so I feed him his breakfast, and we take a nice walk to the park. We walk back home, and I assume I won't hear from Dex until after practice at the earliest. And then I'll hit him with all my questions, starting with the most important one: Are we still faking this marriage in public?

After Jack's nap, I feed him lunch before I pack him up in the car and we head to Desi's.

I ring the bell, and her brows pinch together when she spots me standing on the other side of the door.

"Are you okay?" she asks.

"Is it that obvious?"

She chuckles. "Well, Asher told me you and Dex are having problems, but he didn't seem to know anything else."

I'm not sure how much to say. I don't know who's my friend or who's his or who I can trust in this town. But I need someone to talk to, and she invited me here so the boys could play together, and I guess this is my best option for someone to talk to.

"Can I trust you?" I ask.

Her eyes whip to mine, and she looks nearly insulted by my question. If she is, she doesn't mention it. "Of course. Anything you say to me stays with me."

"I should probably make you sign the same NDA Dex made our families sign, but whatever. Our marriage started out as an arrangement, but it turned into something else. Something more. Something real. And then last night, I was forced to end things with him, but I'm in this for the duration of our contract, and I'm Jack's nanny, and I have to live with Dex when I love him so much but can't be with him, and I just want to go home." I realize how very much I'm babbling by the end, but I can't seem to stop until the entire story is out.

"Oh, gosh, Ains," she says, and she moves toward me to give me a hug. The squeeze feels comforting, and I draw in a shaky breath as I do my best to ward off the tears.

"I'm so sorry," she says. And then, instead of asking what she can do to help, she jumps into action. "Listen, Dex asked Asher if he could stay with us the next few days. Why don't you leave Jack here, too, and go home for a while? I'll watch him, and maybe time apart and away from this town will help you figure out what your next move should be."

"I couldn't ask you to do that," I murmur.

She reaches over and squeezes my forearm. "I know. It's why I offered."

"You're a good friend." I pat her hand on my arm.

"And you're going through a hard time. If you miss home and feel the need to be there, I'm simply opening up the option to make that happen."

"I'll think about it," I say softly. It's so easy for all of these people to just jet off to another town to get away from things for a while. My entire life, I've never had the money to do that sort of thing, and it feels strange that I do now. I'm not quite used to it yet, and I'm still living frugally even though my bank account is growing every two weeks thanks to Dex's generous paychecks.

I can dip into that and go see my family for a few days. But I'm not as sure how to get home to Chicago and avoid seeing Ivy. I'm not ready to admit that things got pretty damn real between her brother and me…especially not now that it's all over. She's my best friend, though. She's who I would talk to about *any* guy trouble, and that doesn't preclude her big, dumb brother.

The boys play, and we chat. She slips something about how she's already starting to show, and I find out she's due in February with her second child.

I hate that I love her as much as I do since he'll win this couple in our split. He works with her husband. Of course they'll side with him. It makes sense that their allegiance will lie with him.

The boys go down for a nap at the same time, around three o'clock, and we keep talking right through naptime.

It feels good to have someone to chat with even if there is likely no future to this friendship. But blabbing my secrets would hurt Dex, her husband's teammate, so I feel like there's a bit of inherent trust there.

The boys both wake, and we're doing some tummy time when Desi gasps.

"Jakey Jakey!" she sings. "Daddy's home!"

My brows dip. "He is?"

She giggles. "I can hear the garage when it opens." And thirty seconds later, the door opens.

My heart starts to beat in double time as I realize Dex is probably with Asher. I didn't mean to stay this late knowing there was a chance I'd run into him, but here I am.

"Hey, there's my family!" Asher says when he walks into the room.

"Da da da da," Jake babbles, and he holds his arms up in the cutest way to indicate his dad should pick him up.

Desi gets up off the floor to greet Asher with a kiss, and I spot Dex behind him but avert my eyes to Jack so I don't have to make eye contact with him.

God, this is complicated.

Dex gets a little too close as he moves in to greet his son. He picks him up and hugs him, and then he asks, "Ains, can we talk?"

"You can go upstairs and leave Jack down here if you want some privacy," Desi says.

He sets Jack back on the play mat where he was having his tummy time, and he holds out a hand to me to help me up.

I don't take it. I can get up myself, and it's like taking a symbolic stand that I can manage on my own, thank you very much.

"First door on the right upstairs," Asher says to Dex, who nods.

I follow him up the stairs, and we turn into the room Asher just mentioned.

"Are you okay?" he asks softly once the door is closed behind us.

"I have some questions, starting with where the hell you were last night." I fold my arms over my chest and brace myself for some snide answer about how it's none of my business.

"That's fair. I went to a club, drank myself stupid, went to a VIP lounge that's not my father's, got into some trouble, got rescued from getting into more trouble, and woke up in my coach's guest room this morning," he says.

At least there weren't any other women, I guess.

"What else do you want to know?" he asks.

I lift a shoulder. "I don't know. How are we managing this mess? Are we still attending events together? Still pretending to be married? What do I say on the reunion show?"

He closes his eyes and lets out a soft breath, and when he opens his eyes, they're dark with sincerity. "I realized how stupid I was, and I want to turn things around, Ains. I don't want to lose you. It was a fight, that's all. It's not the end."

"Then how come it is?" I whisper.

"What can I do to get you back?"

"Nothing. It's over," I say.

"There has to be something." He tugs on the ends of his hair, and I'm glad he's putting up a fight for this. It feels like he cares.

But that doesn't change what split us apart in the first place.

"I've thought it through, and I can't be with you if you're putting us in danger. So unless you give up the lounge, which I know you can't…well, then it's over."

He closes his eyes and shakes his head. "You know I can't."

I press my lips together and nod. I knew that would be his answer, and honestly, there's something to be said for his loyalty. I just wish his loyalty wasn't entirely to the wrong entity. "Desi said she'd watch Jack for a few days. I'm going to head home and see my family while we sort through this. I'll be back on Monday," I say.

He blows out a breath. "At the reunion, you say you're married to me. That was always the plan. It's why we did it in the first place. It doesn't have to change now just because our circumstances have."

"Okay. Then I guess I'll see you Monday."

"Yeah," he says quietly, and I walk out of the bedroom without a goodbye.

CHAPTER 47

DEX BRADLEY

A Shitty Practice

She really left. She really went home to Chicago.

When she said it, I guess I didn't think she was serious. But she's on a plane right now, at least according to Desi, who's been in touch with her.

She didn't text me to tell me she got a flight, but I guess it's no longer my information to have given our situation.

I would've taken her to the airport. I would've given her a little extra time with Jack—which I know she would have wanted. I see the way she looks at him like he's hers, and in many big ways, he is. She stepped into the role of his mother when he no longer had one, and I treated her like the hired help.

I've been such a dick.

But if I could do it all over again, I'm not sure I'd really do anything differently. I wouldn't know *how* to do anything differently. I'm fumbling my way through all of this.

Friday practices are usually lighter ahead of game weekends, but I'm not going any lighter as we run game scenarios on the practice field before lunch.

My job is to rush the quarterback, and Asher's job as the tight end is to stop me in the play we're running.

Only, he doesn't. I plow him down, and when I help him up, he glares at me.

"What the fuck was that?" he demands.

I hold up both hands. "I'm just doing my job."

"We're going light, man. Chill the fuck out."

His words set a fire under me. I realize he's my friend off the field, but in this moment, he's the enemy. Friday practices might be lighter, but if we're running game scenarios, he's my opponent. My single job is to get to the quarterback and take him down.

The quarterbacks rotate during practice, and the team's second backup quarterback, Brandon Fletcher, is in for this play. Asher stops me from getting to him again, and he shakes his head like he can't believe what I'm doing.

I'm just practicing.

On the next play, Maverick Jennings rotates in. He's brand new to the Aces, acquired in a trade from Dallas during the draft, and he'll be our starter this year. Our other starter, Miles Hudson, has been having issues with the ACL he tore a couple years ago, so Maverick will be stepping up to the plate.

Mav has been around a few years and has killer instincts, and I'm frankly shocked that Dallas let him go in the deal. He's an incredible quarterback and competitor, and I'd rather play with him than against him. But he does things his way. He doesn't listen to anybody, and he's polarizing. He makes as many headlines off the field as he does on it, but Coach Nash is confident he can turn this guy around. Nobody is quite sure *how* he's planning to do that, but if anyone can do it, it's Lincoln Nash.

This time when we run the play, I barrel over Asher, and I try to stop myself, but my momentum is too great.

I plow right into Maverick, who lets out a grunt as I take him down.

I don't *mean* to take him down. He's fully padded under his red jersey that signifies not to hit the player, but my instinct to take down the quarterback took over.

"Fuck," Maverick hisses as he gasps for breath, and his hand goes immediately to his ribs, which I plowed into shoulder-first. Always shoulder-first. Never helmet-first. We've practiced that enough over the years that I know it was my shoulder.

But shoulders can bruise and break ribs just as much as helmets can, and the way Mav is clutching his ribs and wheezing…it's definitely broken ribs.

"What the fuck was that?" Asher yells at me.

I turn toward him. I already feel bad enough about whatever I just did to Maverick, and now he's laying into me, too?

"I had too much momentum after taking your ass down," I say to him.

"I told you to take it down a notch!" He's still yelling at me.

Lincoln comes between us a second later—literally. He walks right in between our fight to check on Maverick, who I've clearly just made an enemy of, and then he looks up at me.

"In my office. Now."

His voice is eerily calm, and I know I'm in for a punishment far worse than stadium stairs.

I follow him to his office, and he slams the door shut behind me as I slide into one of the chairs across from his desk.

"What the fuck are you doing out there, Dex? I thought you were pulling yourself together, and now you're plowing down Asher and taking out Maverick? You don't hit the quarterback in practice. Ever."

It's ribs, which will be four to six weeks recovery at most. I feel bad about it, but it's a risk that comes with playing the game. We've been trained *not* to feel bad when we take down our target.

"Sorry," I mutter.

"You know Fridays are light. Why'd you mow down Asher?"

I take a breath—mostly because I'm about to say something really stupid about how he probably wouldn't care if it was Austin Graham or some other tight end that's *not* his brother, but talking back right now isn't going to earn me any favors, so I shut my trap.

"Well?" he prompts. "Why?"

"I couldn't go light. I needed to get my anger out, and football is the outlet."

"If I say practice is light, that means the goddamn practice is light. It does *not* mean you get to do what you want. You put at least two players in danger and injured one, and that's absolutely unacceptable, Dex. You'll stay here while the rest of us travel to New York."

"Coach, no! Don't do this. You need me. You know you do."

He shakes his head. "No. I need a *team* player. Someone I can trust. Someone who will put their personal shit on the back burner and focus on the task at hand. And right now, that's not you."

"I'm sorry. What can I do to change your mind?" Why do I keep asking people that? They've already made up their minds. Nothing I say will change it, so why even bother?

"Nothing. Don't do anything stupid this weekend. I'll expect you in here Monday morning, win or lose, ready to run extra solo drills."

I clench my jaw. "Yes, Coach."

"You're dismissed from practice today."

I grind my teeth, but I don't say anything at all. Instead, I get up and walk out of his office.

Well, that was a shitty practice. Maybe the shittiest one of my life.

I head to Asher's place to pick up Jack since Desi's watching him, but I text her ahead to let her know I'm on my way and I left practice early.

It's not like I can stay at their house this weekend when I'm in town and Asher isn't, so I grab my kid and head home. I'm sure Asher will fill her in on the stupidity that landed me here.

It was my fault. Again. It's all my fault lately.

And as I get Jack out of the car seat once I'm back home in my parking garage, a new realization dawns on me.

I'm glad I get a little extra time with Jack. It's rare it's just been the two of us, and while I know I'll struggle my way through it, it's good for me. But the truth is, we shouldn't have this time. I should be packing for New York, and I'm not.

I don't just need to get my shit together. In order to do that, I need to figure out exactly what my shit is, and I need to figure out what it is I want out of life.

Because this right here? Getting suspended from the first game of the season as a direct punishment from my coach and not getting to travel with the team…this isn't it.

CHAPTER 48

DEX BRADLEY

Can I Stay at Your Place

I manage to feed and bathe my son thanks to the note with the schedule on it that Ainsley wrote for me months ago, and he's currently playing on the floor as I contemplate what to do next.

And as I wander over to my thinking windows, the place I've stood so many times contemplating all sorts of problems and complexities as I looked out over Las Vegas Boulevard, her words seem to come back to me.

Unless you give up the lounge, which I know you can't…well, then it's over.

Give up the lounge.

The words echo in my mind.

Give up the lounge.

It's not something I ever truly considered before. I think it never occurred to me because it was always assumed I'd just do whatever my father asked. That's how he raised us.

But if the choice comes down to my father or Ainsley, it's not my father who will come out the winner.

Give up the lounge.

It's walking away from the legacy. My father might disown me, but I'll still have my siblings.

For just a moment, I wonder if Archer has known about this underground shit the whole time. Is that why he was shunned from the family? Is that why he ran to Vegas and never looked back? Because, man, I tried that. I tried to leave and never look back, but our father somehow has this hold on me that keeps pulling me back in.

But now that I'm a father, maybe things can be different for me. Maybe I can stand up to the people wielding power over me and prove that I'm stronger.

If I want that little slice of the picture-perfect family we were for a snapshot in time, then it's what I have to do.

Almost getting into that lime green Lambo, plowing down Jennings…neither gave me even a tiny glimpse of the sort of thrill I got when I walked into Asher's place yesterday and saw Ainsley sitting on the floor playing with Jack.

Those are the thrills I want now. Not the fast life. Not the risks or the danger.

But love. A deep, emotional kind of love that I never knew existed.

The love I share with Ainsley. The love I have for Jack.

Two different types of love that have developed over the last few months into something far stronger than anything I've ever known.

I know what I have to do.

It's not going to be easy, but I don't have any other choice.

I look at the schedule she drew up for Jack, and I take a photo of it. I pack first for myself and then for Jack, bringing along everything I could possibly need when I realize that if there's anything I forgot, I can just buy it when I get to my destination.

I book the next flight. I may not be going to New York, but I'm sure as fuck not going to sit around at home with my dick in my hand.

I'm going to fucking fight with all my might to get back the life that was just within my reach before I lost it.

I carefully buckle Jack into his carrier, and I text Milton and ask him if he can get me a car to the airport.

He's at the reception desk when I walk down with Jack in his carrier in one arm. I'm dragging my suitcase with the other, and I have a duffel slung around my shoulder, too.

I set the carrier carefully on the floor and walk over to Milton. "I never properly thanked you for getting in touch with my coach on Wednesday."

"You should thank your wife. She's the one who texted me asking if I knew where you were."

My brows pinch together. "She did? I thought the driver texted you."

He presses his lips together. "She was worried about you, Dex."

"I've thought this many times over the years, but I've never said it to you. You're like a father to me, and I appreciate all you do to look out for me."

He nods once, clearly not sure what to say to that, but he doesn't have to say anything. He clears his throat, and then he nods to Jack and my suitcase. "Are you bringing Jack with you to New York?"

I bite my lip before I answer. "Coach isn't having me travel with the team. I went a little too hard in practice when it was supposed to be light and might've cracked Maverick Jennings's ribs."

"Oh, Dex," he says quietly. "So where are you off to?"

"Chicago." I flash him a smile. "Bet you can guess why."

He nods again. "If I may say so, I hope you get her back, sir. It's nice having her around."

I glance at Jack, and then I look back at him. "I agree. I'm going to go put up the biggest fight of my life, so wish me luck."

"Best of luck to you."

I plow into him for a quick hug, and he laughs as he awkwardly pats me on the back.

And then I head to the airport to catch a flight to win my girl back…with a few obstacles in the way first, of course. It wouldn't be my life if it were quite that simple.

Jack sleeps through the entire flight, thank God, and I text Madden when I land.

Me: *Can I stay at your place this weekend?*

Madden: *What the fuck?*

His response is warranted since I'm supposed to be playing in New York this weekend, not chilling in Chicago.

Me: *Long story, but I'm suspended for a game and headed to Chicago right now to try to fix the things I fucked up.*

Instead of answering with a text, he calls me.

"Hey," I answer.

"I'm in San Diego, and my place in Chicago is vacant. Everleigh has a spare key if you need it."

"Are you kidding?" I ask. "I had a copy made when I stayed there last time. I think everyone with the last name Bradley has a key to your place. You should probably change your locks."

"Duly noted. Thanks for the free advice."

I laugh. For the first time in days, I actually laugh. And it feels good. Like maybe there's some light at the end of this darkness. I hope so, anyway. I'm sure as hell going to try.

"So what happened?" he asks. "Why are you suspended?"

The aircraft doors open, and I grab the duffel filled with Jack's supplies plus my own suitcase from the overhead and pick up Jack's carrier while balancing my phone. It's a lot for one guy to handle. "Hang on."

Once I'm off the jetway, I glance around. The airport is crowded, and I'm glad I carried on. I call up a rideshare and head right for the pickup area. My car will be here in seven to ten minutes.

"I, uh…made some questionable decisions. Lincoln Nash showed up to divert me from doing something stupid, so he was already mad at me. Then I went hard at a Friday practice, and the QB might've ended up with some broken ribs because of me."

"Dude! How stupid are you?"

"I hope that's rhetorical," I mutter.

"Why are you acting like this? I thought you were finally pulling your shit together," he says.

"I was. And then—" I glance around to make sure nobody's listening since someone like me can never be too careful, and I lower my voice. "My wife ended it. Took off her ring. Told me she couldn't be with me."

"Why?"

"Because of Dad's fucking VIP lounge." It's not quite that simple, but that's what it breaks down to.

"How?"

I figured he'd ask that, so I give him the truth. If there's anyone in the world who could understand the position I'm in, it's my big brother. "It's complicated. I lied about the underground stuff to protect her, and she got mad when I told her the truth. Said I was putting her in danger, and the only way she could be with me is if I cut ties with the lounge."

"Yeah. Dad's putting us *all* in danger," he mutters.

"Even you?" I ask. I keep walking toward the rideshare area, and I've navigated this airport enough times that it's second nature to know where to go.

"We never talked about how I found out," he says.

"And?"

"He was using Bradley Group to hide a lot of his illegal companies. I found some shell companies on the books that he was feeding large sums of cash to, and I did some digging and ultimately stumbled on the underground casino. I couldn't get in and didn't know what it was, but it was actually you who helped me get in."

"Me?" I ask. "How?"

"Your deepfake. I used it for the facial recognition software."

"Shit. I taught you well." I wondered what the deepfake was for when he asked for it, but I also know better than to sniff around and learn things I don't need to know.

He laughs. "Something like that. He knew within ten seconds of me entering that I found it, and eventually I made him extract anything illegal from Bradley and sign it over to me just before I left for training camp."

I whistle in appreciation for what he did. "Damn, bro. I had no idea you signed the papers."

"It's still pretty recent, and he's wrapping up loose ends."

"So are you retiring at the end of this season to run Bradley?" I ask. It's the question everyone is wondering the answer to.

"To be determined."

"Well, good luck this season," I say.

"Hey, you too. And good luck with what you're there to do. We have to stop letting Dad fuck up our relationships."

"Hopefully either way, we'll end up the winners in the end."

"Yeah," he mutters. I hear Kennedy call his name. "I better go. Clean up after yourself, okay?"

I laugh at my brother's compulsive ability to be a neat freak even from hundreds of miles away. "You got it, bro."

I hang up just as my ride pulls up to the curb. I strap Jack, who's still sleeping peacefully, into the car, and then the driver takes off for the destination I gave him.

I realize Ainsley and I have other problems, and I used the plane ride to think those things through. I reviewed the contract we signed. I came up with some revisions. I emailed my lawyer. And then I closed my eyes and visualized how my next conversation is going to go. I rehearsed my lines over and over.

And instead of going to Madden's place in this Lyft, the driver navigates toward my parents' mansion.

CHAPTER 49

Ainsley Bradley

Aligned

I feel strange going to Ivy's house, but she assured me her parents are out at a dinner party. She thinks the reason I feel off about going to her house is because her parents are technically my in-laws.

I suppose that's part of it.

I've never felt weird going to my best friend's house before, but I've also never gone there when I was married to her brother and we just broke up.

I don't want to go. I don't want to see the photographs of a younger Dex on the walls. I don't want the reminders of everything I just willingly gave up. But I don't have much choice. Ivy was insistent, and she doesn't know the truth.

I guess maybe tonight I'll tell her. Does it really matter now that it's over?

I pull up in front of the mansion in my little old Volkswagen Beetle. It's the only car I've ever owned, and we got it for a good price a little over five years ago when my parents needed help toting my younger siblings around. It's served me well, but it certainly doesn't drive as smoothly as the Mercedes back in Vegas.

Nothing here feels as smooth as life in Vegas does, and maybe that's why I decided to tell Ivy the truth. Maybe she'll be mad. Maybe she won't care. Maybe we'll talk about what it's like to have sex since she's still a virgin. Maybe we won't since it involves her brother, and that could get awkward.

Maybe I'll chicken out and not tell her the truth after all, but she's my best friend. We tell each other everything, and it's not like I can easily hide the heartbreak I'm feeling right now. I can see it on my own face when I look in the mirror, so surely she'll be able to see it when she looks at me, too.

I ring the bell, and Ivy opens the door a moment later.

She looks all around me before her eyes meet mine, and her brows are pushed together. "Doesn't Dex need help with the baby since he has a game this weekend?" Clearly she's looking for her nephew. "Or is he with Everleigh?"

My brows dip together. "Everleigh?"

"Yeah, didn't Dex tell you? She's moving to Vegas. She might already be there." She shrugs.

I shake my head, a little confused. Maybe Dex knew and didn't tell me since we haven't spoken. "No, I didn't know that." I hear the crack in my voice when I say the words, and I'm giving myself away *way* too early.

I had plans. I rehearsed what I was going to say.

But none of it matters now because tears are already falling down my cheeks, and I'm going to have to admit why to Ivy.

"Oh my God, Ains, what's going on?" she asks as she ushers me in.

I pull it together, wiping my eyes and sniffling. "Sorry," I say.

"Did he hurt you?"

"No more than I hurt him," I say, though honestly I don't know if that's true. I don't know if he's hurting or not. He doesn't seem like he is when he stays out all night the way he did, but if he genuinely cares about me and what we built, like he said he did, then he must feel *something* over the loss of it.

She's quiet, and she pulls me in for a hug. "You fell for him." She says the words flatly.

"Very much so, yes." I'm resting my head on her shoulder, refusing to move because I don't want to have to look her in the eyes while I tell her how very much I love her big, dumb brother.

"And him?" she asks.

"He fell, too. Or he said he did, anyway. I wasn't alone. But it's over now."

"Did you, uh…" She trails off, and I fill in the blank.

"Sleep with him? Yes."

"Oh, God."

"I know. I'm sorry."

"I had a feeling when I stayed with you for my birthday weekend. I don't know, you just seemed so…" She trails off again, and this time she pulls back as she looks at me while she says the word. "Aligned."

I twist my lips. "We were. And then we weren't."

"Can I ask why?"

I can't exactly tell her that it's because of her father and this illegal underground casino he's running. We tell each other everything, sure, but that seems off-limits. If her dad wanted her to know, he'd tell her. It's not my news to tell when it involves so many members of her own family.

So I dart around the central issue. "We just have such different backgrounds. It was never meant to work."

"You and I have the same different backgrounds, but this works," she points out.

"Yeah, but we're not romantically involved. It's different. And you're not this NFL bad boy with a history filled with women."

She presses her lips together. "What can I do?"

We're still standing in the foyer, and there's a huge family photograph on the wall. It's from several years ago, but Dex is in it, and it feels like his eyes are on me as I stare up at it.

"Come on," she says as her eyes follow mine to where I'm staring, and we head toward the kitchen. She gets us each some water, and we sit at the kitchen table. "Talk to me, Riggs."

I chuckle a little wistfully. "It's Bradley now."

"Right. Not if you ended it. Are you sure about this?"

"He's a complicated guy. He's secretive, and he claims he keeps those secrets to protect me, but how do I know I can trust him?"

"I feel like somewhere in that question, you're admitting it's not over yet," she says.

"It feels permanent. But you know me, the eternal optimist." I roll my eyes.

"I do know you, Ains. And I know you try to be sunshine and rainbows all the time, but those rainbows don't come without a little rain, right?"

"This feels like more than a little," I point out. "This feels like thunderstorms and lightning and destruction." I twist my lips.

"The storm before the calm?" she suggests, and I shake my head.

"I don't know. He kind of holds the keys, but he has to want to fight back, and I'm not sure he does."

She reaches over and squeezes my arm, and frankly, I'm surprised she's being so cool about this. We never *had* to hide it from her, and she's not even questioning why we did. She just seems to get it, and *that* is why she's my best friend. "He's never *had* to fight before. He might not know how."

I chew on my lip. Is she right?

He's an adult, but he's always lived recklessly. He's always done whatever he wanted that felt good or right in the moment. He never had to think about anyone else. And regardless of what happens with *us*, he'll still have Jack. He'll still have someone else to think about in every decision he makes.

Eventually I head back home. I don't feel any better after admitting the truth to Ivy, so maybe some family time will do me good.

I still share a room with Claire and Holly, my nineteen- and seventeen-year-old sisters, respectively. Claire is attending community college while Holly is a senior in high school, and my brothers—Carson and Henry—also share a room. It's a modest, three-bedroom home with only two bathrooms, and I can't say I miss sharing a bathroom with two sisters. It's probably why I spent so much time at Ivy's house, to be honest.

But I'm back. This is where I lived all through college and even after I graduated last year. I was saving up to find a place of my own, something that's harder than I realized it would be when rents are skyrocketing while entry-level paychecks remain the same.

It's a Friday night, always movie night in the Riggs household, and when I walk in after visiting Ivy, I find my two brothers and my parents on the couch, a bowl of popcorn on my dad's lap as everyone reaches in to grab handfuls. There's popcorn on the floor, and my mom will make a game of cleaning it up once the movie is over. They're watching one of the Marvel movies. I debate heading to my room for a bit just to be alone, but instead, I plop down onto the couch beside Henry. I reach across him to get my own handful of popcorn.

"Where are Claire and Holly?" I ask.

"Claire is out with friends, and Holly's at Becca's," my mom says, naming Holly's best friend.

I miss having them here. These little family moments are always so lovely, even if I didn't appreciate them so much back when I could have them any time I wanted. I've even missed this since I've been in Vegas for the last few months. Maybe I didn't realize how much I missed it until I was back here in the thick of it.

But it doesn't even come close to comparing to how much I miss Dex and Jack.

CHAPTER 50

DEX BRADLEY

Family

Ivy's jaw drops when I walk through the front door. "Dex! You're here! And you have my sweet nephew!"

Her sweet nephew is currently crying his brains out. *I get it, little dude. It's a long trip, and you're ready to get the fuck out of your car seat.* I pull him out and hand him over to my sister, and she coos over him as she tries to get him to quiet down. I grab a bottle from the duffel and head to the kitchen to mix up some formula and water, and Jesus, this is more than I'm used to handling on my own.

But that's the whole thing.

I *can* handle it on my own.

I'm doing it.

Ainsley believed in me, and she was right. She was fucking right all along. Of course she was. Of course I can do this. It's hard, but life's fucking hard, and here I am, doing my best to step the fuck up.

"Is Dad home?" I ask once I'm back in the family room. I move to take the baby, and she shakes her head and holds out her hand for the bottle. I guess she wants to feed him, so I let her.

She walks over to a chair and sits with the baby and his bottle. "No, they went to some dinner party. You know who *was* just here, though?"

I narrow my eyes at her. "Who?"

Jack starts sucking down that bottle, and the room is quiet when Ivy says, "Your wife."

I press my lips together, schooling my reaction.

"What did you do, Dex?" she whispers.

"I didn't fucking do anything," I mutter as I sit in a chair across from her.

She purses her lips. "You messed my best friend up good."

"Yeah, well, she messed me up pretty good, too."

"So why are you apart?" she asks.

"If I tell you a secret, will you keep your trap shut?" I ask.

She rolls her eyes. "Yes."

"I'm here to fight for her."

Her eyes light up, and she sits up a bit, jostling the baby as she moves, but he's so intently sucking down his bottle, he doesn't even notice. "You are?"

Ivy and I have never been particularly close. We're just from different generations with twelve years between us, so we've never built much of a relationship. But considering it's her best friend I'm talking about, I guess maybe we'll start to get a little closer.

"Yeah. I did some thinking, and I love her, Ivy. I fucking love her. She drives me nuts, but it's been two days since she ended things with me, and these have been two of the worst days of my life," I admit.

"Then what are you doing here?" she asks. "Go get her. She just left. She's probably at her parents' house. I'll watch the baby while you go. Go!"

I press my lips together. "I appreciate that, but I have to take care of some other things first. I have to prove I'm serious about her. About us. About a real life together." I don't know what Ivy knows about our father's illegal casinos, so I leave it at that.

"And that somehow involves…Dad?" she asks, clearly confused since I showed up asking where he was.

"It does. It's complicated, but he has me helping with some business-related projects in Vegas, and I'm here to tell him I want out."

"You're here to tell me what?" my father demands, his voice booming as he steps into the room.

Well, fuck.

This isn't exactly how I rehearsed this.

"Can we talk?" I ask.

He looks livid.

"How was dinner?" Ivy asks as my mother steps into the room behind dear ol' Dad.

Mom rolls her eyes. "Awful. The Goddards had the nerve to ask us to donate to their next charity endeavor when they wouldn't shut up about their new villa in the Caymans. We bowed out before dessert. What are you doing home, Dexter? Don't you have a game this weekend?"

I sigh. "Long story, but I'm benched this weekend and not traveling with the team, so I came here to discuss business with Dad."

He lets out a frustrated sigh, and then he tips his head toward his office. I follow him in that direction, and he slams the door shut behind me when we're both in there.

"You want out?" he hisses at me.

I throw my speech out the window and wing it. "Someone was tailing me the other night while my wife and my child were in the car. That's unacceptable, and I can't be putting them in danger even if you don't give a shit that you're putting *me* in danger. I want out."

I left my suitcase in the other room, but this is where I'd planned to pull out the contract and tear it in two.

He runs a hand along his jawline. "Thirty-five, Dexter. We agreed. I'm sorry you don't like it, but that's life."

"Fuck that," I say. "You want me to go to the cops with the contract? Because that's the only other option here."

"Where did I go wrong with my sons? First Madden threatened me with that nonsense, and now you? I thought you were the one I could count on."

"You could until you cost me everything that means anything to me," I hiss.

"So your loyalties are no longer to your family," he says flatly.

"Actually, quite the opposite. My loyalty is to my wife and son. If you try to block me from extracting myself from your illegal activities, you know I have enough on you that I can tip off whoever needs to know. I want out, and I want your word that I'll be protected. That whoever's on your tail leaves me and my family the fuck out of it."

"You know as well as I do whoever followed you could've been anybody, Dex," he says, his tone so logical that it only serves to piss me off. "It might've been a fan. Or an anti-fan. It may have had nothing to do with me. And even if it did, it's not like I can control other people."

"Really?" I scoff. "Seems like you've done a pretty goddamn good job of that where your kids are concerned for our entire lives."

He rolls his eyes. "You know that's not true."

"Because we developed minds of our own, not for lack of trying," I mutter.

"Think of the legacy, Dex. You could have your own empire."

"I'll build my own empire from the ground up, the legal way," I counter. Fuck it. "I don't *want* an empire. I want the simple life I shared with Ainsley and my son. It's not worth losing everything I care about because I'm trying to make you proud of me. Nothing I ever do will accomplish that, and that's why I'm out."

"*Proud* of you?" he sneers. "I can't begin to tell you how *disappointed* I am."

The jab might've hurt before Ainsley ran into me on the Strip, but his words do nothing to touch the pain I feel in having her walk out of my life. "Look, I fucked things up by keeping your secrets, and now my only goal in life is getting back the woman I love and putting my own family back together. I don't care about money or underground gambling. I don't even care about rings and championships, or MVP awards or trophies. Just her, and building a life with her and my son. So what's it gonna be?"

He steps behind his desk, and he picks up the house phone and presses a button. He puts the call on speaker.

"Paul, it's Tom Bradley. I need you to revise the Vegas lounge to write my son out of it."

"Hi Paul," I say, addressing my father's lawyer cheerfully from across the room.

"Are you sure about this?" Paul asks with a sigh.

My father glances at me, and when he sees the look on my face, he says, "Yes. Get it to me by—"

"In the next ten minutes," I interrupt. "I want out, and I want out now."

"Consider it done," Paul says.

The call ends, and I slide onto the chair across from my father's desk, for once feeling like the power in our relationship has shifted.

CHAPTER 51
DEX BRADLEY

Dex Bradley Standing on My Porch

I thought about asking Ivy to watch Jack for a while, but I realize I want him here for this.

My sister tells me she'll give me a ride since I took a rideshare here, and clearly she's all for patching this thing up. I'm surprised, to be honest. I thought she'd be fully against the two of us being together, which is why we didn't tell her.

But I guess Ainsley admitted the truth, and here we are.

With my sister behind the wheel.

Me in the passenger seat. Jack strapped in the back.

Ivy pulls into the driveway of a small house. From the looks of it on the outside, I'd guess it's under two thousand square feet for five kids and two adults.

It has to be cramped in there. I think of Madden's place, where I'm planning to stay tonight, and he's got more space for himself than this family of seven has.

I suddenly want to do something.

But first, I have an apology to make and some forgiveness to beg for.

"Stay here," I say to my sister.

I knock on the front door with Jack's carrier in my hands, and the door opens a beat later.

"Dex Bradley?" a man who I assume is Ainsley's dad says.

I stick out a hand. "Nice to meet you, Mr. Riggs. Is Ainsley here?"

"Yeah, she's right in…jeez." He shakes his head and rubs his hand along his jaw the same way my dad did earlier, but my dad did it in frustration. This guy seems to be doing it in awe. "Dex Bradley standing on my porch. I couldn't believe it when she said she married you. Wait, don't you have a game?"

He doesn't wait for me to answer, and he also doesn't turn in toward the house as he yells, "Ains!"

The effect is that he yells his daughter's name in my face.

I clear my throat, and I hear her before I see her.

"Yeah, Dad?"

"Someone's here to see you." Her dad steps aside, and there she is.

She's in jeans and a black T-shirt, and her feet are bare, and how have I gone two whole days without pulling her into my arms and making things right?

"Dex," she murmurs. "What are you doing here?" Her eyes fall to the baby, and they soften before they move back to mine.

"Birdie." I stare at her for a second, and I draw in a breath. "I came to tell you I'm sorry. I came to say that—" I cut myself off as I glance at her dad, who's standing behind her listening to my every word. I see movement behind him, and I guess we have an audience as I see two younger boys and an older woman who looks to be Ainsley's mom.

I blow out a breath as those five people stare at me, and Ivy's probably in the car staring at me, too.

Fuck it.

I came here to win her back, and I'm not leaving until I know she's coming with me.

I clear my throat. "I came to say that you were right, and I could've told you this over the phone, but I had to go see my father first in person." I glance at her dad, and my eyes move back to hers. I keep my words vague, knowing well enough that she knows exactly what I'm trying to say. "I tore up our contract, Ains. I'm not hosting at the lounge anymore. I'm done with it. All of it. I told him I couldn't work for him any longer because it was coming between me and the people I care about."

Her jaw slackens, but before she can get any words out, I plow forward.

"I came to tell you I love you, Ainsley May Riggs Bradley, and I will do anything to prove to you that we belong together. You were right. I was putting you and Jack in danger, and I came to tell my dad I'm out. The only family I care to be loyal to is the two of you. I walked away from my father, from the legacy, from the money. It's behind me. I know I fucked up—"

I hear Mrs. Riggs clear her throat at my curse word in front of her two younger boys. They look to be teenagers, and I would venture to guess they toss that word around casually. Besides, this is a private conversation that they're standing around listening to.

But I'm not here to make waves.

"Sorry," I say. "I screwed up, and I want to be clear that I didn't do this to look good. I did it because the two most important people in my world were put in danger because of me, and I will never put you in danger again."

"You walked away from your father?" Ainsley asks quietly.

I nod. "I told him I didn't want any part of the lounge. It was the one thing you said you needed from me, and I'll do whatever it takes for you to know that you and Jack are my only priorities."

"Oh, Dex," Ainsley sobs, and she rushes for me, tossing her arms around my neck. She buries her face in my chest as I set the carrier down.

"The only legacy I care about is the one we build together, Ains."

She moves to her tiptoes, and her mouth collides with mine.

It's a quick kiss that's far too short-lived when we hear an audience clapping, and then my sister clearly rolled down her window because I hear whooping coming from the direction of the car.

I laugh, and then I lean down and kiss Ainsley again.

She pulls back. "We have other issues, Dex. Things between us that aren't quite so simple. The age difference. The difference in backgrounds. The things we spend our money on."

"I know. And we'll compromise. We'll work together and figure it out because when it's this important, that's just what you do." I look between her eyes, and she looks a little uncertain.

"Come home with me," I beg.

She finally swipes at a tear, and then she nods resolutely. "Yes."

"Oh, and you left this at home," I say, and I pull the ring out of my pocket and slip it back onto her finger where it belongs.

I pick her up and twirl her around, and she's giggling and her parents and brothers are clapping, and somehow this all feels about as picture-perfect as that goddamn breakfast at Coach Nash's house.

And it's only getting started.

CHAPTER 52

Ainsley Bradley

Elementary Education

I tug on his hand. "Come in."

He picks up the carrier, and I wave Ivy in, too. She gets out of the car and walks to the door, and her grin is wide on her face as she follows behind Dex.

The credits are rolling on the movie. I guess we missed the ending.

But this was worth it—wholly and totally.

I got the ending *I* was hoping for, too. I once told him the only thing he could do to save our relationship was to give up the lounge, and two days later, he's standing on my front porch to let me know he did exactly that.

If that doesn't scream of his sincerity—of his *love*—I'm not sure what would.

"Popcorn duty!" my mom yells to the boys, and they race to see who can pick up more popcorn. The loser has to do the winner's chores tomorrow.

The adults sit in the kitchen around the worn table while the boys race, and I can't help but stare at Dex.

I'm still in shock that he's even here. It feels surreal, like this is some dream and not my reality.

We sit and chat with my parents a while longer, and my mom holds the baby.

"So if you're his stepmom, does that make me his…" She trails off, and Dex fills in the answer.

"Grandma," he says.

My mom looks at Dex, and then at me, and then at Jack, and she swipes away a tear that falls onto her cheek.

"Oh, my sweet baby," she coos to Jack, and I feel myself getting a little emotional seeing her with the baby.

He's not mine by blood, but it's starting to feel like he's mine anyway. And that's pretty damn special.

We chat a little longer with my parents and Ivy, but it's already getting late.

"Ivy, would you mind taking us to Madden's?" Dex asks, and she agrees. Twenty minutes later, we're pulling up to a lakefront tower and taking the elevator up to the penthouse.

These Bradley boys sure know how to pick places with views.

He shows me around the place, and we get Jack down to sleep in one of the guest rooms. We end up on the balcony overlooking Navy Pier as Dex reaches over and grabs my hand in his.

"I didn't just tear up my father's contract. I also revised ours. My lawyer sent it digitally if you'd like to take a look."

Her brows dip a little. "Can you tell me what you changed?"

"A few things. I took out you being his nanny. I don't want to pay you to nanny for him when you're his stepmother. You were right about that, and if anything positive came out of the past few days, it's knowing that I could do this. I want to strike a balance where you get your time and I get mine, but we also get family time. And since you're my wife, you don't need a paycheck. My lawyer is ordering credit cards linked to mine in your name."

My jaw drops.

"I could see you getting bored at the penthouse, Ains. I want you to do whatever it is that's going to make you happy, and I want you to be able to do it without limitations. If we need to hire a nanny so you can work somewhere else, so be it. If you want to farm butterflies on the balcony, I'm on board. If you want to open a kiosk at the mall where you write names on grains of rice, you have my support."

"Farm butterflies?" I repeat with a giggle.

"What? It's a thing. My point is that I want you to be happy, and I want to facilitate life in a way that allows you to do whatever you want."

Tears heat behind my eyes. I'm not sure how I deserve all this, but it's somehow mine anyway.

"I want to go back to school to get my degree in elementary education," I blurt.

He turns to look at me, and he pins me with that hot gaze for a few beats. "You do?"

"It's always been a regret that I went into communications instead of education, and I could go the route of a master's degree in education, plow through a program in as little as a year, and start next school year in the classroom. It would have to come together quickly, but I think it could be done."

"Then do it. I'll do whatever I can to make it happen," he says.

"Really?" I ask, and he nods.

"Of course, Ains. But only if you promise to get one of those slutty teacher outfits to wear for me on the weekends."

I laugh, but then I move in and press my lips to his, and I pull back to say, "Oh, I'll even wear it for you on a school night."

He thrusts his hips to mine, and I can tell just the thought of me in my slutty teacher outfit has him ready to go.

His mouth opens to mine, and he kisses me with urgency and need, as if it's been months since we were last together and not just a couple of days.

He pulls back, his eyes hooded and dark with desire, and then he grabs my hand and pulls me inside. We walk past Jack's room, and he leads me into another guest room.

He closes the door, and less than ten seconds later, we're both naked as clothes fly in every direction, and we're both very clear on what's about to happen.

This is it. My first ever makeup sex.

He gets on the bed first, and he lies on his back. He fists his own cock and strokes himself a few times, and I watch with rapt attention as the searing throb pulses tightly between my legs.

"Climb on top of me and get that cunt over my face," he demands. "Face away from the headboard."

The ache throbs harder as I leap into position, following his instructions. I'm practically sitting on his face, hovering as I rest on my knees, not sure what's going to happen next.

"Now lean forward and suck my cock into your mouth," he says, and I lean forward, take his cock from his hands, and pump my fist up and down a few times before I take him into my mouth. He yanks on my hips to pull me down over his face, and then I feel his tongue as it swipes through my pussy.

I jerk over him, and I may bare my teeth a little on his cock, and he grunts, his sound giving the effect of vibrating against my pussy. It only serves to drive still more pleasure toward me, as if I wasn't already on the brink of an orgasm.

Hell, just him showing up today, giving me everything I asked for…that's climax-inducing all on its own. I was three-quarters of the way there when I walked into this condo, if we're being honest.

"Fuck, Ains. That feels so goddamn good," he murmurs as I slide his shaft in and out of my mouth. He sucks on my clit, and my legs start to tremble as the release builds.

I suck on him harder, and completely and totally without warning, I feel his finger as it slides through my wetness and right into my ass.

Oh my God.

I've never felt anything there before, and he's inched close to it a few times. But to have his finger there, moving in and out…it's such a strange sensation that feels somehow forbidden and sexy at the same time.

I moan loudly and push my hips back to let him know I like it, and he keeps doing it while his tongue starts to move in and out of my pussy. It's so many sensations at once with his cock in my mouth as his grunts and groans telling me he's enjoying every second of this as much as I am. His sounds continue to hum against me, pushing me into an orgasm that seems to explode over me completely out of the blue.

I keep sucking his cock as I come all over his face, my pussy contracting over and over as the wetness nearly turns into a damn waterfall coming out of me, and he stays with me beat for beat.

And just as my jerks start to calm, his begin.

"Fuck yes," he groans. "Baby, I'm about to come," he warns, and I keep sucking on him, wanting him to explode in my mouth and give me every last drop just as much as I want him to explode inside my pussy and give it all to me there.

I want to spend the night naked, with him slipping into me whenever he wants, to make me his sexual toy to use. I want to take the pleasure I've been missing my entire adult life until I met him. I want to make up for lost time as we make up for nearly ending what's growing to be the most important thing I've ever experienced before.

And that's what we'll do. Because we have time now. We've proven to each other that this is what matters, and nothing and no one can ever take that away from us.

It may have started as a play fake, but it's ending with the happily ever after I never saw coming when I flew to Vegas to take part in a reality television show.

Ainsley Bradley

The Reunion

Three Weeks Later

"Ainsley!" Drew, the host of *Speed to the Altar*, says as he introduces me. All the couples are seated together, and he announces Jordan next. "Jordan!"

I got a louder cheer from the crowd than Jordan did. In fact, I think he even got some boos.

It's a small audience that's gathered here today, but it's all people who've already previewed the show.

We haven't seen it yet, though we know how our own story ended.

I didn't *have* to show up today since they already pulled my pay, but I definitely *wanted* to be here. I have a whole hell of a lot to say.

And I'm lucky enough that my *husband* is sitting in the audience today, here to support me. I suppose I got lucky on that front. Filming is happening in the evening after he happened to finish up at practice, so he's able to be here.

Drew finishes introductions and makes a little speech about the first season of the show. Instead of starting with the three couples who actually ended up married at the end, he decides to begin with those who didn't make it.

"We're going to start today with one of our contestants whose name has been all over the news lately," he says.

Cheers rise up from the audience, and he continues, "Ainsley. How are you?" he asks, turning to me.

I wave, and I think about his question. How am I? Well, I'm a hell of a lot better than I was. Thanks to my husband, I showed up today in a gorgeous—albeit expensive—dress that I'll donate later. I was able to get my hair and makeup done, and I don't just feel great. I *am* great. "I'm great. Better than great, actually."

"Let's take a look back at your wedding," he says, and my face appears on a large screen in front of us. I look happy and hopeful, but even I can see that it's not quite there in my eyes.

Not the way it is now, anyway.

We watch as I say, "I do," and then as Jordan says, "I don't."

When the clip ends with me running, Drew turns to me again. "Take us through what happened when you ran out of the chapel."

"I was devastated. I felt like my heart was shattered. But the further I ran from the chapel, the more I started to realize it wasn't heartbreak. It was embarrassment. I knew this would be aired, and everyone would get to see that rejection."

"So you married someone else?" Jordan asks. His tone is demanding and rude, and I open my mouth to answer, but he plows forward before I can. "I tried calling her. I tried working things out," he says.

That little liar! I can't believe him. "You never called me," I say, rolling my eyes.

"Were you with Dex before you went on the show?" he asks. "Because it's only been three months, and you're already married."

"I wasn't. The truth is that he's my best friend's older brother. We'd known each other for years, but never in the romantic sense. One thing led to another, and, well…" I hold up the giant rock on my hand, and gasps fill the audience.

"I see him here in the crowd," Drew says. "Would it be all right with you if we introduced him?"

They asked us ahead of filming if they could mention him by name, and he agreed. After all, this was the whole point of our marriage in the first place even if it shifted into something else entirely.

I nod, and the cameras pan toward the audience.

"I'd like to introduce Dex Bradley!" Drew says. "Dex, come on up."

He doesn't smile as he walks up the stage, and he sits down right in between Jordan and me. He slips his arm around my shoulders, and I love how he's taking up more of the couch than he needs to in order to give Jordan less room. It may be petty, but it's also hot as hell.

I slip my hand onto his thigh, which is tight with tension since he's sitting beside someone he hates simply because I do.

"Take us through what happened between the two of you," Drew says, and Dex nods at me to take the floor.

"When I ran out of the chapel, I ran into Dex. Literally. He was out for a run, and I was running, and we slammed into each other on the street. Once he realized who I was, he took me back to his place. I wasn't ready to give my final interviews here, but he was gracious enough to listen to me. He was there for me. He's the one who helped me see that I never really loved Jordan. He's actually the one who taught me what true love really is."

"And what is it?" Drew asks, maybe because he wants to know what I think or maybe to educate some of the people here who don't seem to know—like, for example, Jordan.

"It's following through. Doing what you say you're going to do," I begin. "It's not just the cliché of being there for each other because sometimes you physically can't be. But it's really listening and truly working to understand what the other person needs from you and then giving them that. It's balancing life but doing it together. It's having fun with and relying on the one person you feel like you can't live without."

"And that's what Dex is for you?" Drew asks.

Dex answers before I do.

"It's what *she* is for *me*. Look, when she asked for a place to lay low after she ran from this show, I opened up my home, no questions asked. I wasn't looking for love. Trust me. I was happy with the way my life was. But when you live with someone day in and day out, you get to know them pretty quickly. We fell hard and fast, and we both knew it was right. She came to Vegas with the intention of finding her happily ever after, and she got it. But sometimes the things we need come about in ways we don't expect. That's what happened for us." He turns to Jordan. "So I guess I have to thank you, man. Because if you weren't such an asshole as to lead this gorgeous woman on, I might've missed my chance."

Jordan sputters a little, but then Dex kisses me, and the crowd goes wild.

Drew asks Jordan some questions, and Mariah, one of the contestants who didn't end up at the altar, interrupts to tell Drew that Jordan tried hitting on her at a bar a couple of weeks ago, and it all sounds pretty messy.

I'm just glad I don't have to worry about that anymore.

Dex is right. Sometimes the things we need come about in ways we don't expect, and as it turns out, that's what he is for me just as much as I am for him—and Jack is for both of us.

I may have come to Vegas with the intention to *Speed to the Altar*, and I did—just not in the way I expected. And when I did, I ended up with an instant family that turned out to be even better than I ever could have dreamed. It extends further than just Dex and Jack now, too. Everleigh moved into our building, and we've gotten close over the last couple of weeks. She was hired by the Vegas Aces to rebrand Maverick Jennings, and so far, it doesn't sound like it's going very well.

But as for Dex and me? Now *that* is going well.

As the saying goes, when one door closes, another opens. I'm just happy that it was Dex Bradley standing at the door that opened for me.

The End

Want more Dex and Ains?
Scan this QR code to download a bonus epilogue!

Scan this code to join Lisa on Facebook
at Team LS: Lisa Suzanne's Reader Group!

Acknowledgments

Big thanks first as always to my family. Thank you to Matt for the love and support and to our kids who all this is for.

Thank you to Valentine PR for your incredible work on the launch of this book.

Thank you to Valentine Grinstead, Christine Yates, Billie DeSchalit, Serena Cracchiolo, and Patricia Rohrs for beta and proofreading. I value your insight and comments so much.

Big thanks to my ride or die bestie, Julie Saman. We'll always push each other to hit those deadlines no matter how impossible they may seem!

Thank you to my ARC Team for loving this sports world that is so real to us. Thank you to the members of the Vegas Aces Spoiler Room and Team LS, and all the influencers and bloggers for reading, reviewing, posting, and sharing.

Thank you to my ARC Team for loving this sports world that is so real to us. Thank you to the members of the Vegas Aces and Vegas Heat Recovery Room and Team LS, and all the influencers and bloggers for reading, reviewing, posting, and sharing.

And finally, thank YOU for reading. I can't wait to bring you more sports romances where swoony superstar heroes ride emotional roller coasters to their happily ever afters.

Cheers until next season! We're heading back to Vegas with Everleigh Bradley's story, RED ZONE! What happens when she's hired as a brand strategist for the Vegas Aces' newest bad boy quarterback?

xoxo,
Lisa Suzanne

About the Author

Lisa Suzanne is an Amazon Top Ten Bestselling author of swoon-worthy superstar heroes, emotional roller coasters, and all the angst. She resides in Arizona with her husband and two kids. When she's not chasing her kids, she can be found working on her latest romance book or watching reruns of *Friends*.

Also by Lisa Suzanne

Grayson & Ava

Spencer & Grace

Asher & Desi

Tanner & Cassie

Miller & Sophie

FIND MORE AT
AUTHORLISASUZANNE.COM/BOOKS

www.ingramcontent.com/pod-product-compliance
Lightning Source LLC
Chambersburg PA
CBHW021023310726
48969CB00006B/1518